PICKY

JULIE T. KINN

For Bethany Cockburn, who picked out my first strawberry

Contents

The Menu

Apples
Carrots
Bread
Chicken
Cereal
Granola bars
Milk
Peanut butter
Potatoes
Rice

Chapter One

There's a one-in-ten chance Cheerios will be my last meal. This is my deep thought while I spoon dry cereal into my mouth and choke for a second. I recover and knock on a wood cabinet for luck. I can't die at age twenty-three full of toddler kibble. I'd rather exit life with one of my more mature options.

A habit I need to break is going without a spoon entirely and using my tongue to trap and pull up cereal like a frog catching flies. Efficient and mess-free, but a higher choking risk. When I'm eating that way, I keep a spoon on hand, just in case Paula catches me.

I call her "Mom" to her face because she's my mom, but I like to think of her as "Paula my roommate" to feel more like other adults in their twenties. Within the year, I'll have my first real-live roommate, my boyfriend, Cliff. Paula's holding my move-out money for me, and she promises to fork over the dough once I'm ready.

But her definition of "ready" keeps changing.

After the cereal takes the edge off my hunger, I preheat the oven for our usual Thursday dinner of tater tots and chicken strips. My many years of practice with reconstituted potatoes and frozen chicken has taught me that 385-degrees Fahrenheit is the magic temperature that works for both tots and strips without leaving too much raw or burnt.

Paula gets home from the family medicine clinic she manages and talks to me loudly from the entryway while she changes out of work shoes, into home shoes, and sanitizes her hands.

"Anyway, did you see the news today? About that girl in Indiana?" she asks, as though we're in the middle of a conversation. She makes her way to the kitchen and continues. "Or Iowa. It was one of the I states. Did you see that one?"

"No," I say and wonder what's next. Knowing Paula, this won't be a happy story about someone winning the lottery twice in one week.

She kisses me on the cheek and washes up while I slide the baking trays into the oven. Paula's animated while she tells me about the woman's abduction and murder. She closes with, "Can you imagine?"

I can.

My imagination is way too good for these stories. I easily picture myself in that unfortunate young woman's situation. Helpless. Hungry. Hurt.

My fear rises like bile in my throat, and I picture it as a crayon doodle. Brown and red and lime green all battle inside me like a poorly drawn map of the nervous system.

It's an old habit from when I'd share my worries with Paula as a kid. I wasn't good at describing emotions, but I could tell her when I felt scribbly inside like pencil scratches or calm like watercolor.

"But I have a strategy," Paula says brightly.

"For what?"

"Abduction. To prevent it."

Whatever idea she has is going to suck ass. But my imaginary doodle gets smoother and less clashy. It's comforting to have another person to plan things out with.

"Want to tell me at dinner?" I ask as I put away the cereal and sponge off the counter.

"Let's talk now." She sits at the dining room table and asks, "Tater tots or fries?"

"Tots."

She sighs, even though we haven't had tots since Monday. She knows there's only so many ways to make my dietary habits interesting. I feel guilty enough about the weirdness without any accusatory exhalations. Zillah, I say to myself, moms are allowed to sigh.

My nutritionist Eleanor will sigh some four-letter words when I add processed potatoes to my food tracker. She's Cliff's cousin, and he bribed me with Pentel Graph Gear Pencils to work with her. "Try it for a while.

Just once a month," he'd said. "You don't have to eat anything you don't want to eat." I've only met her once so far, and her comment ("Ten foods? I can't tell if you're joking.") is still ringing in my ears.

"I'll take any tots that come out half-crunchy," I say.

"But back to abduction—"

"Increasing it or preventing it?"

She ignores my sass and makes her pitch. "Using the computer website to see where you are isn't good enough. Your *phone* could be at school, but your body could be *anywhere*. So, we'll take pictures of the car any time we park. Not just the car. A selfie picture of you or of me in front of the car."

"'Selfie picture' is redundant."

"Don't get smart. We'll send the pictures to each other by text message. If we don't hear from each other, or if the Find my iPhone program isn't working, then just *think* how good this will be to help the investigation."

"Investigation?"

"Whe— *if* one of us is abducted." She gets up and continues the pitch while she gets out things to set the table. "Of course, you have nothing to worry about. It's much more likely we will get in a car accident or lost or maybe in a what-do-you-call-it. Tsunami? What's a big watery mess in Chicago called?"

"I don't think we have those here." I imagine a post-apocalyptic wave off Lake Michigan that sweeps up the Magnificent Mile.

"Then a tornado."

"Is there a different way we could check on each other?"

"No, no, no," she sings. "This is what the experts recommend." She opens the oven to investigate dinner status. "Consider how reassuring it will be. I'll send you mine, too."

I think about the selfies while Paula complains about the quality of the in-progress tater tots and chicken strips ("Are these the garbagy generic ones? Too salty. I like the name-brand ones better. I don't believe that nonsense about them being the same product with a different label. What do you think of that one?").

I *do* worry about her.

A lot.

If she's home fifteen minutes late or if her phone doesn't connect to our family location-tracking app, I assume she's dead or at least mangled and in the *process* of dying.

She has the same, if not worse, worries about me and I'd like to spare her some of the hours of anxiety she spends on me each week. I usually keep her posted, but sometimes I get wrapped up in things with Cliff.

I'll be moving in with Cliff in a few months, if I get my real estate internship. Paula has promised that once I get a placement, I can have the five thousand dollars my dad gave her when I turned eighteen. He meant for it to help me move out, but I doubt he expected it to take me this long. Paula's also going to give me a raise for the part-time admin work I do for the clinic she manages. That, plus occasional babysitting and maybe student loans, will be enough to pay rent once we get a place. But she holds the keys to the money from Dad I'm planning to use to pay the deposit, first month's rent, and last month's rent that all these Chicago slumlords demand.

Cliff works as IT support for University of Illinois at Chicago, convenient since I go to UIC and we can go to campus together when I spend the night. It pays okay and he's got rich parents to fall back on. He's been willing to pay more than his half so I can get out sooner, but I don't want to be a freeloader. Plus, I know myself — I'd turn into the housecleaner to feel like I'm earning my keep. I want to enter the next phase of our life together on even ground.

I can stand this for now, knowing it's temporary. Paula's safety measures are annoying, but they come from a good place. And they soothe my fears, too.

"Yeah, let's try it for a few weeks." As soon as I agree, I feel a visceral relief. I hate how good it feels to have a safety plan.

And I ignore the little voice saying that other twenty-three-year-olds don't need to know where their mommy is every second of the day.

After dinner, I sit at my desk and organize my study-music playlist.

Paula opens my door without knocking and walks in while sorting a small pile of mail.

"Zillah, you have a few things, but it's all junk." I reach out to take it, and she lifts it over my head, out of my reach. "Did you finish your internship cover letter yet?"

"I'm working on it," I lie. "Are you withholding mail as punishment? That's a federal offense."

"No, my doll." She hands me the small stack. "Just want to see if you could reach."

Despite seeing me every day, Paula always seems amused by my growth plateau at a smidge over five feet as a teenager. Now, at twenty-three, there's no hope for a late adolescent growth spurt. At least being the shortest makes me easy to remember at such a large university.

Being tiny also helps me look young, which is nice since I'm usually the oldest in my classes. My friends from high school and freshman year have almost all graduated, but I'll still be chugging along for at least another two years to chip away at my business degree so I can become an appraiser. It's the number one most secure job in the United States, and it pays well, too.

It's a solid goal, but my college pace is complicated. I like UIC, but too many of the classes I need are scheduled at times that I can't accommodate and so I've ended up taking extra years to fulfil my requirements. I don't travel in the dark, so that rules out classes that start early in the morning or would require me to stay on campus too late. I also can't fill up my days with too many classes in a row because then I wouldn't be able to come home to eat and use the bathroom. A lot of my time revolves around the toilet; a major reason I did homeschool until I was sixteen. But Cliff convinced me I needed a real high school experience before college. And his parents helped convince Paula.

Dad's paying the bill for college, and he doesn't mind that I'm going so slow. He doesn't mind *anything* about my life. If he has opinions, he's keeping them to himself. Once in a while on our monthly phone call he'll ask, "You thinking about moving out soon?" But that's the only hint I get that he questions my choices. I get more advice from strangers on the train. It's always been like this. I love him, but when he left us, he let Paula take on one hundred percent of the parenting.

I've had to put off the internship so long while I filled requirements that I'm on my last chance. If I don't get a placement for this summer, then I'm out of the real estate program and lose my scholarship. I could still finish my degree in business, but we decided real estate appraiser is the way to go. Plus, Paula would deem that I'm certainly not ready to move out if I fail that big.

She leaves me alone and I navigate online to my internship folder, open it, then close it.

I think about that murdered girl.

Why'd Paula have to tell me that story?

Our world gets a little smaller every time we make a new ritual or safety practice. Eventually, we'll just huddle in a closet with a toilet bucket and wait for the apocalypse.

I turn to my phone for the solace of distraction. None of my usual feeds are appealing today. I start a text to Cliff, but I can't describe why I feel so bad. If he was here, I'd ask him to brush my hair or give me a back massage.

A woman speaks.

It's my new, loud neighbor on the other side of our shared apartment-building wall. Our building is a horseshoe-shaped structure, that's really like ten three-story walk-ups smushed together. Each of the ten walk-ups has its own stairwell leading up to six apartments with two on each floor. I never realized how thin the walls were between us and the apartment on the other side of the wall until this family moved in last fall. I haven't seen them yet since we don't share the same stairwell, but I hear them all the time. This one says, "My life revolves around fear and the fear keeps me stuck here at home."

I get ready to knock on the wall to communicate, "Shut up please," as her words sink in.

She continues, "I want my adult life to begin."

Yes. Exactly.

Another voice, sounds like it's coming through her phone or computer, asks her to explain.

I don't knock on the wall.

I sit.

A realization sinks in — this is online therapy. I'm eavesdropping on therapy.

And I'm hooked.

Chapter Two

"I haven't left the apartment since Christmas," the neighbor says. "Mom makes me go out to get the mail and sometimes I go with her or Ben for food, but usually they bring it back for me."

"What's the fear?" the therapist asks.

"What if I'm waiting in line somewhere or on the bus and I can't leave, but I know I'm going to throw up? Or, like, what if I try to ask for something in a store and I feel a panic attack coming? Everyone would look at me. Everyone would know I'm weird. And I might say the wrong thing and look even more stupid."

I've heard the family since they moved in around Thanksgiving. They must have lived in a house before, since they have no idea how to be quiet for apartment life. But have I seen her in person? I haven't noticed any new girls in the laundry room or the courtyard. I picture her as undersized like me, but with huge anime eyes.

This is better than reality TV.

And way better than working on cover letters for my real estate internship-placement applications or my nutrition homework. Fuck if I want to write about how I ate as a toddler. I move closer to the wall.

No, this is bad.

I need to go to the other room or shout through the wall. But hearing someone else talk about fear and feeling stuck is energizing. It's like taking notes and learning from a fellow criminal's prison escape.

Most of the session is about leaning into fear instead of avoiding it. "Your anxiety is like a dog that barks at scary things, but also barks at the UPS truck, a man with a baby stroller, and an old lady, just in case they're threats, too," the therapist says. "It's soothing to avoid the things that scare us, but any fear we avoid just grows stronger." The things I'm scared of are legitimate fears, but I see how this applies to the neighbor.

And maybe a couple of my quirks.

The therapist and my neighbor make a list of things that make her panic (saying the wrong thing, meeting strangers, going to new places, being in crowded places she can't leave, feeling out of breath, feeling nauseous) and pick a couple to practice together.

On purpose.

For her "homework", the therapist asks the neighbor to try two things she usually avoids. She chooses to work out in the apartment gym and to send three text messages with typos. Without apologizing.

They finish up, and I make a note of their plans for next Thursday at five o'clock.

I wake up in the morning and think about the neighbor while I text with Cliff. "`Meet for lunch today? Feeling wired.`"

I meant "weird," but I don't notice my autocorrect fail until he replies with emojis and, "`I'm confiscating your caffeine pills. Drink coffee like the rest of us.`"

I've never thought about apologizing for a typo before. That would be a lot of extra texts. How does the neighbor live like that? At least she's trying self-improvement.

My home is too safe. Paula and I spend hours keeping each other feeling calm. I need to test the limits so I can get out.

While we both get ready for our day, I ask Paula whether our insurance covers therapy.

"Now you need a therapist on top of a nutritionist? What kind? Physical therapy or crazy therapy?"

"The brain kind." I choose not to antagonize her about her dated word choice. Instead, I sanitize the kitchen counter and sink while she finishes her breakfast.

"You don't want therapy." Paula puts away her breakfast things. "I tried it after your father left and it was a waste of time." This is news. Details about that time are rare.

"I bet a therapist could help me get ready for my internship and do adulty stuff. Like getting ready to move out." I don't want to see her reaction, so I work a spot on the backsplash with a scrubby sponge as though there's a resistant stain I can only vanquish with dedicated concentration and elbow grease.

Paula is silent for a few seconds. That's like a minute for everyone else. She asks, "How?"

"I heard therapists help you make a list of all the things that scare you and then you go through the list and change them." I hope she won't ask how I know so much about therapy all of a sudden. Those BetterHelp ads never get this specific.

"My doll, that's called 'being an adult', and you don't need to pay some therapist to do it for you. Just figure out what you want to change and do it."

While I wait for the 36 bus, I open the notes app on my phone and make a list of some of my fears:

- Being alone overnight
- Yuck Food
- Yuck Food touching my food
- My finger touching Yuck Food
- Seeing Paula eat Yuck Food
- The stairs
- Kissing with tongue
- Peeing if anyone is nearby
- Pooping in a public toilet
- Sharing a cup

It's not a complete list, but these are the biggies. And I don't want to try to overcome any of them. Unlike the neighbor's fears, mine all make sense.

Except the stairs. That's one I've slowly been outgrowing, anyway.

We've lived in this apartment since I was a toddler, and I've always been scared of the stairs. I drove Alexi, our building manager, insane with all the ways I've tried to make it safer. Extra salt in the entryway. Colorful bathtub stickies on the steps. Good luck charms on the walls. He complained I made the three flights of stairs to our landing *more* dangerous. When I was in high school, we compromised. He let me put silicone grippy tape on the handrails as long as I promised to take everything else down.

The grippy tape had worked. The stairs looked crappy, but I felt safe. Maybe I've even saved lives for the other five apartments that use this stairwell.

But no one has ever fallen down any of the other nine stairwells in our building as long as we've lived here. Plus, the tape is curling in places and now our entryway looks even crappier.

I know *logically* that I'm not going to fall down the stairs. I go up and down stairs in other places all the time and it's not a problem. It's just *these* ones that turn my insides to paint blobs.

Could I take off the grippy tape? Over the past few years, I've practiced not holding the rail, but I liked knowing the tape is there just in case.

I think about it throughout the week. Sometimes it sounds easy and other times I get nauseous, like there's a clump of mud in my stomach.

On Thursday, I make a deal with myself: I can only eavesdrop on the neighbor's therapy if I do the therapy homework beforehand.

I put it off until about 4:30, and then I go down to the bottom of the stairs and consider how to remove the grippy tape.

The staircase has eight steps in each segment, with a landing in between, and two segments per floor. I start with just an inch at the end of the bottom handrail.

It's already peeling off, so no biggie.

I pull off another few inches.

It peels off easily and doesn't leave residue. How many people's hands have touched this? I should go up and get gloves.

No, you chicken. Just do it. Just start with a small section.

I peel more, and about a foot comes free with a satisfying "shlup" noise. I go halfway up and pull all the rest off this banister segment and consider my work.

It's only eight steps, but the stairwell looks better. Can I walk back down?

I move with deliberation and hold the nude handrail tightly. Left foot. Hand slide. Right foot. Hand slide. I repeat back up to the landing.

I break a sweat but remind myself that I climb stairs at school all the time.

And it's just eight steps.

I go up and down four times total, and even approximate non-zombie movements.

Am I out of breath from fear or because I don't do enough cardio?

I had planned to remove tape from the entire staircase to our third-floor apartment. But this is progress.

Therapy homework? Check.

I'm so ready to be an adult living without supervision.

I go to my room and get my desk set for the neighbor's therapy session. I've got my water bottle, my laptop for maybe taking notes for my econ paper, and drawing things in case I get bored.

Our ancient apartment door announces Paula's arrival home.

I swoop into the hall and shout-whisper my lie, "Hey Mom, I have a study-group call in a minute." I sneak back on quiet feet while she's busy sanitizing her hands. I can't get into a thing with her right now, or I'll never get away.

"I'm running to the store in a few," she calls. "Text me if you think of anything we need."

Is there a polite way to say, "Time for you to go, and please be quiet so the neighbor doesn't figure out how thin these walls are"? I close my door and creep back to my desk, where the acoustics are best for my eavesdropping.

I wrap my electric blanket around my legs burrito-style and pull my laptop toward me. Maybe I can work on internship cover letters while listening to the neighbor's therapy. If I don't pair the writing with something fun, I'll never get around to it.

And if I don't get an internship placement, there goes my apartment with Cliff.

I can't think about that now.

It's my time to relax and enjoy someone else's therapy.

I need a distraction from thinking about the stairs.

I google "death falling down stairs".

Big mistake.

My stomach turns into a Jackson Pollock, and my pulse rises.

Fuck. What did I do?

After this session, I can put the tape back.

With this decision, I breathe easier and focus on the discussion next door.

The session finally gets going. The therapist and my neighbor check their volumes. I hear the neighbor clearly, but the therapist's voice is a little muffled through the wall *and* through the neighbor's computer speaker.

I turn up the heat on my blanket. Thanks to chronic anemia, not only do I look so pale that I edge into goth, but I'm always cold. Chicago in January is the worst. The gray days and early sunsets make me feel like a half-defrosted chicken breast: soft on the outside, with icy tendons holding it all together.

If I move away from the Chicago region right now at age twenty-three, it would take at least until age thirty to thaw completely.

Rugs over the hardwood floors would help. I add these to my checklist for my someday-apartment.

My neighbor must also have bare wood floors since the acoustics are ideal for my eavesdropping. She doesn't seem concerned about privacy and speaks to her online therapist through the computer speaker instead of using a headset. As long as I sit at my desk, I can hear them easily. It's the one reason I'm grateful for our apartment's crappily insulated walls.

The therapist and neighbor laugh about something. I missed the joke. Why is therapy funny?

They write a story that describes the neighbor's worst fears. It's depressing. I rearrange my desk items by color instead of size while trying to come up with justifications for my eavesdropping. I grab my colored pencils and sort them by complimentary colors, then triad, then tetradic, and back to complimentary.

What are ways I can compensate for my sleazebag behavior? What do normal neighbors do? Baking something for her is out of the question and I don't have a lot of practical skills. Can I draw her something anonymously?

The answer is obvious: stop being a creep and swear off eavesdropping.

But I'm not a good person.

Plus, comparing myself to the neighbor helps me feel normal. The neighbor's life is even more fucked up than mine. The therapist helps my neighbor on the other side of the thin wall discover ways to taste independence and I want a slice of that, too. If I can't eat the cake, I want to smell it, at least.

My phone vibrates. When I fish it out of my blanket burrito, I see I've missed a call from Paula.

Odd for her to call instead of text.

While I draft a text to see what's up, she calls again.

"Mom?"

"Zillah!" Her voice is strained and echoey. "Call an ambulance!"

"Where are you?" I shout.

"Home. Here," she says in a breathy voice, like she's carrying too many groceries. "Don't talk. Just listen. I'm in the building. I fell," she says. "I fell down the stairs."

Chapter Three

"Ambulance on the way! I'll be down in a sec!" I shout down the three flights of stairs.

"Careful!" her warning echoes upwards. "We don't need us both injured."

"Fuckfuckfuck," I whisper and walk down the stairs as fast as I can while holding on to the handrail like a lifeline. Even though I only removed the grippy tape from the bottom portion of the handrail, the entire staircase feels doom-flavored. Any moment I'm going to step wrong and lose my footing. Was the handrail always this slippery? Is it sweat or did Alexi oil it today in celebration of me taking off some of the grippy tape?

Paula's at the bottom of the stairwell, sitting against the wall in the small vestibule that opens out onto our courtyard — not sprawled with her limbs in crazy positions like I'd feared. She's cradling one arm and squints her eyes shut as though that will block out pain.

My confession spills out in a rush. "It's my fault. I took down the grippy tape. How far did you fall? I'm so sorry. The ambula—"

"I think I broke something in my arm." She inhales deeply. "And maybe my ankle."

I try to make her comfortable while a record in my head spins around with too many thoughts for me to consider.

Maybe she broke her hip.

Shouldn't I keep her still in case she broke her spine?

What if she's bleeding internally?

My mother might die.

A couple of neighbors join us in the vestibule and offer help, while we wait for the ambulance. We know one of them, and the other is a youngish dude I've noticed recently because of the satchel he always wears. It looks like it's made from repurposed paint-by-numbers and seatbelt straps, and I've wondered if he made it himself. If he wasn't handsome, I might have asked him about it the first time I noticed, but I can get intimidated by hot guys. He's short-ish, at least shorter than Cliff, white, and wiry looking. He's got thick, sandy hair that's short on the sides and swept in a dated side-part on top. He looks like the kind of guy that *could* be a sporty gym rat but instead plays in an ironic kickball league.

Paula opens her eyes a crack. "Oh, Rebecca," she says to the one we know. She's older than Paula and has been here for a long time, although not as long as us. "Can you two watch Wellington Ave for the ambulance so they can find us? You know how it is when people use the apps to find us."

The neighbors leave, which gives me more opportunity to say, "I'm so sorry, Mom." I feel like if I say it enough times, it will undo her fall.

"Take a note on your phone," she tells me. "Bring the car and pay for parking." She lists all the things she wants me to grab from the apartment before I meet her at the hospital (granola bars, her book, reading glasses, her cell phone charger, essential toiletries including "the good lotion and not that chintzy stuff with all the chemicals from Bethany. You know which one I mean?").

If she's giving me directions to calm me down, it's working. I like tasks I can complete.

Rebecca is back at the door and shouts, "They're here!" through the glass. Two, no, three paramedics arrive with a black metal gurney. I let them in, and back up on to the stairs as they collect information from Paula. It's good to have experts on the scene.

The hardest part is getting Paula out the door. She has a minor freakout when they don't let her tap the door in the way she likes every time she leaves the apartment.

"It's our good-luck ritual," I explain. "It only takes a minute."

Paula's eyes tear up and redden when they don't position the gurney so she can tap the way she likes. She says, "Zillah, you'll do it, right? First thing!"

"Of course," I say, so she has a calm ride to the hospital. Well, calm for being locked in a moving box with strangers who jab you with needles.

After the ambulance pulls away down Wellington, I go back to the door of our stairwell and do Paula's tapping for her.

Whenever we leave, we just tap the door out of the apartment building three times in three specific spots. It takes about five seconds and isn't that big of an investment for her peace of mind.

It started the day we moved in. I was a toddler and don't remember it, but I've heard the story enough. Paula gave the door a playful tap each time she left to go to the moving truck or her car, and it just became a habit. "The apartment hasn't burned down while I've been tapping," she likes to say. "So why stop now?"

After a while, it just didn't *feel* right to Paula, so she changed it to tapping in three specific spots. When I was eight or nine, Paula changed it to *three* taps in each of the three spots while I was at my first sleepover at my aunt Bethany's house. I actually didn't end up sleeping over. I called Paula to pick me up around 10. She must have had a rough time too, because she introduced me to the new ritual as soon as she brought me home. Such a small thing to feel safe.

Someday, after Cliff and I move in together someplace secure, maybe I'll sleep by myself overnight if he's out of town.

Maybe tapping does keep our building from burning down.

Maybe it's a waste of time.

Maybe it will help her heal up fast and forgive me.

My two seconds of hopeful calm pass. What if I did it too long after she left and she bleeds out in the ambulance? What if I just killed her for real? Did I do it wrong? It doesn't feel right.

I tap a second time, but something's off. I try it again. And another time.

In the glass, I see someone behind me, and when I turn around, the satchel dude from earlier is standing a few feet away from me. He looks at me with curiosity, I guess, but behind that I'm sure lies pity and judgment.

"Thanks for helping," I say in the least-friendly tone I can manage. I'm not so good at being deliberately cold. He nods and leaves.

Who the fuck is this asshat to judge me? I rant to myself as I unlock the door and stomp back up the stairs to get supplies.

I may have misread the look on his face. Maybe he just wanted to help more. But I like having a target for my anger. Easier than experiencing my worry.

Inside, I take off my boots and grab a canvas bag from the pantry. I rush as fast as I can from room to room, grabbing everything we might need. I devote my backpack entirely to snacks we can share, just in case she has to stay overnight and they don't have any of my ten foods there.

I sit on the entryway bench to lace up my boots and re-read my note to make sure I have everything.

At the top of the stairwell, I take a few deep breaths. Theoretically, I want to get down the stairs as fast as I can to get to the hospital. But I need to be logical.

Paula's with experts.

I can't let myself fall, too.

An extra thirty seconds isn't going to *extra* kill Paula.

I make my way down with deliberation, one step at a time. What do the morgues look like at Illinois Masonic Medical Center? If she's dead, do I get to see her before they move her? Do I have to identify her like on TV? My thoughts are dark, but at least they distract me from the fear of falling.

I enjoy an imaginary fight with Satchel Dude while I speed walk to the apartment building a couple of blocks away on Barry Ave, where we rent a garage space. I understand he's just a hapless bystander, but this is a good distraction. I prepare all the mean things I can say to him if I run into him again on the way.

Well, I'd *like* to have mean things to say, but my bitchy muscles are out of practice and the best I can come up with is, "Who the hell do you think you are?" I sound like a suburban dad watching kids walk across his lawn. I need a cruel way to convey "Mind your own business" and

"Just because you're good looking doesn't mean you can butt into other peoples' lives."

Too long. Taunts need to be pithy.

I stop in front of the bike shop to adjust the straps on all the bags I'm carrying. The owner waves through the window and I give a small wave back. I even manage a little smile.

Why do I put so much effort into being nice? Paula could be dying right now.

Wouldn't *that* make Satchel Dude feel bad! I imagine a scene where he asks in a snarky voice, "How's your mommy?"

I'd look him straight in the eyes and say, "She's dead, you fuck."

I get about half a second of joy out of imagining his shock, but I think about the reality of Paula's death and I'm back where I started.

I can't think about her dying. My insides are charcoal squiggles.

"She's with the experts," I whisper to myself once I'm in the garage. "They would have had me ride in the ambulance with her if she was dying." I heave everything into the hatchback of our car and take deep breaths to calm myself before driving. No sense in getting in a wreck. "Maybe she didn't even break anything," I whisper while I check the mirrors. Check the locks. Check the seatbelt. Check left-turn signal. Check right.

I drive on Wellington toward the hospital and use hands-free calling to leave Cliff voicemail. "I need you. Paula's hurt and we're going to Illinois Masonic. I fucked up bad." A woman in a nicely structured pink tweed peacoat stands still on the sidewalk looking at her phone. She's so calm while Paula might be dying.

I give her the middle finger because she exists and I'm jealous of her coat. She doesn't look up from her phone.

Cliff texts me instead of calling. "`Be there asap. Call me with updates.`"

I try to stay calm on the short drive, but two different metal bands play in my head at the same time. I blame this cacophony for why I park in the wrong lot at Illinois Masonic and have to hunt for the ER.

Getting around the hospital to find Paula is like a new level in a dungeon-crawler video game. I'm low on life points from the long day and the added stress of the upcoming battle. I rush to reach my goal in a time limit to save the princess, but I also need to orient myself to figure out what the hell is happening.

Illinois Masonic Medical Center at least has human helpers to assist panicked newbies like me.

"Emergency room?" I ask the elderly greeter. I hope my slight bouncing on my toes conveys my rush. He's probably moving at normal speed, but he seems to take forever to raise his arm and tell me which way to go. How do I signal "please stop talking and release me to my next stage of hospital hell"? I start a side shuffle in the direction he points and say some "uh-huh"s and "yeah-yeah"s.

I escape my prison of etiquette and find Paula in the beige-and-blue waiting room. "Zillah," she says loudly, and then "This is the one," she says to another woman in the waiting room. "She's the one in business school." The woman looks a bit older than Paula and she smiles and nods at us.

Instead of hugging her, I just move my face next to hers and breathe in her mom smell of lemons, paper, sweat, and wool.

She's alive. My mother is alive.

The thoughts are a relief, but my body is still ready to fight dragons.

"You tapped the door?" she asks.

"I tapped. What do the doctors say? Have you been through triage?"

"Yes, but it was a big nothing. They took my temperature and vitals for all the good that does. I didn't even see a real doctor yet."

My inner scribbles turn from thick oil pastels to fine pencil lines.

I sit next to her and show her the offerings I collected for her at home. We settle in together to wait for the sound of staff calling, "Paula Scriven."

I try to make myself useful by telling Paula how well-rated the hospital is and looking up all her symptoms for her on our go-to favorite medical websites. But I have trouble keeping the warble out of my voice while I try to reassure her. I guess I'm more annoying than helpful when she says, "Okay, enough." She announces she's going to rest her eyes, and I'm left alone with my dark thoughts.

Chapter Four

Here are lessons I learn about the Emergency Room.

Lesson one.

They don't call it an Emergency Room anymore. Now it's the ED, Emergency Department. But every time I see that signage, I think *erectile dysfunction.* Someone should have put that through a focus group.

Lesson two.

There's nothing gory like on TV. No bones busting through people's legs or gunshot wounds.

Lesson three.

There's so much waiting. The evening and night have a drawn-out procedural feel, like going through lines at the airport.

If Paula wasn't injured and trying to rest, this would be a good time for me to interview her for my nutrition assignment. I'm supposed to find out how my eating got this way. I already know the essentials: I've always been picky. From the time I could eat solids, I rejected almost everything. Apparently, I used to freak out if someone put something new in front of me. I was a complete hellion and would make life miserable for everyone around us.

I wish there was video of that.

But the nutritionist Eleanor wants me to dig deeper: what kinds of food did Paula try to get me to eat? Did I play with them and put them in my mouth before rejecting them? Or did I refuse any contact with the foods like I do now? How did I react as a young child when Paula ate other food in front of me? And why did she decide she would *also* eat the way I do?

Paula hates talking about the past, so I'll have to pick the time carefully. *If* she recovers from whatever's wrong with her after the fall. Am I worrying a normal amount for a 23-year-old or is this excessive? How the hell am I ever going to move out if it means I can't go to her for reassurance? I wish I wasn't so creative. My imagination takes off and I can think of at least ten ways this fall will lead to massive devastation.

In between meeting with providers, I text Cliff and my Aunt Bethany with updates and photos.

When we get put into a room.

When we see the first nurse.

When two police officers escort someone past her bed.

After X-rays.

When we learn the treatment plan to reset her dislocated elbow.

I'm not allowed to be in the room for the actual procedure to reset her elbow, thank the Universe. But Paula wants me alongside her for the rest of it, "Just in case you ever have an injury like this, God forbid, then you'll know what to expect."

I go back to the waiting room while they put her under and do whatever. She also has a mild concussion and a twisted ankle, but there's not much to be done about those other than rest and time away from screens (for the concussion) and elevation and stabilization (for the ankle).

I can't find a comfortable position in my chair. What sick people touched it before me? I'm not too germophobic, but the thought *pink eye* enters my mind, and now I just want to rub my face.

Thanks, Brain.

My heart rate is jacked up and I'm so energetic I could jog around the hospital even though it's late.

Sit still and act like an adult.

My self-pep talk works for about thirty seconds and now my leg jiggles with energy and my backpack bounces on my knee.

Time to send Aunt Bethany more texts to keep myself busy until Cliff gets here, which should be about ten minutes according to his latest text.

Bethany's the perfect person to get my blow-by-blow since she gets the subtext of innocuous messages like, "Mom's nurse washed her hands for a few seconds before taking her `vitals again.` " To anyone else, this might seem like an unnecessary detail sent by an overenthusiastic notetaker. But Bethany understands that what I'm saying is, "Paula might have a fit because she's afraid her nurse is contaminated with Typhoid."

Bethany replies with empathetic responses, and we plan for her to meet us at the apartment. I ask her to go buy supplies for the coming days and stock our fridge with Paula's preferred beverages and snacks. Knowing Bethany, she'll also get some of my favorite treats, like frozen chocolate-chip waffles. I may be in my twenties, but there's no rule against being spoiled by an aunt for life. And chocolate-chip waffles are a delicacy in our home.

It's hard not to compare the two sisters. Well, half-sisters, since they had different moms. Bethany is like an older and messier version of Paula. They look similar, both average height, each with a slightly pronounced overbite that I also inherited but had braces to correct. They both wear their hair short, which increases their resemblance, but Bethany is almost a decade older and her hair is fully gray, whereas Paula's is just "10 percent witchy" as Bethany describes it.

As kids, the sisters had spent holidays and long vacations together at Myrtle Beach with their shared dad. But they never lived under the same roof or even the same state until Bethany moved to Oak Park when I was a kid.

Bethany's mom must have been a free-love hippy type since Bethany's so out there. She's always in the middle of a dramatic and dangerous enterprise, like traveling with people she barely knows or learning an expensive craft she's going to abandon. She carries Narcan in her purse in case she sees someone who might have overdosed.

Bethany is our cautionary tale.

When it's just Paula and me, we say, "Sure, Bethany" in a sarcastic tone when one of us considers something risky like taking a new route to get somewhere, trying a different brand of cereal, or going out without a mask in our pocket.

Even though she's reckless, I like being with Aunt Bethany. She tells me stories about her few memories of her time with Paula as kids and secrets that Paula won't discuss. She tells me sweet things but also hints about the bad stuff. Like how Paula once needed to live with her father for a couple of months while her mom was out of the picture. What would Paula have been like if her father had kept her and raised her instead of her mother? As much as I blamed Paula's mom, who I never met, I blamed her dad just as much. He didn't care enough to check on her before the ill-fated move or to insist she stay with him afterwards. Yeah, *my* dad left too, but he knew I wasn't stuck with a crazy lady.

Thinking about my dad reminds me I should text him about Paula's injury. We keep each other posted about major events, and this counts.

I'm drafting the text when I realize the woman from earlier, Paula's waiting-room acquaintance, is trying to get my attention. She's fifteen feet away from me, sitting several seats down.

"What's that you're eating?" she asks over the heads of the other patients and family members while leaning so forward toward me she might topple out of her seat. I've been mindlessly eating a snack I'd had buried in my backpack: squares of Wonder bread wrapped around leftover French fries.

I point to my ears and shake my head "no" as though I'm wearing earbuds. I *should* be wearing ear buds. Stupid.

I have zero desire for a one millionth conversation about my odd snacks. I need to stay focused on the hallway that leads to Paula's room.

The woman gives up on trying to befriend me and I go back to my Paula-watching vigil.

"**Here**," Cliff texts. I stuff my snack back in my backpack and scan the area to make sure I have everything before I meet him at the entrance, so he doesn't have to bother the staff.

"I got you," he says when he sees me and pulls me into a strong hug. His coat smells unwashed and musky like an ashtray, but it doesn't bother me tonight. Cliff is comforting and strong. His brown hair is pulled into a tight ponytail and it's wet like he just took a shower. Did he take time for a shower instead of rushing here? "It's gonna be okay. She's going to be fine," he says gently while holding my hand and following me through the maze of chairs.

"You don't know that!" I turn on a dime from cool blue relief to magenta rage. Cliff backs up a step, and my words come out in a tangled flow of all my fears.

I want Cliff to be worried like me. His assurance that everything is just peachy is infuriating. He needs to take things more seriously.

I get up close to him and crane my neck to make eye contact. Stupid height difference. In an attempt at my normal volume, I say "You should have been here already instead of– instead of whatever you were doing." How long does it take to get to Lake View from Logan Square? Thirty minutes at most?

"Do you want me to go?" He doesn't look pissed. More like a man holding a potentially venomous snake.

"No?" I say like a question.

"Let's sit down and you can tell me everything." We sit on chairs away from Paula's nosy acquaintance. "Here's some stuff." He hands me a plastic grocery store bag, and I peek inside to see a box of our favorite peanut butter granola bars and some applesauce in little single-serving squeeze packages. It's thoughtful, even though neither Paula or I will eat the apple sauce since that brand he bought also has lemon juice in it.

"I'm sorry." And my diminishing rage is swept away by regret for being an asshole and my sadness for this horrible night. "I really am."

"Okay," he says, which I take to mean that my apology doesn't work, but this isn't worth rehashing now. I've known him so long that I can take him for granted and lash out as though he's family. We met at a weekend Art Institute camp when I was thirteen and he was fifteen. Bethany had paid my tuition as a combined Christmas and birthday present. Cliff's family had bought his spot at a fundraising auction for the museum, and he was more interested in flirting with the short, homeschooled kid than actually creating art. Worked for me. I liked the attention, and I didn't know many boys.

We stayed friends afterwards, in part due to Paula. When I was with Cliff, Paula let me do more things and go farther on public transportation ("Such a strong young man to protect you!"). She liked his practiced manners and his clean-cut look (before he grew out his hair and cultivated a goatee). And both Paula and I were taken by the sheen of wealthy glamor his parents carry so easily they don't even realize they have it. He grew up in Evanston in one of those very Evanston houses. White brick. Black shutters. A staff to maintain the grounds, prepare meals for the family, and clean up after everyone. His parents often tell me they love that I'm responsible and driven. They nurture our relationship, and they tolerate Paula. We fooled around after a few years and sort of dated on and off, but things have been serious-serious since I started college.

We got especially close when his mom was battling breast cancer. He practically moved in with us for a while, and both Paula and I were his listeners, sounding boards, safety net. His mom has been in remission for two years, but Cliff is still like a Scriven family member. He depends on us for the emotional talks and connection that his polite but distinct family doesn't provide. We're more smothering-and-entangled, but he likes it.

We both look at our phones while we wait.

When I'm finally let back in Paula's room to help her collect her things, she looks like she's been dragged behind a horse. She lies on her hospital bed with her eyes closed. Her arm is in a beige cast and there's an air-brace on her ankle. Her clothes have a wrinkled-and-shoved-in-a-bag look. I should have brought her something else to wear.

I sit in the folding chair next to her bed. "Hey," I say gently, in case she's sleeping. "How you doing?" I pick up her uninjured hand.

She gives my hand a little squeeze and opens her eyes. Her mascara's runny. Has she been crying or rubbing her eyes? The thought brings pricks of tears to *my* eyes. Somehow her hair still looks like it had this morning: a short grayish cut that apparently is ER-proof.

I mean ED-proof.

I have a moment to myself when I go to get Paula's car from the lot and pull around to pick her and Cliff up. I take deep breaths and try to force my thoughts to become a light-blue painting instead of the black scribbles pounding inside my head while I wait for a nurse to wheel her to the exit.

Everything will be normal again soon.

Chapter Five

Bethany's waiting at the door to our apartment stairwell with a book tucked under her armpit and glittery reading glasses on her grey hair like a headband. We huddle quietly out in the courtyard while Cliff helps Paula get up our three flights of stairs.

"How're you doing?" Bethany asks as she scans my face like I may be hiding secrets.

"Me? I suck and it's all my fault, but I'm fine."

She folds me in a hug while I cry and asks in a playful voice, "Did you push her down the stairs, you little murderess?"

I choke-sob-laugh at the same time and then break into a coughing fit.

"Later you can explain how you take all the blame for gravity," she says. We go upstairs and she takes over Paula care so Cliff and I can get to sleep in my room.

From the moment I wake up in the morning, I'm itchy to re-secure that damn stairwell. It nibbles at me like gross pedicure fish. During all my tasks, the cloud of an unfinished task hangs over my head. It's like a constant voice asking, "What was I supposed to be doing? Oh, right, fix the deadly stairwell."

Re-securing the stairwell is harder this time around because I don't have time to special order the tape. Instead, when stores open, Cliff tells his boss he needs to come in late for work and then he and I drive around in Paula's car to all the hardware stores in Lakeview to search.

After I declare that the third store is a fail, I say, "Want me to drop you off at work? I can do this on my own."

"Nah. What are they gonna do? Fire me?"

It's a good demonstration of how our backgrounds affect the way we think about money. I would never jeopardize my work, but in Cliff's view, there's always another job to be had.

After failing at all the nearby stores, Cliff and I brave the giant Menards on Clybourn, and I find what I'm looking for. He smokes a cigarette in our courtyard while I apply the tape.

Now the stairwell looks stupid because I had to get a different brand of tape and it doesn't match, but at least Alexi hasn't complained to me.

And no one else has fallen.

You're welcome, neighbors.

Not that anyone has thanked me.

Chapter Six

I t's been a week since the accident and Paula says the pain isn't too bad. She's using over-the-counter meds instead of narcotics, so I feel okay leaving her alone when I go to class or out shopping.

The hardest part is coordinating with her doctors for follow-up visits and her many, many questions for them.

"I have an idea," I say when she directs me to make yet another call. "How about we wait until this afternoon, and you tell me if you have any other questions so I can just ask them at the same time?" My voice fades at the end of this brave speech as Paula's eyebrows lift and her forehead tilts toward me in that mom way. "Never mind," I say. "Stupid idea."

"It isn't a stupid idea. It's a *lazy* idea," Paula says. She motions me over and I help her prop up on our couch with pillows to support her injured limbs, and every concussion-safe entertainment within arm's reach on the coffee table. I've laid out the two different kinds of granola bars we buy: peanut butter and plain. We normally buy one at a time, but I splurged to create a sense of variety. And we'll eat them eventually. I also put out a sleeve of saltines and sliced up a fuji apple.

She closes her eyes and leans on the pillow behind her head as though a fresh wave of pain has seized her. "I need to know about the vitamins *now*, since we always take them in the morning."

"Yup. Agreed." It's not worth arguing this point. She's grouchier than normal, but I get it.

A blessing is that we are compliant patients. If a medical provider tells us to do something, we follow all instructions faithfully.

Except, of course, if they tell me to change my diet.

Eleanor, the so-called nutritionist, doesn't understand how improbable her advice is: eat a serving of fruit with each meal? I'm tiny! How many apples does she think I can fit in here?

It's not that I hate food. I would eat more kinds if I could, and it would save a lot of trouble in social situations.

When people offer us food, Paula says, "Zillah can't eat that," or I say, "We ate earlier." Neither of these are strictly lies. Sure, she implies I'm allergic, but if I *did* try to eat a new food, I'm sure I'd freak out and ruin everyone's day. And we *did* eat earlier — probably at some point that day. It's better than getting into all the details and dealing with questions.

At least I use medicine when I need it, even though that's sort of food, and we both take lots of vitamins every day.

Life would be easier if I could be one of those people who eats any food they come across. No scouring the menu for one of our ten foods. I wouldn't turn down invitations to friends' homes for dinner. I could travel. Maybe Dad wouldn't have gotten so frustrated with how Paula set things up to make me comfortable. She'd be able to eat anything she wanted, we'd have a normal home, and maybe he'd still be around.

A highlight is that today's Thursday, so I get to eavesdrop on the neighbor's therapy as usual this evening. It's going to help me jumpstart my adulting. How the hell am I ever going to be comfortable moving out if I can't even *pretend* to be a normal person? I'm hoping the neighbor's therapy opens a door, especially since my plan to work through my fears backfired. If Paula had died, would that have been involuntary manslaughter?

No matter how good my internship applications are, I still need to prepare for the actual experience of having a sort-of full-time job. I'm fine with the work aspect of a real estate internship: shadowing my mentor, drafting initial documents, researching zoning issues, assorted grunt work. I can do grunt work all day. It's the other aspects that get me: Eating near other people. Holding in my poop. Not tapping doors when I'm nervous.

I'm getting the hang of the therapy routine. Sound check. Homework review. Torture. Assign new homework. Does the therapist follow the same pattern with everyone, or is the neighbor special because her anxiety is so severe?

"Did you remember to bring a straw?" the therapist asks.

"Yeah," the neighbor says.

"Good! Good! We'll use it in a few minutes."

God, she's chipper.

And tricky.

What does a straw have to do with anything? And do we have one?

I hurry to the kitchen and rummage through our pantry. "What are you looking for?" Paula asks from the couch.

"A straw." I shift aside our surplus of cleaning wipes. I *know* Bethany gave us a set of reusable stainless-steel straws with a tiny wire brush.

"What? What did you say? Come over here and tell me!" she calls.

I find the straws and say, "I gotta head back for my call." Please don't ask me follow-up questions.

I come back in time to hear the neighbor describing her experience using the small gym in our building's basement.

"It started okay." After a pause, she continues. "I went with Ben, and we had the whole gym to ourselves." The "whole gym" is one treadmill, free weights, and a yoga mat. "I did about a minute on the treadmill, but I got that sense again. I knew something bad was about to happen." I nod, as though they know I'm there. Like I'm a third person in a group therapy session showing empathy for the weirdo on my left while I wait for my turn to talk.

The therapist says, "Your brain pairs your breathlessness, your increased temperature, and your heart rate with fear. When you're on the treadmill, your brain thinks, 'Huh! I'm not breathing too easy. Must be something scary going on.'"

"Maybe. But it felt real. Like a premonition."

"Thus, the straw! We're going to hyperventilate by plugging our noses and breathing in and out quickly for one minute." The therapist sounds delighted to tell the neighbor to suffocate herself. "Let's see what you notice, okay?"

I hyperventilate along with them. It's hard, but not scary. I feel ridiculous, especially when I catch sight of myself in the mirror.

"Zillah, I have another kind of straw for you. Zillah!" Paula knocks on my door once and comes in. Privacy is an unknown concept to moms.

Fuck.

Fuuuuck.

But I don't hear any "what was that?!" from the neighbor or her therapist.

I swoop over, grab the straw (same kind I already have in my hand), and quietly encourage her back to the couch.

Hopefully Paula's voice was muffled through the wall. But she's so goddamned loud.

My mouth is dry, and I slurp water and listen to them debrief.

The neighbor says that at first it was funny. Then weirdly scary. And then just annoying. She doesn't mention anything about hearing me and Paula through the wall. The therapist says, "Perfect!" So chipper. "Your brain figured out you were breathless because of your weird therapist and *not* because of a real danger. Annoying is good. What else do you think can cause us to mistake our body's reactions?"

I quietly organize the items on my desk by size while they go on like this for a while.

"Coffee," the neighbor said.

"Yes! And sex, of course." I stop my fidgeting and look toward the wall separating us as though that will help me hear better. "Sexual arousal has several of the same features as fight-or-flight. Sex and masturbation bring on those warning signs for some people."

I sometimes get that danger warning when I touch myself. At first it feels fine, but then I think about terrible things, or I get cold all over. Cliff teases me that I do it wrong, and he's offered to buy me all sorts of gadgets. But he's got a dong, so what does he know? I can get off if I'm home alone with loud music, locked doors, and five or six other conditions. Even with the stars in alignment, I've never had an earth-shaking orgasm. Just nice little rumbles. And, occasionally, terrifying fear.

I bet this therapist would cheerfully assign me to practice finger-painting my personal O'Keefe. Except she'd call it clitoral stimulation.

They move into quiet time while they look at images together that increase the client's anxiety, so it's not as entertaining as usual. I wish I could see what they're looking at. She's supposed to rate her anxiety on a scale of 1 to 10 when she's scared, and then just suffer without distraction until it's half that number. It takes a couple of minutes, sometimes less and sometimes more. Each time I clench my teeth and hold my breath, waiting for Paula to pop in and ruin everything.

I assume the therapist is trained and has advanced degrees, but this seems wrong. Paula's anxiety has picked up since her fall, but the thing that works for her is the exact opposite of what the therapist is making my neighbor do.

Instead, I listen to Paula's worries, take her seriously, and we problem solve.

For example, she wants to know my schedule so she can reach me at any moment. Like, my exact, precise, minute-by-minute schedule, so that she doesn't accidentally interrupt my classes "because your education is more important than anything I could ever need, even if I fall on the floor and dislocate my elbow again." Now that Paula has graduated to a sturdier cast, that's unlikely.

But I get the point.

To help ease her anxiety, every morning since her fall I send her an email with my exact plans, including travel to and from destinations and any errands I'll be running. It's only an extra five minutes of my time, so it's worth the trouble.

Annoying? Sure. But it's a way I can show my love.

It's what we do for each other.

One of my earliest memories is when I was sick with the flu and had been delirious with nightmares. I can still see my vivid vision of clowns and mean people riding a steamroller on their way to get me. They shouted my name over and over in a scolding tone like I was doing something wrong. I ran to Paula's room in a panic and slammed her door shut, sure I was still being chased. I had shouted, "They're chasing me, and they have whips!" I knew they were right outside her door, steamroller and all.

Paula had treated me seriously, as though I had identified a logical threat, not anything irrational and silly. She had gotten up and looked in the hall. She came back and tucked me into her bed. She assured me everything was fine and that she would protect me forever. She took my temperature, saw I had a fever of 103, and got me Tylenol. I don't remember the rest, but knowing Paula, she probably rubbed my back or told me quiet stories until my fever broke and I fell back to sleep.

Paula has always been kind about fear. That's what I want to do for her. Because I love her and because I won't be able to move out until she's less worried about me. She won't think I'm ready until she feels ready.

While I wait for the therapy appointment to get interesting again, I draft a list of all the little things I could do around the apartment to help ease Paula's worries and stabilize her anxiety. I sort it into categories of personal safety, cleanliness, shopping, organization, and medical. Where do I put things like fear of causing bad luck? I make a catch-all category, "spiritual".

I pause my Stabilize Paula Plan to listen to the therapist and my neighbor take turns singing the phrase, "Everyone remembers my vomit," to different tunes. Yankee Doodle, You'll Be Back from Hamilton, Row Row Row Your Boat, and something operatic I recognize from old cartoons.

If all therapy is like this, I can understand why Paula didn't get much from it when she tried it twenty years ago. I take a break from my list to google "therapy singing about fear" and then "weird therapy techniques anxiety". I skim the results from a reliable medical website. The therapist is either doing "exposure with response prevention" or this thing is a sham.

Reading about treatment sends a sharp stab of guilt through me. Why do I listen? This is not what good people do.

I clean up my desk and listen to the neighbor's session wind down. They agree on homework: torture with a straw twice during the week and picking another item from her fear hierarchy. The neighbor agrees to compliment one stranger each day. She plans to jump start by taking a walk right away and complimenting the first stranger she sees after the session.

The first stranger?

I'm a stranger.

It wouldn't take *me* that long to run outside and be in the right place to meet the neighbor.

I'll be a nice stranger!

I can be the nicest fucking stranger she's ever met.

I can balance out the ledger a bit to make up for eavesdropping and entertaining myself with her worries.

I grab my parka and scarf and tie my combat boots with a double knot in case I need to run. I'm not sure why this becomes important, but I *need* to meet the neighbor and maybe help her.

This is what guilt does to you.

Halfway down the stairwell, I got a hit of inspiration. I run back up and untie my knotted boot laces. I try to run as quietly as possible through the apartment to my room to grab my sketchpad and pencil pouch, and head back out the door, down the stairs, and into the small courtyard. I look up and check Paula's bedroom window. The view from her desk is out into the courtyard, but I can't tell if she's sitting there due to the glare on the glass.

It's not until I tighten the cord around my hood that I realize I don't remember holding on to the railing at all. Gods, I'm lucky I didn't fall.

Unlike me, the neighbor doesn't rush to get to her therapy homework. I wait for a couple of minutes. Is she chickening out? Even though it's cold, my armpits are sweaty. I should have skipped the layer of long underwear today.

Alexi, our building manager, is scraping caulk on a window across the horseshoe courtyard. We wave hello to each other, and I'm grateful he's far enough away that he won't strike up a conversation and prevent me from seeming approachable to the neighbor. There's no way she would walk over to *two* people to give out compliments.

I check the time. I'll give her three more minutes and I'm going in.

My breath is back to normal after running around, and I'm more relaxed. I begin a sketch of a crocus bud peeking its way up and out of a rectangular planter box next to one of our courtyard's two benches. My shoulders lower and my pencil grip loosens as I focus on the plant. I'm up to adding texture and my hands are getting numb from the cold when she comes out of the door of her stairwell. Out of the corner of my eye, I see a figure leave the building. *Can you go a little faster, please? Some of us are getting frostbite.* I resist looking up at her, but I feel her getting closer.

People always peek over my shoulder to see what I'm drawing, even when it's just so-so. I correctly predicted this would help the neighbor with an opening.

After an excruciating long minute, I hear a tentative "Excuse me."

She's different from what I imagined. She's about my age, maybe younger, but tall. Like, actually tall, even though everyone looks big to me. Light brown hair escapes her hood in frizzy clumps, and the tip of her white nose is already pink from the cold. She has terrible posture and everything about her screams, "Look the other way! Nothing to see here!" The only exception is the large purple frames of her eyeglasses. Her voice is much higher than it is in her sessions, and she's scratching her wrist under her watch.

"Hi," I say, and feel sad and proud for her. In therapy, the neighbor had practiced compliments like "Nice hat," and "I like your shoes." Now she has forgotten the casual attitude she had studied and instead is acting far too formal.

"May I see what you're drawing? Oh! It's good!"

"Thanks. Do you draw?"

"Yeah. I mean, no. I do other stuff."

As we chat, her voice almost returns to its usual register. Her name's Lise, and she asks me to spell "Zillah" to make sure she heard me correctly. Lise's also in college, in an online program.

"Do you like it?" I ask.

"It's okay," she says and stares at me for a second, looks at the door to her stairwell, and then back at me as though just waiting for me to continue making conversation.

A little help, please? I think.

"Are you from here?" I try again.

"Indy. I mean Indianapolis." She pauses but then gets her conversational stamina going. "We just moved here in November."

"We?"

"My mom and my brother."

"I live with my mom, too."

I'm pulling every sentence from her. But I do the active listening thing of nodding and making eye contact. Inside I congratulate myself on being a decent human being.

I did a good thing.

If I believed in heaven, I'd be a bit more assured about my entry ticket.

The conversation picks up when she asks, "So what are you studying?" and is more natural until Lise's eyes dart to something behind me. I turn around and see Paula leaning against the screen in her opened window while she shouts to Alexi.

"Did you get my email about the electrical outlet in the laundry room? Alexi, I'm talking to you! I emailed you last night, and I *thought* residents were supposed to get responses within two hours for emergencies."

Alexi puts down his tools and walks with resignation toward Paula. I appreciate that he doesn't shout back. That would have just escalated things. He's a pro.

Paula continues her shouting with a brief, "Hello, Doll. Are you warm enough?" to me before she turns back to her target with recriminations about fire hazards and faulty wiring.

"My mom," I say to Lise as we heard the unmistakable threat of "—call your supervisor."

Lise nods and turns red in the face. Not a blush, but a cartoony I-just-ate-a-hot-pepper red.

"I should go," I say at the same time she jumps in with "How long have—"

She keeps talking while I put away my pencils "Oh! Yeah. Yeah. You should go. I mean, I'm not telling you what you should do. I mean—" She takes a breath and continues, "I think the cold made my brain pause."

"I totally get that. I'm like that when I'm hungry. See you soon?"

Lise stays while I walk back to our doorway, I guess to keep up the pretense that she was just coming out to enjoy the grey, mushy day. I hope she's not paying attention to whatever Paula's shouting now.

And that was that.

I almost made a new friend.

Are all moms this embarrassing? What would it be like to live in a place where no one knows her? Where I'm just "Zillah" and not "that Paula's daughter."

I've got to finish those internship applications. The sooner I can prove I'm ready, the sooner I can move out.

I leave the courtyard and walk into the small vestibule at the bottom of our stairwell, grateful for the strong door that dampens the sound of my mother's complaints.

Chapter Seven

After two weeks of recovery, I'm still pushing our lives back toward normal. On paper, things look good. Paula's ankle and brain are solid enough that she's able to go to the small medical clinic she manages in Rogers Park. She's worked there since I was in elementary school, so at least ten or something years.

She wasn't always in charge. She moved up the ranks from a part-time biller, then admin, then to full-time and then up to manager. She does well with details and is almost always diplomatic and able to deal with the difficult situations her bosses, the two married doctors who own the clinic, prefer to avoid. And they let her hire me for administrative tasks like record management checks. Other than kerfuffles around COVID protocols and sanitation, they've been awesome about Paula's quirkiness.

Fortunately, she can do what she needs to do with her arm in her cast. She's just slower.

And grouchier.

Her temper has a hair trigger these days. Paula treats me like the world's best daughter until I screw up. And then I'm in the doghouse. Today I didn't cause her bodily harm. I just invited her sister over for dinner next week. She acted like this was a betrayal, even though we have Bethany over maybe once a month or two.

"Of course I'd like to see Bethany, but the apartment is disgusting," she'd said while she gathered her things to go to work this morning. If the apartment is disgusting, I'm to blame since I've been doing all the housework. And I'm definitely to blame for that, since I'm the one who crippled Paula. I'll do a second pass at mopping the floors. If they aren't clean enough for Paula's inspection, she can kiss my bucket.

I'm grouchier, too.

I should get my iron levels checked. My anemia is a long-term problem that has unpleasant secondary effects. To counteract it, I take a crap-ton of iron. Iron causes constipation (yay), so to counteract the iron, I take a crap-ton of stool softener in order to actually have a ton of crap.

A benefit of my old homeschooling days was the close proximity to a familiar toilet. Nowadays, going to class and sticking around campus needs to be timed with any poop-inducing supplement.

My grouchiness could also be from less sleep. I've been setting my alarm ninety minutes earlier than usual to clean and organize. I'm low on sleep from the chores around the apartment, from driving Paula around town, from the extra errands (like when she needed a set of worry dolls from Guatemala like she had as a child), and from all the other crap on my Stabilize Paula Plan. Is this what it's like to have a baby?

At least my plan has worked. Her anxiety *is* better. She hasn't come up with any new safety routines for us, and she seems okay with going up and back to work instead of just teleworking here. And, until I invited Bethany over for dinner, she hadn't had a major freak-out.

I text Aunt B, "`Hey, can we postpone the dinner for a week or two?`"

I hope this all goes down in Scriven family lore as that Time Zillah Proved She Was Ready to Move Out.

Most important, I finished a draft cover letter for my internship application package. I don't have to turn everything in for another two weeks, but I don't want to take any risks on something this high stakes. I've got a good shot, and my materials seem solid. To celebrate, I allow myself to just goof off by looking at apartment listings and cheap furniture websites while I listen in on Lise's therapy and eat a peanut butter sandwich (smooth on the generic version of Wonder Bread) with carrot sticks on the side. It's the same thing I had for lunch, except I had crunchy peanut butter then. I like to switch things up. At least Eleanor, the nutritionist, will be happy to see vegetables on my menu twice today. Three times if

I have corn with dinner. She doesn't count potatoes unless they include skin. Unfair.

Lise's session begins the same as always, with the therapist asking about her homework. I grin goofily when Lise says, "I complimented five people aaaaand I met someone with friend potential!"

I didn't think of her as a potential friend since she was kind of boring when we met. But I guess boring-ness could have been a result of her being anxious. I can give her another chance if I run into her in the real world. It's not like I have a ton of other friends taking up my time. There's Cliff, of course. I get along with people in my classes, but we don't hang out. It would be interesting to have an actual *friend* friend, especially here in the building. Even if she is weird.

Guilt floods me as they start their next activity: repeating, "Everyone thinks I'm weird," about twenty times and then saying it in silly voices and accents.

I'm such a dick for judging her.

During the debrief, Lise says it helped.

How? How can this possibly help?

"It's not going to get rid of the thought, but next time it might not stick quite as much," the therapist says. They talk about practicing and I consider what *my* sticky thought would be. Maybe "I have to eat a banana," or "There are germs on my mouth," or "Adults have to tongue kiss."

Of those three, the kissing one is the worst. I'm okay with kisses on the cheek by family since I can rub them off with my shoulder when the kisser turns away. Paula sometimes gives me a kiss on the top of my head, but she's the cleanest person I've ever met, so no biggie.

The kissing issue felt normal when I was little. Watching grown-ups on TV kissing with tongue was disgusting, and it had been okay to shriek and turn my head. My friends and I used to make each other laugh by pretending to vomit or die in horrific ways if a kissing scene happened on screen. My friend Suzanne had been the best at this. It wasn't a big deal until the other girls experimented more with boys and with each other in middle school. Even Suzanne had said kissing was fun and that tongue was the best part.

Disgusting.

Disgusting and terrifying, since kissing was the gateway to the other fun stuff. You had to start at first base before you could do the other things.

I wasn't afraid of boys. Or girls, although I've never had a chance to try dating a girl or a nonbinary person. I'm lucky I found my life partner early.

I like the thought of someone's body up against mine, and hands on my breasts and my butt. It's just the tongue and mouth aspect that shuts down my fantasies.

When Cliff and I were still just friends, I remember one flirtatious conversation we had at the Lincoln Park Zoo. We were sitting on a bench watching the human primates. I had brought my knees under my chin and was trying to get close enough to him to show my interest and far enough away to keep from breathing his cigarette smoke.

We had a couple of minutes for him to smoke until we risked scolding by a park employee. So, he'd huffed down the cigarette while I admired his rebel look. Fourteen-year-olds are idiots for sixteen-year-olds.

I tried to think of an adult and sexy topic of conversation.

"Do you think the macaques have their own version of the bases?" I asked.

"What?" Cliff had finished his cigarette, rubbed the butt on the bottom of his sneaker, and tossed it in the trash. We walked in a random direction, going where the crowd wasn't.

"Like, do they start with kissing, then feeling up, then down, then sex?"

"They just go for it." He'd put his hand on my shoulder to guide me back as a group of tourists had come by. I loved this feeling. I don't know if it was just because it was a guy touching me, or because I was being protected against the roving horde.

"Yeah, and they don't kiss, anyway," I said. I had thought about this often.

"Good point."

"Could you get together with a girl who just wanted to skip right to second base?" The bravest question I'd ever asked.

It had worked, though. Cliff was up for the challenge.

We did *talk* about tongue kissing, but Cliff had been patient. After six months or so, we agreed on dry pecks on the lips that I wouldn't wipe off (until he was out of sight). That had felt like a huge step toward real adult intimacy, even though we'd already had sex at that point. Sex had been much easier to negotiate since condoms were involved and it didn't take long. Plus, it reduced the pressure on the kissing issue and other mouth stuff.

So, in the here and now, while I sit safely at my desk, listening to Lise and her therapist talk about schedules, I consider the thought.

Adults have to tongue kiss.

I repeat it silently, my mouth moving along with the words.

Adults have to tongue kiss. Adults have to tongue kiss.

I think about the time Cliff had tried to surprise me with a real, open-mouthed kiss. He held my head in a way he thought was romantic, but when he put his tongue in my mouth, all I could think was, "I can't get away." I remember his rough goatee and stale cigarette smell. My throat was filled and I knew I would never breathe again. He only tried this once, but then, like now, my gag reflex kicked in.

Adults have to tongue kiss. Adults have to tongue kiss.

This is not working. My ears pound, and I'm lightheaded. My guts feel green and rancid, and those half-digested bites of peanut butter sandwich feel like rocks in my stomach.

I rush to the bathroom and slam the door. I lean over the toilet, but nothing happens. My stomach seizes, but no vomit.

"Zillah? Are you okay?" Paula calls from her room.

"I'm okay," I say, my voice shaky like I'm on a wobbling funhouse floor.

I almost go to her for comfort like I had when I was little. I want to complain to her. I want to hand her my worries and say, "I'm going to throw up. I'm scared."

She would let me sit on her lap and tell me, "I've got you." She would rock me and repeat, "You're safe. You're safe. You're safe."

But I would also be a few steps backwards in proving what an adult I am.

I feel grimly superior for trying to comfort myself.

Eventually my stomach unclenches, and I feel like erased pencil.

I check my face in the mirror.

My mascara is everywhere. I don't even remember crying. I wash up. Does this ever happen to Lise during therapy? It's kind of amazing that someone so scared does this weekly. By choice. I can respect that.

I re-apply everything. This second coat of mascara is symbolic. It shows I'm confident that I'm done crying for the day. Maybe forever.

Chapter Eight

Sometimes I'm so empty that nothing can fill me up. It's an appetite that's different from my usual hunger. It's a void. A bottomless pit inside me.

This is when I turn to weird combinations. With ten different foods in my diet, along with a few additional sugary things we don't count, there are a large but limited amount of permutations.

Today I wait until after Paula goes to work to make one of my favorite bizarre snacks since it grosses her out: rice with corn and minced apple and smashed up potato chips on top for crunch.

From constraint comes creativity.

It's okay, but it doesn't ease the topsy-turvy neediness inside.

I'm glad Paula gets to branch out with other food when she's at work.

The snack takes a while to prep, but I don't have any classes until this afternoon. I'm excited to relax. I should finalize my internship applications, finish a metrics report for the clinic, and start a paper I'm avoiding, but I've earned time to draw and binge shows.

I flip through the movies and shows that my algorithm suggests while I eat my unique risotto.

I wish we had Ritz crackers.

I imagine the mouthfeel. Crunchy, but not too salty. Almost sweet.

Now it's all I can think about.

New plan: I'll walk to Safeway, get crackers, and then have an amazing cracker and Netflix party.

That will cure what ails me.

I'm stymied in my shopping adventure when I see Lise on the sidewalk outside our apartment's outer gate. With one hand, she's holding a large black dog by the collar while scrolling on her phone with the other. I'm no fan of dogs, but I have to walk near her to get out. As I get closer, I realize she isn't holding a dog collar. The dog is wearing a flowered orange purse, and she's holding the strap.

I try to make sense of what I see when she notices me.

"Zillah, right? Can you help me?" I go over, and Lise explains that she found the dog without a collar or tag. She's going to take it to the vet to get its microchip scanned if no frantic owner comes back soon. Her purse is the closest thing Lise had to a leash, "But look, he's not running away! I think he likes me. He's such a good boy!"

"It looks nice in your purse."

Lise is different now. She's talking in complete sentences and not afraid of the large dog despite all the teeth. She even pets it and *ohmygod, did that dog just lick her with its actual dog tongue near her mouth?* Lise laughs and coos nice things again while she strains her neck to look around for an owner.

"You stay here with it," I say. "I'll go down the block and see if anyone's searching for a wild beast."

I walk around the block to Broadway and don't find anyone frenzied. I even ask in a few stores that might appeal to dog-people (the bike store, the rustic cafe that specializes in pour overs, my favorite consignment shop) but I don't get any leads. By the time I get back, Lise and her furry friend look calm.

"Just a sec," she says while texting.

I get a better look at the dog. It's all black and smaller than I first thought. Bigger than a cat. It could fit under a laundry basket, but just barely.

"Okay," Lise says. "There's a vet four blocks away that will scan him for us." She's bright with energy and then catches herself. "Are you in a rush? I'm so sorry. I trapped you." Redness creeps up her neck. "You can go if you want."

I would love to go on my way. The dog is filthy, and it has that short dog hair that looks like a buzz cut slicked down. The kind of dog hair that gets everywhere. Paula would insist I strip upon re-entry.

That said, my craving for Ritz crackers has subsided and here's the opportunity to do another good deed. I think of the phrase "friend potential" and I feel a jittery warmth. I say, "Yeah, let's go."

Lise looks relieved once she realizes I'm up for dog rescue shenanigans. We start at her apartment to find a leash.

"We always had dogs until we moved here," she says and holds the door open for me. "Oh, you can keep your boots on. Will you hold this guy and my purse? We have a leash and collar someplace." She gets on her hands and knees, and roots through a bin in her front closet.

Lise's apartment has the same general layout as ours, but backwards, and hers has an additional bedroom. It's disorienting because of the reverse layout and because the entryway looks like a crime scene from a craft store robbery gone wrong. Several dozen empty mason jars line the hall; a cardboard box full of tissue paper, feathers, and assorted stationery; and a few reusable grocery bags filled with wrapped snack cakes and crackers. No Ritz. "We're doing a project," she says as though that explains everything.

"Let's check the utility space." The dog and I follow her. "Our old pupper died, but during the pandemic it was hard to find any dogs that needed homes, so we've just been waiting for supply and demand to switch."

After searching for a couple minutes more, she raids her brother's room and comes back triumphantly. "Belts!" She fashions one into a collar by doubling it around the dog's neck and threads the buckle of the second to be a leash. "Perfect is the enemy of good, right?" Sounds like something her therapist says.

"Wait, let me get a picture for my mom before we go," Lise says, posing me and the dog. "I'll send it to my brother, too, and caption it, 'Found a man who could do your belt justice'. Too much?"

"I've never had a brother, so—"

"He'd kill me if I took his stuff without asking, but maybe not if it's for a dog."

It's windy outside, but we walk north on Broadway and so we're protected from the cold by the buildings except when crossing the road. Our Lakeview neighborhood is mostly residential, with stores on the ground level of buildings that line the busier streets. Our horseshoe apartment building is tucked in a side street between Broadway and Sheridan, so we get the benefit of being close to the bus routes, but also the park.

Once we're on the way, Lise gets quiet except for occasional mutters to the dog of "It's okay" and "There you go" as we pass pedestrians.

A dad and kid approach us after they have a quick conference. The kid is bundled up with a scarf wrapped around their face, and their hood pulled tight to keep it in place.

"Can I pet your dog?" the kid asks, taking off a glove.

I expect Lise to get flustered, but she gets down next to the dog, so she's at eye level with the child.

"I'm sorry, but I'm just watching this dog, and I don't know if he's safe with kids," she says. The dog sits on the sidewalk and looks at each speaker like it's a spellbinding play.

"Come on, Anderson," the dad says. The dog watches them go and then trots alongside Lise again.

"What do we do if there's no microchip?"

"We can ask at the vet. They deal with this all the time." She stops to wipe her glasses on her scarf. "I don't know if the shelters here are no-kill." Her tone changes when she addresses the dog. "We can't risk that, can we? You with your beautiful black coat! Maybe he'll just stay with me while I look for his family." Lise's more comfortable with this slobbering hellhound than with me.

I ask, "What if it has a disease communicable to humans?"

"No use bleeding until I've been cut." I know with one hundred percent certainty that *this* saying was from therapy. It's one of those things the therapist said a while back that had made no sense. If you could do things to prevent being cut, wouldn't you? Or wouldn't you want to plan how you'd care for the wound so you can have all the right stuff around?

I wonder about Lise's family. "Don't you live with your mom? Isn't she going to freak out?" The plan to keep the dog sounds childish, like hearing a kid decide to dig a swimming pool in their garden patch.

"She'll have fun until we find the owner. Look—" She shows me her phone, with several texts. All of them are from her mom in response to the dog's picture.

```
I'm in love!
Don't name him! You'll get attached.
But just in case, what about Reggie?
Scout?
Noah! Too human?
Let's ask Ben for ideas.
Ben Junior?
```

At the vet, Lise takes small steps toward the front desk like an invisible hand is pushing her. I help explain what we need, and it doesn't take long for a vet tech to scan the dog with a little machine like at the grocery self-checkout.

No microchip.

It takes less than a week for Lise's family to adopt the dog and name him Halsted.

Chapter Nine

"Do you have time to hang out before we go to UIC?" I text Cliff on the next Friday. Fridays are a magical day when the timing works well for me to use Paula's car to drop him off at work before I go to class. He can return the favor once he has his suspended license back. I usually take public transportation since we're so close to the bus lines and multiple elevated trains, but while Paula's out of commission with her ankle, I can use her car as much as I want.

I'm spending extra time with him to make up for being a raging badger since Paula's fall. When I'm stressed, Cliff is extra irritating. Everything he says annoys me, and we keep getting into little stupid fights like when he tried to convince me that sharks are immortal ("You never hear about a dead shark, right?") or when he claimed he gave me the design idea I used on a recent flyer for his roommate Rik's band.

But he tries so hard.

We spent one afternoon this week watching old British comedies with his roommates. And then yesterday he surprised me with a new journal. It's double-sided with a daytime illustration on one cover and a nighttime illustration upside-down on the back so I can flip the journal over for two kinds of entries. Plus, it has two long ribbons for keeping my spot and gilt decoration along the edges of the paper.

I'm using the daytime part of the journal to write about positive things like ideas for our future apartment and places I'd like to travel to within an hour from home (safe come-back-to-poop distance). I'm also keeping a list of times I've successfully sat near other people while they ate disgusting things. The nighttime part is for writing about daily frustrations and all the things I'd like to say but can't to Paula, Cliff, my dad, and the universe. The nighttime part is filling up much faster.

Last night I wrote in it instead of eavesdropping on Lise's therapy, so that's one huge achievement.

I walk up the steps to Cliff's converted 1900s Logan Square house, where Cliff and a few friends rent the first floor. I have a spare key (handy for helping Cliff and the other boys when one gets locked out), but the front door's ajar. I feel a stab of rage for their carelessness. Anyone could have just walked right in. My apartment building has three layers of security. And even if one of our neighbors is an ax-wielding homicidal maniac, they still have to get through our deadbolt. I reassure myself that the peeling white paint on Cliff's porch, along with the carcass of an ancient potted plant supporting an empty Goose Island beer bottle, would deter thieves.

Once I'm a real estate appraiser, I can own a house like this and keep it nice.

"Make sure your door latches when you close it!" I shout to whoever is around. I hear a muffled "Thanks Mom," from a roommate. Neil or Rik. I can't tell them apart.

I poke my head in Cliff's room, but he's not there. Five or six coins are scattered on his bed, along with dirty tissues, and a sock. I put the coins in a little pile for him on his desk. I move my sleeve over my hand so I don't have to touch the other stuff and push it to his floor. I adjust his blanket and give it a quick sniff that verifies he needs a laundry day. I take his pad of sticky notes, draw a couple of cute cartoony whales with a heart between them, and stick it on his pillow.

When we were first becoming friends, I couldn't believe I'd found a boy almost as neat and clean as me. Cliff's messiness was an unpleasant revelation when he went to college and no longer lived in his parents' house and had a cleaning crew.

In the living room, two roommates are eating snacks and looking at their phones on mismatched couches. Jerzei is the one I know best because he works with Cliff. The other is the Neil-or-Rik one. I nod my head toward the bathroom and ask, "That Cliff in there?"

"I think so," Jerzei says, and offers me a Starburst.

"No, thanks." I pick up a few things off their floor (an empty chip bag, two cigarette butts, cellophane wrapping from something), make a trip to the trash can, and scrub my hands at their kitchen sink while I try not to look at the mess in there.

Cliff is still occupied, so I empty their ashtray and organize their coffee table. Two remotes, rolling paper, a water bottle, USB-C cord, Don DeLillo's *Libra*, a Nintendo Switch controller, an adjustable wrench, a scrunchie.

When Cliff emerges, I can see he's put in extra effort today. He's pulled his long hair into a tight ponytail, trimmed his goatee, and even waxed his mustache. I like Cliff's looks, but he's self-conscious about his peaked eyebrows and his pockmarked skin from severe acne during his teen years. I didn't even notice his skin until he pointed it out to me. I wish he wouldn't obsess so much. He's good looking enough. But sometimes I wonder if his low self-image helps keep him tied to me. When he says things like "you're the only girl who'd like this face" I wonder how much he's with me just for the security of *having* a girlfriend and not needing to *find* a girlfriend.

Cliff gives me a kiss on the top of my head and asks Jerzei for a Starburst. He gets a red one and announces, "Zillah's never eaten a strawberry."

I try and fail to communicate "Shut it!" with a fierce look. Cliff sits on the edge of a recliner and unwraps his strawberry-flavored candy. He only has to wait a moment for his roommates' reactions.

"What?"

"How? How do you get to your twenties without eating a strawberry?"

Cliff turns to me and raises an eyebrow.

"We should get going," I say.

"We got time." Cliff relaxes into his chair and follows up with a crowd pleaser. "Actually, she's never eaten *any* berries."

The reactions are loud, and Cliff holds court. He takes questions from his roommates (another, Mike, joins the group after hearing the kerfuffle).

"Not even a blueberry? Is she allergic?"

"Nope."

"No raspberries? Blackberries? Not even one?"

"Nuh uh."

I don't need to hear this, and my stomach and throat feel coated in chalk. I hate knowing people are talking about me. I get up and go to the bathroom. It's disgusting in there, so I head back to the main room and hope they've gone back to their phones.

When I reappear, Jerzei turns the conversation back to me. "Zillah, you have to try blueberry pancakes." Heads pivot to me. "Or just a ripe blueberry. I'll pick you a perfect one!"

"Maybe," I say.

Neil-or-Rik asks, "Is that why you're so short?" All eyes are on me, evaluating whether my stature resulted from genetics or malnutrition. Their faces are evaluative rather than unkind. Like the face one would make when trying to guess the number of hairs stuck on a brush.

Thanks, Cliff.

"See you in the car," I say and stomp to the door.

Cliff joins me a minute later. He climbs into the passenger seat with a grunt as he bangs his knee on the glove compartment. He adjusts the seat backwards to man-distance for his long legs.

"You mad at me?" he asks.

"Yup."

He slides his hands in between his seat and the console, feeling for my charging cord. This just makes me angrier. Maybe *I* want to charge my phone.

"It's in the glove compartment," I say.

He plugs in the charger, and we drive in silence while I replay the incident in my head. I try to come up with the right words to help him understand.

"I don't like to talk about the food stuff," is the best I come up with.

"It's interesting," Cliff says.

"It feels like you're making fun of me. Like I'm an exhibit."

"No, Z. I love you how you are. You don't ever have to eat anything you don't want to. When we live together, you're going to be so comfortable. We're going to have the best place."

"Yeah. Just—" I'm not sure of my exact complaint. "Just don't brag about how weird I am, okay?"

"Have you talked to your mom about moving out?" He puts his hand on my leg. It's distracting and doesn't feel good while I'm pissed, but I don't say anything.

"Yeah, but she acts so nervous when I bring it up. I can't get her to commit to a specific date. Want to come over tonight for dinner and the three of us talk? I can pick you up after your shift. You're her favorite." We kiss goodbye and he gives me a quick shoulder squeeze before he leaves.

I wait for traffic to clear so I can pull out and think about tonight. If Cliff is there, the conversation will go smoother. Paula is thrilled that I'll be part of his family someday, with their big house, prestigious jobs, and actual social skills. It's like she wants to release me into their care, so I don't flounder on my own.

Infantilizing, yes. But I can use it.

Moving in with Cliff will be hard for Paula, but good for us as a couple. I love the thought of moving out and living like a real adult. I want to decorate my own home. This is the next natural progression toward a happily ever after.

And in a few years, once I have money coming in from a job as an appraiser, I can hire a housecleaner. Maybe I could hire one for Paula, too, since I won't be able to do my share of the chores at home.

She'll adjust. She knows how to go to YouTube to learn new things. And it's not like we're moving out of the city. She'll always have me. And Bethany and Cliff, too. Maybe without me to talk to, she'll work on making friends.

Or maybe she'll flounder. While I drive to the parking garage on Harrison, I envision the worst case scenarios. Paula crying by herself over breakfast. Paula refusing to speak to me. Paula hiding in fear under her blankets.

A panicked magenta floods through me and I sweat and breathe fast. I rub at my eyebrows and temples trying to make these images disappear.

"It's gonna be fine," I tell myself out loud. Then I try it really fast. "It'sgonnabefine. It'sgonnabefine. It'sgonnabefine. It'sgonnabefine."

My face is burning with the tears I'm trying to hold back. "Chill the fuck out, Zillah," I command. I need to calm down and get to class. I turn my music up and count my breaths. I get to seven and feel more like a functioning grown-up human.

Good enough for today, but how the hell am I going to move out if I'm worried about Paula surviving on her own?

"Do you want to stay at home forever? Are you going to back out?" the argumentative side of my brain asks.

No, I respond to myself and grab my parka and backpack from the back seat. This is the right thing to do for all of us. It's time. We'll talk at dinner and I'll feel better once I see Paula's response.

Chapter Ten

Today I have my favorite class for this semester, User-Centered Design. It's bittersweet, though. I've been able to take courses from the graphic design curriculum to meet some of my elective graduation requirements, but after this semester I need to be all business about business. Dr. Underwood asks me and another student if we're applying for the Fox fellowship, a summer Usability and Design bootcamp on campus, and it hurts to say no. I can justify taking a few design courses and playing with the software in my free time, but it's not a career that makes sense and I need to let it go.

I'll feel better once I'm into the fun parts of appraisal. Like when I get an internship and get to work hand-in-hand with professionals. Aunt Bethany says that if I find myself on a team with kind people who are excited about appraisal, I'll have a good time.

After class, I sit in Paula's car to do my call with Eleanor the nutritionist. We discuss my latest tracked meals (she's not pleased) and I learn my next assignment: Decide on one new food to integrate into my diet.

After I catch my breath, I tell her, "I'm not going to do that."

"Zillah, you're doing great so far with tracking the baseline. Let's just set one small goal, okay? What's a simple food you might enjoy? I'm thinking pears."

I can't even touch Yuck Food. And she wants me to put some of it in my mouth? I say, "Eleanor, um, can you just send me some links to read or something? Like a podcast I can listen to?"

She's silent for a bit and then, "Zillah, don't you want to eat more food?"

"No. I really, *really* don't. You said yourself I get enough calories."

"A healthy meal plan is more than calories. You don't have regular periods. Your iron is still low. Your bowel movements–"

"I think I'm pretty okay as I am."

More silence. "You can get in touch with me if you ever change your mind, okay Zillah?"

"Thanks, Eleanor." As far as break-ups go, it was a pretty nice one.

Afterwards, I try to work in the library until Cliff's shift ends. Normally, I'm calm like freshly sharpened colored pencils while I'm there. I love the UIC library and all the hidden desks up in the stacks. But today I'm irritable and jumpy.

I text Cliff when I'm outside Technology Services and I don't have to wait long. I also don't have to worry about making conversation since Cliff is upset about system updates at work and talks about it the whole way home. I concentrate on the road and imitate active listening until he asks, "Can we go out instead of eating at your place?"

He *has* been eating at our place a lot, and I guess there's only so much peanut butter and chicken he can take. I give him credit, though. Cliff is patient with my food restrictions. I hope he takes it well when I tell him I dumped his pear-loving cousin.

We brainstorm places Paula might also be willing to go. It has to have our food, of course, but Paula will only eat at a place with seats that can be thoroughly sanitized. In other words, no fabric upholstery.

I haven't been hungry all day, and nothing sounds that great. I feel that churning sensation that means I haven't eaten enough, but the thought of actual food sounds terrible until he suggests Clarks on Belmont. I picture their waffles and suddenly I'm starving.

"Clarks is perfect," I say. "I've got a waffle deficiency." My appetite is back with a vengeance. "Will you look in my backpack for a granola bar?"

"No, don't eat before we go out," he says, but he looks anyway. Hangry Zillah isn't delightful. "Nothing."

"Can you text my mom and see if she's up for going right away? We can pick her up from her clinic and save time."

When Paula joins us outside her office, she refuses Cliff's offer to give her shotgun. "No thank you, Cliffy," she says as she gets in the back seat and buckles in. "But you are *such* a gentleman for thinking of it. So like your father. How is your mom? Oh! Speaking of which, I meant to call her to warn her about those dishwasher pods she insists on using. I'm almost positive that those are the ones with the microplastics that can clog up the garbage disposal. Cliff, does she still use those blue and white ones or has she switched to some other fad?"

Cliff admits he has no idea what kind of dishwasher pods his family uses. "And I think Dad orders all the cleaning stuff."

This curveball stumps Paula but doesn't silence her for long.

"And while we're on the topic," she continues inaccurately, "thank you so much for coming with us to dinner! It's a delight to be with both of you children. A delight!"

We find parking close to Clark's. Paula and I love this place because of their waffles and amazing hash browns—two foods we have never recreated at home with satisfaction despite trying several varieties of frozen imitations. Plus, the menus have become an inside joke with their "Oh my, you should eat!" graphic. Paula loves to say this when she's in a silly mood.

We get a table without waiting too long. The host seats us next to a man and woman who might be in their seventies. They're sharing a newspaper, with her working on a crossword puzzle and he reading the comics.

We look over our menus while I eavesdrop on the couple.

"This is you. Read this," he insists, shifting his section of the paper over hers.

She reads the comic, chuckles, and says, "You ingrate."

He laughs and pulls the paper back while she asks him for help with a crossword clue ("What's a six-letter word for a thin lotion?").

We all order, and I can't avoid the reason for this cabal any longer.

"Mom, Cliff and I are going to look for apartments pretty soon."

"I know, I know. It's all you talk about," she says without making eye contact. She unfolds her napkin and adjusts it several times. "Cliff, do you like bacon better than sausage? I've never noticed you ordering bacon before. Isn't that something?"

"Mom, I want to make sure the timing works for you to feel comfortable, and you change the subject every time I bring it up."

Cliff looks around the restaurant, perhaps plotting his escape from us Scriven women.

"You want to talk about it? Fine. It's too soon. We're not ready."

"Mom, you'll be fine. We can—"

"I know I'll be fine," Paula snaps at me. "I've lived on my own before. But is Cliff ready to take care of you and your special needs?" She uses her fork to point at Cliff. "It's a lot, Cliffy. Are you ready for this?"

"What do you mean?" I ask. "The food?"

"Yes, Zillah. Of course, the food."

"Paula," Cliff breaks in, "I know what it takes."

"You guys. The food isn't that big of a deal," I say.

"It's a huge commitment, Cliffy, and you're a young man."

"I understand, Paula."

"This is bullshit," I say. Apparently, I'm loud, because even the elderly couple look up from their conversation. I return my voice socially-appropriately-low. "Mom, is there a reason you don't want me to move out? Is there something else that's making you—" I want to say, "an asshole about this," but I settle for, "hesitant about this?"

She takes her time answering, so she's trying to be diplomatic. "Zillah, you've never been on your own without me there to help you. I trust Cliffy. But what if it's too much and you break up or need to move out, and then where will we be?"

"Cliff isn't Dad," I say.

But, I'm not a part of this conversation anymore. The two of them discuss how best to manage me and my deficits. I interrupt again.

"You're treating me like a kid."

"Well, you're acting like a child right now, aren't you?" she asks. "Zillah, please go to the restroom and compose yourself, and we can discuss more after dinner. This is unfair to the other diners."

I embrace my childish side as I huff, push back my chair, and stomp my way to the bathroom. Once there, I regret leaving my phone at the table. I don't want to be alone with my thoughts.

I look in the mirror and give myself a quick pep talk. *This is just Paula's trauma about Dad. Just because Dad left us doesn't mean Cliff will.*

Dad's never been shy about the fact that he couldn't stand the safety protocols we follow. My food situation probably caused a lot of tension, too.

"I don't know how you do it, Zillah," he said when he stayed with us a few years before the pandemic, sleeping on the couch to save money. He'd sat next to me at the kitchen table, watched me eat a peanut butter sandwich and carrot sticks and said, "Eating the same thing day after day after day."

I remember holding back my tears and feeling swamped with guilt. "Yeah. I get it."

"You do get it, right, Z?" He'd put his giant dad-hand on my shoulder. "The food, and the cleaning, and the rules." He got up and looked in the fridge as if expecting new ingredients to have magically appeared. None had, so he came back and sat with me again. "If you ever get tired of this, you could join me after you graduate high school. I'd get a bigger apartment, and I'd have a spare room for you. I'd find other work so I could stay put."

Dad moves around a lot, opening new locations of a major chain of convenience stores. He rarely lives in the same place for over six months at a time.

We get along, and I like being with him when he comes to town. I'm fine with the fact that he's not part of my life because that's too big a wound to dress. Much better to just cover it with Band-Aids and be grateful for what I *do* have.

I have Paula and I have Cliff.

Cliff knows what he's getting into, and I don't do all the crap with safety rituals like Paula does. Not *nearly* as much. Cliff would never decide I'm too much trouble. He gets me. He even forgave me for ditching his cousin Eleanor.

Anyway, Cliff needs me as much as I need him. I help him stay organized and on time. He can talk to me about feelings. I make him feel handsome and sexy. We joke that we're ruined for other partners. That's just what happens when you find your partner when you're a teen. We've forgotten what it's like to try to impress someone.

I take deep breaths and wash my hands. Before I dry them, I trace a little design and a sad face on the mirror with my wet pinky nail. My version of tagging.

Gods, I'm hungry. I shouldn't have started the conversation on an empty stomach. When's the last time I ate?

I return to our table just as our server delivers our meals. Cliff's looks like art. Colorful and fresh.

Paula and my plates of hash browns and plain waffles ("No butter, no syrup, and no garnish, please.") look dull. Like a stage prop of food made of cardboard or papier mâché.

I lean close to Cliff and stare at his fruit salad.

I can sometimes distract and calm myself by looking at pretty colors. There are five, no *six* types of fruit in there. What is it like to order without wondering if there is anything gross in it? The colors are so vibrant. Especially the strawberries. They're small and pretty like in pictures even though it's early spring and so surely these came from Mexico or California.

I use my fork to stab a strawberry from Cliff's plate so I can inspect it from close up. He looks at me with eyes wide and says, "You can have it."

I look at the strawberry close up. Eleanor, my ex-nutritionist, would cheer me on if she were here.

"Zillah," Paula says so loudly that the old couple turn to look again. "Don't eat that. It's a Yuck Food!"

"I'm just looking." The seeds are so orderly.

I run my index finger along the side of the strawberry. I can't feel the seeds. Interesting. I assumed it would feel rough and bumpy. I sniff the berry and get a faint reminder of my Strawberry Shortcake doll, but I can't smell much over the other scents at the table.

Hell yeah. I just touched and smelled a strawberry!

It's a small thing, but I'm proud of myself. I'm about to put it down when Paula's scolding gets more frantic.

"You give that back to Cliff. We can't eat that." Her voice is screechy with a panic I don't understand. Why can't she just say, "You can do it. Try it!"

Sometimes you need to be your own mother.

I consider licking the outside of the berry. I have a napkin, just in case I need to spit or vomit. There's a pounding in my chest and the other usual warning signs that panic is approaching. But that could be because of Paula's screeching.

I embrace my inner mom again. What do I have to lose? I could put it in my mouth and spit it out. I can drink water to wash out the taste.

I think about Lise working so hard. What am I afraid of? The discomfort of having something slimy and foul in my mouth?

"Put that down and we can hear about Cliffy and that system he's installing on the school computers," Paula urges.

Cliff uses his fork to spear a strawberry, too. "Wanna do it at the same time?" He uses a soft voice, like I'm a scared horse he's trying to coax. "Want to watch me eat one first?"

Paula pushes her chair back and stands up, leaning over the table as though she's going to grab my fork.

I want to pop it into my mouth and surprise her.

But I look at it again and see it ooze like a wound where the fork has pierced it. It looks ready to burst open and spill its innards and I don't want that mess in my mouth.

I put the fork down.

I imagine the slippery spatter and viscera in my mouth. Invading my throat. Choking me. Leaving a taste I won't be able to get rid of. My head is pounding and I'm seeing red. My stomach tightens like I've drunk from a cup of dirty paintbrush water. It flows through me, turning me to brackish yuck.

Paula's scolding breaks through. "Zillah, how will you eat with coworkers if you look like you're going to vomit all the time? For goodness' sake! And you claim you're ready to move out!"

This time I remember to bring my phone before I flee to the respite of the toilet.

Chapter Eleven

I was in a rage last night after we got home from dinner, and it's still simmering. I'm mad at Paula for being right about me acting like a child, but I'm even more furious at myself for not being able to approximate adulthood. That's the worst kind of anger — when you can't even blame someone else because it's all your fault.

I start the same chapter about income tax four times without any information sticking. Instead, my brain keeps trying to puzzle out a solution to the big question: how do I convince Paula I'm ready to leave? If she never agrees, would I have to sue her in small claims court for the money since Dad meant it for me?

Fuck it.

Without realizing I've picked up my phone, I'm watching video clips to dull my thoughts. Nope, nope, nope.

I text Cliff instead. "Hey what's your day like so far?" and then "Mine sucks."

These remain unread, so I'm not getting immediate gratification. But now that I'm expressing myself, I can't stop.

"I keep replaying dinner last night over and over in my head."

"Wasn't she so weird?"

"What's the weirdest thing your mom has ever done?"

I send a few more until I see that he's finally reading my messages. Cliff responds, "I'm working. Sorry. Talk later. Use your journal?"

Around mid-morning, I move to the couch. I swear I'll finally be productive. But first I watch updates from a comedian I like. This will motivate and inspire me, for sure. Twenty minutes in, I'm still on social media.

Until I get a text from Lise, `"I'm at your stairs. Can you come down?"`

Distraction? Yes, please. I text back a thumbs up.

"Hey," I say when I open the door. "Come on up."

"Hi." Her voice is high-pitched and squeaky. I guess she needs to warm up to me again. "This is from my family." She hands me a pie tin, heavy with something warm. It will go right in the food waste bin, but she doesn't need to know that.

"Thanks." We go inside. I show her where to take off shoes, show her the hand sanitization station, and I put the pie on the counter.

"Want to come over and say 'Hi' to Halsted?" she asks hesitantly.

"Now?"

"You don't have to."

"No, it's good timing." Better than trying to scroll to the end of the internet.

Lise's home is cleaner this time and I get a look around. Her family has a selection of abstract paintings on the walls that scream Ikea. Mass-produced, but colorful. They work together.

Am I just casually hanging out with the neighbor I spy on?

"Is this Zillah? Hello, hello!"

"This is my mom, Vivian."

Vivian is tall like Lise, with the same air-dried frizzy hair, just grey instead of light brown. She's stuffed into two different telecommuting looks: navy cardigan straining at the buttons, cream blouse, and chunky statement necklace on top with striped leggings and colorful running shoes on the bottom. It's a chaotic and comfortable look. "It's so nice to meet you! Thank you for helping our little guy."

"I was just there to witness the drama."

"Ben!" Vivian shouts toward the back. "Let Halsted come out and see Zillah!"

I hear a man call, "Give us a minute."

A moment later, a hallway door opens and Halsted comes over to us, wearing and tripping over a pink skirt.

"Ben, he's going to hurt himself!" Lise shrieks and tries to capture him.

This family is so loud.

Vivian says, "My, don't you look lovely today, Halsted! Is there something different about you?" She and Lise give him pets.

It's so ridiculous that I don't feel too threatened when he comes over to sniff me. I just hold still in case he's forgotten me. I even touch him on the head, but he licks my hand. I'm happy to notice that I don't get scared of the germs. Just grossed out.

"Sorry. He licks," Lise says.

"Yes, you do! You are a lickety-loo, aren't you?" Vivian coos. Then, "Zillah, you're so tiny I want to carry you around!"

Vivian takes Halsted to "help" her fold laundry.

The brother comes out of the bedroom from where Halsted made his entrance.

I recognize him. He's that satchel dude who wanted to help or judge or something the day Paula fell.

So *that's* Ben. It's hard to reconcile this guy with the protective brother Lise sometimes talks about in her therapy sessions.

He gives me a nod. Is he just a quiet guy or is this his minimal acknowledgment that I exist?

I rub my hand on my jeans and look around for a place to wash.

Ben moves to the kitchen counter and gathers things from the refrigerator. He tosses a dishtowel over his shoulder, presumably to protect his clothes while cooking, even though he's wearing a well-worn t-shirt advertising the merits of roller derby. I pass by him to wash my slobber hand in the kitchen sink.

"Will I be in your way if I just wash for a sec?"

"You're not in my way." Most of his sandy hair is short, but the top bits (do boys also call them bangs?) are a little longer and seem to irritate him by the way they flop in his eyes. I appreciate the way he uses his upper arm to shift them off his forehead instead of his hands. Less chance of hair in the food. Also, less successful at clearing vision. "Can you hand me that hat?" He motions to a blue baseball cap on the counter.

I hand it over and Lise sits on a stool while she watches us interact like we're live theater.

Ben pauses his work, eyes me, then gets back to work. He says, "You look very Anglo for someone named Zillah."

"Oh my god, Ben. You're 27. Learn some manners," Lise admonishes. Then, under her breath, "Family is the worst."

I sit next to her. "It's a protective name," I say. "It means shade." I toy with my evil eye necklace. "I'm generic white American, but my mom goes all in on cultural appropriation if she thinks it might bring good luck."

"Interesting strategy," he says and goes back to prepping vegetables.

I have a theory that handsome men get away with having terrible social skills.

From the rear of the apartment, Vivian shouts, "Call Halsted!" Her tone is like a delighted child.

Lise calls, "Halsted! Come here, baby!"

Halsted ambles over. The skirt is gone and instead he is wearing men's boxer shorts. They're backwards, with his tail through the crotch hole like a furry boner.

"That's a good look," Lise says. She lays down right there on the floor and snuggles the dog.

I ask, "Are you always so brave with animals?"

"Unless they're humans. Then she's—" Ben starts and fades without finishing his thought.

If this were a sitcom, there would be a record scratch.

Lise's face is red, and she turns her head away from me.

Ben should pretend nothing odd had happened so it could blow over. Instead, he apologizes, which makes it worse.

Dumbass.

"Shit. Sorry." He wipes his hands on a dishtowel and comes over to Lise. "You can't bring over a girl and not expect me to be an idiot."

I grab a box of tissues from a bookshelf and hand it to her. It must have been so hard for her to invite me over and I keep hearing that term, "friend potential."

"Let's go back to my place," I say and instantly regret. I don't feel like hanging out anymore. This is a pity invite. But it's too late now. "I'll show you what I did with that crocus drawing."

Ben shoots me a warm smile that reaches his eyes and he seems so much more human. I feel like he's going to say something, but instead we hold eye contact for a bit until I look away. I'm not here to make friends with hot, knife-wielding men.

Lise follows me home like another lost dog. At least we're getting in cardio from going up and down all the stairs.

When we get to my apartment, we take off our shoes in the entryway, and I direct Lise to the hand sanitizer station again.

"Come look," I say and lead her to the kitchen where my laptop is on the kitchen island. I open it and say, "Remember this?" I show Lise the digitized version of the crocus sketch I had made on the day we met.

"That's good," she says. "You major in graphic design? Is that a major?"

"It's just my hobby," I say and open my portfolio file. I love having an audience. "I'm going to be a real estate appraiser, but I'll be able to use the same techniques for sketching property and floor plans." I flip to a sample website I'm working on and point to some of my favorite designs. "I did this one as a final project for an advanced visual expression course last year. I take as many graphic design and visual arts classes as I can while I have the chance." I ask Lise what she's studying.

"Maybe psychology or education. Or both. I'm twenty-one, but I'm only a sophomore because I took a break. I need to declare my major soon, though."

"It's brave to keep going through college without knowing what's in the future."

Lise gives a quick laugh and says, "I am the scarediest person you will ever meet."

"You wrestle with wild canines, you move to new cities, you approach random artists and make them join your adventures."

"You have no idea how hard that was." I don't know what to say in response. Instead, I open the dishwasher to see if we need more rinse aid. To my back, Lise says, "I have bad social anxiety."

"Oh, yeah?" I try to be casual, like she had said "I'm wearing mismatched socks."

"Yeah. It's hard for me to talk to people outside the family and do normal-person stuff."

"Everyone has something, I guess." Maybe that's not empathetic? "I don't mean to say it isn't bad. It sounds like a hard way to live. It's just that–" I stop talking and concentrate on filling the rinse channel in the dishwasher door without spilling any. I squeeze too hard, and rinse-aid overshoots on to the cabinet next to the dishwasher. "I have fear, too. Stuff that keeps me from doing normal-person stuff."

I don't know if I'm saying this to make Lise or me feel better. I never talk about my own weirdness.

But it's all that's on my mind.

Lise brings over a sponge from the sink to help get the drip off the cabinet. It's the wrong sponge for this task but sometimes doing something with your hands makes difficult things easier to talk about, so I don't mind.

She says, "I'll tell you one thing about me, then you go. Deal?"

"Okay."

Lise hoists herself up and sits on the counter. I pray Paula doesn't come home right now to see this. "I can't go to the grocery store," she says. I look up at her and she continues, "I mean, I can go *to* one. I just can't go *in* one." I want to ask follow-up questions. Like, what part of it is scariest? The choices? The fruit? The carts? The check-out? But it's my turn.

"I'm grossed out by tongues. Like when someone licks their lips? I want to vomit."

Lise kicks her feet a little but doesn't seem uncomfortable by my admission. "You must miss COVID masks."

"Oh my god, I do! It's weird but having everyone cover their pie holes for months and months was the best thing." I love that someone understands this. "I mean, of course I hate COVID. Boo, death. But some of the restrictions were delightful. Your turn."

Lise says, "I don't use the bus and the L. I can only do it if I'm with my mom or Ben."

"Oof, that's hard." It must be limiting, especially once the weather is nice and there's so much free stuff to do. I feel for Lise, who is bright pink in the face and so I decide to share a big one. "I'm a picky eater. Like *really* picky." I take a deep breath. "We have ten different kinds of food here and we always get the same ones."

"What do you mean?"

I walk over to the fridge and open the door. I point to the items. "Apples, sliced bread, skim milk." I do the same for the freezer. "Potatoes, chicken, corn." Then the cabinet. "Peanut butter, rice, granola bars, cheerios."

"Always the same ten? Like forever?"

"Well, technically it's more than ten. I'm being dramatic." I open the freezer again. "We get variations, so we have chicken strips *and* chicken nuggets, and lots of kinds of potatoes." I close the freezer. "We branch out with potatoes." Lise stops kicking. "Hash browns, fries, tots. I also eat different kinds of bread products. Like once in a while, we get crackers or even waffles and things like that if we're eating out." I wipe a speck on the counter. "I also eat vanilla ice cream, sugar cookies, and a few kinds of candy and chocolate. But we don't keep sweets around. Chocolate is our special occasion food. See? It's actually way more than ten. Probably almost twenty."

"I have so many questions," she says.

"I'm used to that." I gesture toward the couch. I need to get her off the counter.

We sit by the coffee table, and both play with the chess pieces on our board.

"So even when you aren't home—"

"This is it." I finish for her. "This is what I eat every day." I glance up to see how she's taking it. I never spell it out like this. It's a story people piece together after knowing me for a long time. "My mom eats the same way around me to help me feel comfortable. It's just that I'm picky and...

And I'm scared to try new food. It grosses me out just being near it or thinking about touching it."

I wait for the usual questions and suggestions ("Have you tried—"), but Lise surprises me. "Do you like it this way, or is it a problem?"

"What do you mean?"

"Like, if you had a magic button that could take away your fear, what would be different? Would it be better?"

"It would be better. But it's impossible," I say, thinking of Eleanor's attempt to help me.

"Well, we're both weird, I guess. You can talk to me about it if you ever want. I can even help you make a fear hierarchy."

I pretend I don't know what that is.

"It's a list of the stuff that scares you. I can send you one."

"Maybe someday." I want to be polite, but I'm not interested in letting a friend play therapist with me.

About an hour later, Lise texts me a template of a fear hierarchy. The sections have inconsistent capitalization and odd typeface choices. The whole thing has the flavor of a handout that therapists or social workers had copied over many times with no thought toward graphic design and usability.

I copy the text into InDesign, make the instructions easier to read, add subtle graphic elements and colors to separate the sections and reformat the document to be a fillable PDF.

I keep all the text the same, but with better design. My version looks less like something handed out in an institution and more like a learning tool.

I send it back to Lise and try to be patient while I wait for a response. I'm always like this with creative work. I need instant gratification. I wish I could bottle up this enthusiasm and use it for my internship applications.

Lise texts back with exclamation points and hearts.

About ten minutes later, she sends it back all filled in and texts, "Don't judge me!"

I look through her hierarchy. It's intense.

There are predictable items ("Ride the bus by myself") and bizarre ("Lie down on the ground in public place").

It helps me appreciate how *not* messed up I am. Sure, I'm a picky eater and I don't poop in public, but those are pretty normal compared to all of this.

She texts, `I have to do some of these with friends or family… want to try #3 soon?`

I check #3. "Ask strangers for things." Vague and weird. I like weird and I can handle vague.

Maybe I'll learn something by watching her peck a hole in her shell.

`"I'm in,"` I text back.

Chapter Twelve

Lise and I planned our adventure for today, Saturday. I have about an hour before we meet up, and I'm going to get adulting stuff done before then.

Paula is once again out of the apartment when I get up. She's spending extra time at her office, and I don't know if she's behind on work, stuffing herself with non-Zillah food, or avoiding me and my bad moods. But I'm grateful for the space, even though it means I'm back to public transportation with her using the car again.

The good news is that Cliff has his driver's license back, so I'll get some rides.

I finish folding laundry and some organizing, and it's time to walk around with Lise and "ask people for things", whatever that means. I've been looking forward to this because I get warm feelings from Lise and I like the thought of a friend who lives so close. I'd settle for a friend who lived far away, too.

I wish it were a day I was feeling better, though. I'm not sleeping much, and the sleep I *do* have is lousy. Every time I almost drift off, I wake up and remember something to add to my list of things to do or a bullet point for my resume. I tell myself, "Don't worry. It's fine," but my idiot self never believes me, and I wake up in a panic every ninety minutes.

I eat unsweetened applesauce and a spoonful of peanut butter and then take half a caffeine pill to pep myself up and meet Lise outside in the courtyard.

"How does this work?" I ask when she joins me there.

"I do something scary, and I rate my anxiety from 1 to 10. Then I wait until it's half that number," she says. "Rinse and repeat."

This is sounding less and less fun.

"What do you do while you wait?" I ask.

"Depends." We walk up Broadway, peek in at a comic book store and a boba shop and size up pedestrians. "Sometimes I focus on the bad thought, like whatever I'm scared of. I lean in and make it worse. Sometimes I get bored and think about random stuff like lunch or that bird," she says, pointing at a crow. "It doesn't matter as long as I don't try to make myself feel better."

"Logical," I say, nodding.

There's not much foot traffic until we reach Belmont. Then we stop people window shopping at the vintage store, taking pictures of the churches, and playing in the small park.

Lise doesn't freak out with the first couple we stop. She says, "Excuse me, do you know what time it is?" I can tell from her pink ears and high voice that she's nervous, but I don't think a stranger would know.

"Well?" I ask.

"Not as bad as I was expecting," she says.

"I'm next."

We take turns. We ask the time, ask for directions, and ask people to take pictures of us. It's not as bad as I predicted. Lise's fun when she's less nervous, and compared to all the strangers we're talking to, I'm practically her bestie.

My phone is at about fifteen percent charge, and I switch it off to save power. "I'm turning my phone off, so we'll need to use yours for the rest of the pictures, and if we need directions. My battery's busted."

"Or it's a user issue," she says.

"When you talk to people, which is scariest?" I ask Lise. "The photos? The directions?"

"Asking for the time, since they know we could look at our phones." She swings a shopping bag around while she talks. We had stopped for origami paper. "But none of it's hard with a friend compared to trying by myself."

She thinks of me as her friend. With that thought, my chest tightens like a too-small bra is hugging my ribs. "Also, I don't want to let you down," she says. Lise swings the bag too hard, and the handle detaches. "Poop." She slides the bag into her purse, trying not to bend the pack of paper. "Anyway, the hardest thing I've done this week was send you that fear hierarchy with all my stuff on it. I was like, 'Great. Now Zillah knows I'm a freak'."

"It was brave. My list would be freakier," I say. I point to the Chicken Hut on the corner. We cross the road.

"I was *not* brave. I sent it and said, 'Zillah knows I'm a freak' over and over until the words wore off."

"Did that work?"

"Yeah, after a minute I was like, 'Meh. Fuck it.' That's what I try to get to with all my fears."

"Meh. Fuck it?"

"Yeah. The goal is to get to be someone who thinks, 'So what if everyone thinks I'm weird? I'll survive. Fuck it'."

This makes sense for Lise, but there's no clear analog to my manifold issues. I'm fine with people thinking I'm weird. I need a neighbor with mommy issues to spy on so I can learn a new set of skills to help me grow up and separate from Paula.

Chicken Hut is the best place to eat in the entire world. Or at least as much of the world as I've seen. So, the best food within an hour of Chicago. It has six things on the menu, and I can eat half of them (chicken, pita, and corn). Plus, it's *so* good.

Lise's glasses fog up as soon as we walk in. After she wipes them on her cardigan, I point to the rows of spit-roasting chickens. "This is my heaven," I say with a sigh. We have to wait in line, but it doesn't take long to order and get our cardboard cartons heavy with food.

We sit at an empty table and pull orange chairs in with a squeak.

"Isn't this good?" I'm evangelizing, but I can't help trying to get more Chicken Hut converts. I had been scared it would fail during the pandemic and relieved once it had survived. I need to keep its base strong for the next global catastrophe.

"So good," Lise says. She tries cutting into her chicken with a plastic knife and fork and then gives up and uses her hands. "Can I ask more about your food thing?"

"Yeah." She can talk about anything she wants while I have Chicken Hut.

"Are there any foods you kind of *want* to try?"

"I looked at a strawberry close up yesterday, but I couldn't do it. Everyone seems to like strawberries." I think for a bit. "I don't want to eat more food, but it would be good to be more comfortable around it. Like if I'm at a work lunch or something. I don't want to have a panic attack at my internship if someone offers me something gross."

"People are so pushy with food," Lise says. "When I was little, I hated being at other people's houses if I didn't like what they were having for dinner. It was always like, 'Oh, I noticed you didn't finish the disgusting green things. What's wrong with you?'"

"Or 'Oh, you didn't take the stuff that looks like poop?'" I get up to get a refill of soda. Should I bring home more chicken for leftovers?

I feel that warm chest tightness again when I walk back to the table where my *friend* is waiting.

After I sit, Lise gets pink in the face and says, "Well, let me know if you ever want help with trying things, okay?"

"Okay," I try to say with warmth but not *too* much warmth so that she won't keep asking.

We clean up, and I gaze at the dead chickens. Once we're outside and walking home, she says, "I have a food thing, too. Hummus."

"Ugh," I say.

"Yeah. When I was a kid, like ten or eleven? I had a bad experience."

"What happened?" The traffic is loud, so I have to lean toward Lise to hear her story.

"We used to think I had a sesame allergy, but it may have been misdiagnosed? Or maybe I outgrew it. Anyway, we were at a tiny Greek restaurant in Indy, and I was eating hummus on pita and my mom remembered hummus has tahini in it."

"Is that a sesame thing?"

"Yeah. And mom was yelling at me to stop eating. She was shouting to the server to call 911, and she was expecting me to, like, go into anaphylactic shock and stop breathing."

"Oh, shit."

"And she stuck her fingers in my mouth and down my throat to make me puke and everyone was watching and I vomited everywhere. Like, all over myself and on our plates."

"Oh my gods."

"And it was this tiny little place, right? With all the tables super close." She pauses her story while a bus passes. "And I can still see everyone's faces looking at me and, like, grossed out and so much pity."

"Did you stop breathing?"

"No, I was fine. It's how we found out that I'm not allergic. But it was the single most embarrassing thing that ever happened. Like, I know it wasn't my fault, right? But I felt so guilty for ruining everyone else's meal and making them see my vomit. Every time I see hummus, it's like it just happened. Does that make sense?"

"We're not missing out," I say. "There's no benefit to hummus. It looks like chunky semen that's been left out for a couple of days."

"Zillah, you've made my hummus aversion even worse."

"I don't remember this one in your fear hierarchy. Do you *want* to try it? Or are you okay with hating it?" This is a very Lise-type question to ask.

"Maybe if I were on a desert island? But it's not limiting my life like my other anxieties. It's been so long that it feels impossible to change."

"That's how I feel about Cliff," I say. Fuck. I want to swallow my words back.

"Your boyfriend?"

Ugh. Why did I do this? The post-Chicken Hut food coma plus Lise opening up about her hummus situation made me let down my guard.

"Yeah. He's great. He's *so* great. But we've been together forever and we're stuck in our patterns." It's surprisingly easy to tell her these things. It even feels good.

"Are you, like, breaking up?"

"Oh gods, no. We've broken up before, but it's been two years since the last time. We just sort of didn't have anything to talk about and I got bored. It seemed like we needed a break. But after a couple of months, I realized we belong together. We have so much history." We're almost to Wellington and my bladder somehow can tell I'm near an available toilet. Since we're almost home, I turn my phone back on. "Anyway, the thought of being with anyone else is terrifying."

"Hm."

I can hear the judgement in her "Hm." It's like she's silently asking, "Is fear a reason to stay with someone?" Fuck me.

My phone has finished restarting and I see a shit ton of texts and even voice messages waiting for me.

"Fuck." I need to broaden my vocabulary.

Paula is freaking out.

"Can't see your location. CALL ME NOW."

"Are you ok? Are you babysitting? I called the Schatz family and the Woods, but they don't know where you are."

Thanks for making me look unreliable to my babysitting clients. The Woods are my best tippers, and the Schatz girl is so fun it's like being paid to hang out with a friend.

"THIS IS UNACCEPTABLE."

"Called Bethany and Cliff and they don't know where you are. Calling UIC security."

"Fuck me with a pogo stick," I mutter while I call Paula. She picks up on the first ring.

"Where are you?" she asks.

"I'm fine. Jeez, Mom. I'm out with my friend. I told you about it."

"Still? That was hours ago. Is it that new girl? The tall one?" She's so loud, I'm sure Lise can hear her, but she's trying to look disinterested and scrolls on her own phone.

"I'll see you at home in five minutes, okay?"

"You tap the front door when you get back!"

"Fine."

I disconnect and Lise brings up some innocuous other topic, so I don't have to come up with excuses to make that conversation sound normal.

Once we're in our courtyard, I say, "Well, thanks for a weird afternoon." I can only be heartfelt in limited quantities and I'm back to silly snark.

"Thanks for teaching me the mysteries of Chicken Hut."

I walk up our stairwell. Even though we've been walking for miles, I'm energized after spending time with Lise. That's a good sign. And she made me think. What *would* a first step be to getting comfortable around food? Not eating it but being okay with being near it. Okay enough that Cliff and I could have a dinner party someday. Okay enough to feed my future child food I don't eat.

Maybe I should start by looking at pictures of more food?

I think back on Lise's bravery today. How she was uncomfortable but still asked people for things for almost an hour.

What would Lise do?

I plan my first exposure.

Chapter Thirteen

I expose myself Lise-style at the grocery store on Tuesday afternoon after I finish putting in my clinic hours.

Usually, I get our standing order of groceries brought to Paula's car. I bring our trolley cart to customer service if I walk there. This time I go into the store to check out the produce close up. While I'm here, I can see if they have any headphones with a mic in the small technology section. Maybe if Lise has a headset, she'll stop listening through her computer mic and I'll be less tempted to eavesdrop.

It's early afternoon on a weekday, so there's not too many shoppers.

I walk through the produce section and notice the colors of all the fruit and vegetables. If I let my vision double and blur, it could pass for a flower market instead of food.

Exposure time.

There's a small display of melons. Some for sure are watermelon, and a small sign informs me the others are cantaloupe.

I approach one and think about the inside of a cantaloupe. I've been up close to this fruit before when Cliff has had it in with his food at restaurants, but I always scoot away and avert my eyes. If it cracks open, there will be slimy orange goo and threads of flesh.

I'm not nervous yet and for this to count as an exposure, I have to get my fight-or-flight going. I need to kick my amygdala in the balls.

I imagine sitting in a grand meeting room in a fancy real estate firm. My future boss hands me a bowl of fruit and I have to sit in front of it. I imagine putting cantaloupe chunks in my mouth and what the goo and threads would feel like sliding down my throat and choking me.

Yup, that does it.

My pulse pounds, my insides are dark green and spikey, and I consider my fear. A seven or eight out of ten. My bile rises and my chest is tight. I close my eyes and imagine what Lise's therapist would say, "This is your amygdala preparing to run away from a lion. What can you tolerate?"

I stand there with eyes closed imagining the mush in my mouth. Minutes are probably ticking by, but it's hard to tell. Eventually I feel it — that loosening of the grip on my insides. I still feel like crap, but maybe a four or five on the scale now.

I open my eyes and rest my hand on a cantaloupe. I'm touching a Yuck Food. For real! And it's not sticky like I expected. I pick it up. Heavy! It's like a burlap sack tightened over a bowling ball. I smell it, and it's not terrible. It's like a Bath and Body Works store. Why did I think it would be sticky? No slime is escaping from the interior. Maybe the interior is firm?

I stay by the cantaloupes and other melons waiting for my fear to spike up again. I still don't like being here holding this weird ball of goo, but it's enough. My insides are back to mostly normal colored. My heart is still racing, but this is a success.

I touched a cantaloupe.

And lived!

A shaggy looking employee makes eye contact with me and comes over.

In her therapy sessions, this is always the part Lise says she fears about exposure – getting asked what the hell she's doing by randos hanging around. I don't care about that. I'm more concerned about whether his beard hairs fall in the food.

I ask, "Can you help me pick out strawberries?"

"Sure." I follow him to the strawberry area, and he hands me a clear plastic case after looking at the bottom and sniffing it. I don't like how close his beard got to the berries.

"Thanks." I walk around the store holding the berries. They don't look delicious like Cliff's had the other night at Clark's on Belmont. I'm not hungry now, and these still have their green leaves on the top.

I don't like green things.

I hold the container up to the light and consider what I'm going to do with these. My heart's beating fast, and I feel the familiar warmth in my armpits: a combination of being anxious about eating something Yuck and wearing my parka indoors.

Oh! I could use whipped cream as a vehicle! I'll dip a strawberry in a ton of whipped cream, and then I could eat a cookie super fast to cover the taste. I get a can of ready-to-use whipped cream and then I go to the cookie aisle and get some vanilla wafer cookies. This will be an expensive outing, but less expensive than therapy. While I'm here, I look at all the flavors and kinds of cookies I've never tried.

But after a moment I sink back into Scriven reality. Who am I kidding? I will never put a strawberry in my mouth. I can't even try a strawberry-flavored cookie.

God dammit. Why am I such a basket case coward?

I don't want to disappoint the produce guy who picked these out, so I put the strawberries on the cookie shelf near the Chips Ahoy. Now I feel guilty about them going bad, so I take them back and sneak them over to the produce section where some normal adult can buy them.

I put away the whipped cream and wafer cookies, too. I'll come back and buy those as a treat when I've submitted my internship applications.

I've missed two calls from Bethany while not buying strawberries and I call her back on my walk home.

"Hey, Sweet Z," she says when she picks up. "How are you holding up?"

"Whadya mean?"

"Isn't this crunch time? For your applications?"

"Oh. Yeah."

"I wanted to see if you'd like another pair of eyes. I'd be happy to give your materials a look."

"Maybe. I kind of want to do it on my own."

"I'm here if you need me, Zillah," she says. "Whether it's for school, or work, or relationship stuff. Whatever you need."

"Yeah, I know." Be polite. "Thanks, Aunt B."

"And Zillah, keep me posted about Paula. If she's— If she's not coping well with her recovery."

"Yeah."

"We could do a tracking system where—"

"No thanks, Aunt B. Gotta go."

It would be easier to turn to her for help and advice if she wasn't always so serious lately. She used to be fun, but now she treats every interaction like a Very Special Moment.

I scroll through Instagram to see if there's anything to distract me for the rest of my walk home. It's cold, but I'm dressed warm. I switch my phone back and forth so my hands can take turns in a pocket.

I get home and realize I messed up. I put the strawberries and stuff back but didn't get the standing order of *regular* groceries. Goddammit. I don't want to go back to the store.

Safeway isn't a far walk, but it's cold and I'm tired and I hate my fucking life, and I want to snuggle under my blankets and watch a show or die or fall asleep. I wish I could convince Paula to get delivery for the winter months at least. I would risk home invasion from a violent delivery person if it meant I didn't have to walk outside.

The front door announces Paula, and I check my phone. It's not even three, so something's up.

"Mom?" I walk to the door and see her hanging up her coat. "Everything okay?"

"Yes, yes," she says. I follow her into the living room, and she puts her purse on its assigned hook. "Why are you following me around?" Then, in her high-pitched mocking voice, she says, "An adult is allowed to come home early once in a while without it being an emergency."

"I know." I hate it when she uses that tone with me, as though I'm unreasonably concerned. Especially from the woman who asks about the color of my urine at least once a week.

"I have to go back later for a special project, so I'm home to have a snack and relax."

These words are normal. They're just unusual from my mother. Relax?

I sit on a stool at our kitchen island. "What kind of project?"

"I'm trying out something new with our electronics. The new printer, and our monitors. I'll have dinner at the office." She's still wearing her gloves.

"Are your hands hurt?"

"Just dry from the weather."

As a chronic over-washer, Paula often has dry hands that sometimes get chapped. It's worst when she's stressed about germs. They're better than they were during the first year of COVID, but it's still something I keep an eye on.

I go to my room to do my own form of relaxation: On my phone I look at organizational ideas for small apartments while I watch shows on my computer. About halfway into a nineties romcom she texts me, `I don't want to interrupt you in case you're working. Love you. See you tonight!` The front door opens and closes again, with Paula leaving to go back to her office.

Again, maybe this is the way other moms interact with grown kids, but not mine. No double checking to make sure I'm doing what I said I'm doing? No last reminders about murderers, thieves, and new COVID strains?

Hours later, Paula still isn't back from her "Special Project."

None of this makes sense. Why did she even come home earlier? To shit?

At nine o'clock I call her to check in.

"Hi Zillah." She sounds busy and not happy to hear from me.

"You still at work?" I can see her location, and I know she's still there, but I'm not sure how else to start the conversation.

"Yes. What do you need?"

"I wanted to make sure you're okay."

"I'm fine. Do you need to talk, or can I get off the phone and finish this task?"

As though I'm the biggest imposition.

"Yeah. See you soon, Mom."

Later, I watch our location app and see her dot move in her usual path on her drive home, with an exception where she circles a block at Briar Place twice before she continues to our parking spot.

She does this often, and I suspect she's eating non-Zillah-style food in the car and needs a few extra minutes to finish. Or maybe she's listening to a story on NPR and doesn't want her drive to end yet.

By the time she gets home, it's almost 10:30. On most nights, I stay up until 11 or so, but she's an in-bed-at-9 kind of lady. I'm waiting on the couch when she gets in.

"You're home." I try for a casual tone when she walks into the big room. "How's your project?"

"I had to stick around to unplug the copier and the two tableside lamps in reception," she says. She goes to her bathroom and returns with hand lotion. She offers me some and I shake my head no. Her hands are red and so chapped in places that maybe blisters have formed and broken. "Those lamps were a terrible purchase. Pure garbage, and the plugs always feel warm to the touch. Nobody else cares, and so now *I* pay the price."

"I can't believe Sid wants you to do that." I try to sneak a closer look at her hands. Ugh. Painful. How much is she washing?

"Oh, he doesn't care at all. He said there's not going to be a fire and stop worrying about it. Can you believe that? He said I can't turn off the printer while people are still working, but if I must unplug things for my peace of mind, I can do it after hours."

"Wait—"

"My peace of mind," she repeats. "How do you like *that* one? And tonight was a disaster because Jennifer and Ori worked late, so I had to stay even later. But there haven't been any fires yet and I don't plan for there to be any fires ever."

"So, you went back to the clinic just to unplug things?" I ask.

"I did some paperwork while I waited for them to finish."

I have follow-up questions, but I keep them to myself and instead we say goodnight.

If she's this strung up about electrical fires at work, it's going to extend to home soon despite my Paula Stabilization Plan. It's like the early days of COVID all over again. She'll never agree for me to move out if she's seeing danger around every corner.

I need to call in the reinforcements. I text Bethany, "When's a good time to call tomorrow?"

Chapter Fourteen

In the morning, Paula's gone before I wake up. Maybe back at the office to plug the electronics in before other staff arrive.

Her fear of fires isn't new, but this thing about plugs is.

We unplug our toaster, TV, microwave, and other electronics when they aren't in use, but we've been in people's homes where things stay plugged in all the time. It's never seemed to bother her before.

I talk to Bethany while I wait for the Brown Line train.

"She promised I could have the money Dad saved for my apartment as soon as I'm ready, but now she's saying no because she thinks I won't be able to deal with Cliff eating like a normal person."

"Hm," is Bethany's noncommittal response. I'm sure she has plenty of opinions about my diet she'd love to share. Before she moved to the area, she stayed with us for a couple of weeks to find the right neighborhood. I remember her surprise at how I ate and even more surprise that Paula ate the same way to make me comfortable. She was the first person who said "this has to change" out loud, and I'll never forget how that felt like a punch to the gut – that my cool aunt thought I was weird. Paula shut the criticism down, though. I remember raised voices in Paula's room and the taste of canned corn turning to dirt in my mouth. She's never mentioned my food rules since then, but I keep an eye on her face when she's near us at mealtimes. Her reactions show what she thinks: my eating is wrong, and it's wrong for Paula to limit herself, too.

"Bethany, I've got to move out of here."

"Paula's money isn't your only option. I can help, and your dad—"

"But I won't feel right leaving if she's a mess and she's been extra—extra *Paula* since her fall. She's talking about electricity a lot, and her hands are so bad. And did I tell you about how she's going to her office late to double-check everything?"

"We've got to get her into therapy, Z."

"Hm." My turn to sound doubtful.

"Well, can I at least pitch my idea for tracking?" she asks.

"Fine," I say, snappish to indicate that it's certainly *not* fine.

I hear a short pause before, "Let's make a Google doc or a spreadsheet and you can have the date and whether she's okay or needs support." Her voice is excited like Paula's gets, and a sticky ball of sadness rises in my throat. "If there's too many bad days in a row, we can check in and discuss whether we need an intervention."

I clear my throat. "Like what?"

"Like therapy, or medication. Or you both moving in here with me for a little while." She pauses for breath. "Or even her getting more serious help."

"More serious than therapy?"

"They have therapy that's once a week and therapy that's more frequent. I'll send you a link."

"The train's coming," I warn.

"Call me later!"

I find an empty pair of seats and sit by the window with my backpack on my lap like a good citizen.

I look at the buildings through the window and like always try to see inside the apartments we pass.

My phone vibrates with a text from Bethany. It's a link to an "Intensive Outpatient Program" where a person comes in the daytime like a temporary job and goes home at night. I skim the website and pick up on words that I know will shut down any talk with Paula: avoidance, OCD, agoraphobia, trauma, reassurance-seeking, exposure, and, most threatening of all, group therapy.

Bethany sent this so fast that she must have already had it bookmarked. How long has she wanted to rehab my mom's brain?

Paula needs my help for all her anxiety. She needs to feel safe and cared for. Not whatever *this* is.

I text Bethany back. "`I'll keep a tracker, but just on my drive. Not to share.`" She sends back a wall of text with several emojis that don't really work for the context.

While I wait for class to start, I set up a simple document. I make a space for the date and whether Paula is her 'N' for normal self or 'W' for weird self.

This will do.

Lots of Ns and hopefully very few Ws.

It will be evidence that things are getting better, knock wood.

Chapter Fifteen

For the rest of yesterday, Paula earned a "N for Normal" on my new tracking spreadsheet. She's odd, but it's typical Paula quirkiness like comparing the ingredients on *our* loaf of bread to the ingredients listed on the bread's product page on the Safeway website to make sure they're the same.

This morning, I wake tangled in a top sheet with a sense of dark green dread. It's Thursday, and I don't have any big exams or deliverables due for the clinic. Probably tension from internship applications. UIC matches us with potential firms, but we still need to interview to make sure we're a fit. Most of the internships focus on real estate sales and there's only a few specific to appraisal.

Thinking about it raises my heart rate and fills me with melted crayon. Time to get my ass in gear if I want to get a match.

I kick off my sheets and stumble to the bathroom to pee, shower, and try to plan out the day.

In the shower, I let warm water massage my scalp.

So good.

I want to do this all day.

I *could* wait another day to finish. I already have my letters of recommendation, and I only need to finalize my cover letters. There's no rule that all my submission materials need to be turned in by Friday *morning*.

No.

Zillah, think how it will feel to be done. I'll finish them this morning and have time to relax before Cliff picks me up to take me to my 2 o'clock class. Or, even better, after I finish, I can go to Blick Art Materials and allow myself to spend fifteen dollars on whatever I want.

The plan's good, but my impulse control isn't.

I pick up my phone and text Lise. "`Whatchya doing? Feel like causing mayhem?`"

She replies right away with a thumbs up and, "`I'm watching my seminar but I'll be done in about 45 minutes. How about some civil disobedience?`"

"`Protest or burn our bras?`"

"`I can't afford new bras, so want to just walk Halstead?`"

"`YES. We can collect his droppings and mail them to people in power.`" I *think* she knows me well enough to see this as a joke.

I'm relieved when she sends back crying-laughy face.

I only need to kill 45 minutes. I *could* use this time to do applications, but isn't it better to eat breakfast and read a book or do something else relaxing?

Too bad I can't earn a living coming up with compelling justifications.

Chapter Sixteen

Lise, Halsted, and I walk toward the part of Madrona Field nearby where everyone lets their dogs off their leashes.

Walking a dog is a low-pressure way to hang out for a short while and it doesn't cost any money. An added benefit is that Halsted doesn't lick me so much when we're outside.

I'm almost kind of content. The neighborhood isn't blossoming into color yet, but I see buds. Also, it's still cold enough that we don't have to deal with tourists yet.

When we get to the park, there's already a few dogs there, but none get close to biting me or even slobbering on me.

It's a little drama every time a new dog arrives.

Sniff. Sniff. Play bow. Chase. Pee. Sniff.

"Talking to other dog people is easy," Lise says on our way back home. "It's predictable. 'What's your dog's name?' 'What kind of mix is he?' 'How long have you had him?'"

"How would cat people interact?" I wonder out loud. "You made eye contact, so now I'm going to kick you in the shins."

"Or the opposite. You stood still in a nice way, so now I'm going to rub against your leg and bite you if you try to walk away."

"I could see your brother as a cat. He's hot and cold."

"That's ironic. He calls you—" She presses her lips together and mumbles something to Halsted.

"Tell me." I grab Halsted's leash. "I'm stealing your dog until you tell me. And he'll come with me. I'm peanut butter flavored."

She takes a minute, and I wonder if she's doing some therapy technique. She says, "He calls you my 'hot and angry friend'."

"I don't hate that." The angry part's accurate. I always have a pot of rage simmering. And it's nice when an attractive guy thinks the same about me. I thought I saw him in the laundry room last night and I got excited for a second until I realized it was some other medium-height white dude in a ball cap. The fact that I was disappointed is interesting.

I reach down to pet Halsted and pull my hand back before he can anoint me with his tongue. I like the texture of his fur. Smooth when I pet him toward his tail, rough when I pet him toward his head. Plus, he seems to enjoy my touch. And me. When we wait to cross a road, he stands next to me and leans against my leg. He puts his snout under my hand as though I would think, "What? How did a furry thing get here? Guess I'll pet it!" Making him happy is surprisingly satisfying.

A couple blocks from our apartment, Lise says, "So, there's something I need to talk to you about." She's red in the face and uses the higher-pitched tone of voice I realize that I haven't heard her use since we first met.

We've come a long way.

Oh, fuck. Does she know I've been eavesdropping? My stomach feels smeary with brown and green paint.

"Yeah?"

"I've been keeping a secret." I want to interrupt with a joke to break the tension, but I stifle my impulse. "Remember the day we met? When you were outside drawing?"

"Yeah."

"I talked to you as an exposure. I used you for therapy." She exhales and says, in fast succession, "But I swear we are friends! It was only that first time I talked to you for therapy. After that was because I *wanted* to talk to you. I hope you can forgive me?"

"Lise, yeah. Of course." She looks down at me with huge, watering eyes. "I'm glad you introduced yourself. It's awesome being your friend." And it's awesome that this isn't about my creepiness.

"I meant to tell you forever. I've been so worried about this."

Damn.

If she can be brave, I can be good.

Chapter Seventeen

After class, I don't eavesdrop on Lise. I'm two weeks spy-sober.

Instead, I take my laptop to the coffee shop and finish up the applications. I don't drink bitter brown bean juice, but I like the environment.

These don't need to be perfect, I tell myself every time I want to stop. My grades speak for themselves. Finish them and get them out the door.

Of all the firms I'm applying to work with, Conway & Cranos is the one I'm most gunning for. They specialize in residential and commercial appraisal, and I can take the #36 bus there.

I spend time on their website to collect facts about their founding partners and mission so that I can tailor my letter and convey that I'm obsessed with them and that they'd be out of their minds to skip me.

Maybe they'll pick me, and after the summer they'll give me a job so I can work there part time while I finish school. I'd quit my job at Paula's clinic, and when I graduate, I could already be a part of the team.

And Paula will be so happy that I got the internship that she'll deem me ready.

I'll be set.

Grown up life, here I come!

I submit my application package and get home before Paula. She's late as usual, given her new routine of staying past everyone else to secure her workplace. At least I can cheer her up tonight with good news.

"I did it," I announce when she walks in, even before she gets her coat off. "All my applications are in!"

"You cut that close," she says and hands me her purse and a tote bag. "I hope the firms don't know you were almost late."

"It doesn't work that way."

"I hope not," she says in a dark tone. But she brightens a bit. "Zillah, I want to talk to you. Let me have a comfort break and then let's chat."

A comfort break is Paula's code for using the bathroom, so I give her space until she calls me to her room.

"Have a seat on my bed so we can be cozy." She sits at her desk and turns her chair toward me. She leans forward and takes my hand. She traces my greenish blue veins without talking.

Silences are not typical of Paula.

"I want to talk to you about something that is unlikely to ever happen and there's no need for you to worry about it all, but I want to explain myself so that you understand."

"Okay?" I say like a question. I mentally scroll past topics of conversation and wonder where this is going. Is she dating?

"We've talked before about how a mother would always give her life for a child. Of course, even if a truck was coming, I would push you out of the way and get hit by it, even if it meant I would die so that I could save your life. This is what a mother does, and I would do anything for you, even die. You know that, right?"

"Yeah, we've talked about this." It's a familiar topic.

"Well, let's say a madman captured you and Bethany, the two people I love most in the entire world, and told me I had to pick which one of you could live and which one of you could die. I've thought a lot about this and I've decided." She pauses as though making a dramatic revelation. "I would let you live and Bethany would die."

She keeps talking before expecting me to say anything in support or contrary to this idea.

"I love Bethany," she continues, "but she's had her chance to live. She's older than you are and she's already gotten to experience many joys. So many joys! You're a child, and no matter how old you get, if you're both alive, Bethany will have had more and so it's only right that she should die so you could live." Her eyes tear up and she squeezes my hand.

Holy fuck, this imaginary threat is real for her.

She's suffering.

"Mom, nothing's going to happen to us."

"Oh, I know. I know! We live in such a safe neighborhood, and even though Chicago is such a big city, crime rates have gone down, and it is very, *very* unlikely anything like that could ever happen to us! But I hate to think what you might think about me afterwards if this *did* happen and I had to choose for Bethany to die and maybe I would be killed in the struggle, and you could run free."

She's thought this out.

She continues, "And Bethany and I would both sacrifice our lives for you, and I worry about what would you think of me afterwards? Would you think I'm a cold, heartless person who sacrificed her very own sister?"

She's hurting my hand, but there doesn't seem to be a kind way to pull away.

She wants reassurance.

"You're not heartless," I say.

"You understand that I'm doing what a mother does?"

"Yeah." I disentangle myself and bring her a box of tissues.

When she's calmer, I go to my room and lay on my bed. I look up at my ceiling and try to visualize peaceful watercolors up there.

What kind of world does Paula live in? What is her inner life like, where killers make horror-movie threats to single mothers about murdering their daughters and sisters?

I pull my laptop over to myself and open my spreadsheet.

Paula earned her first "W for Weird".

Chapter Eighteen

Lise and I stream an old episode of *Hoarders* while I help her untangle a mess of embroidery thread. It's cathartic to watch people on TV with worse mental health problems than ours.

Ben joins us and looks at his phone while occasionally paying attention to the show and offering his commentary, despite Lise shushing him.

The next episode starts, but Lise skips past the first few minutes. They always give away too much in the overview, and we like to be surprised.

When I come back from the bathroom, Ben asks, "How does someone so small stomp so loud? You walk like you're Godzilla, about to take down Tokyo." He taps his chin in faux perplexity and looks me up and down.

"I'd rather be Godzilla than Benjamin," I say. "It sounds like a toddler's name." I make big eyes at him. "Do you need a nap, widdle Benny? You seem fussy!" I like the safe, and fun flirty tension I have with him. Safe because I know it will go nowhere. And fun because he's got the same dry, sarcastic tone I cultivate.

Although I'm much better at it, of course.

"Aren't you supposed to be at work?" Lise asks him, setting aside a plastic bobbin with pale blue thread.

"On a Sunday?" I ask.

He says, "I need to finish a proposal." He groans and asks Halsted, "You think I should quit, right boy?" He announces, "Halsted said to quit."

Lise summarizes the situation for me in a quick voice, like she's recapping an episode of her family. "Ben needs to quit his job. He's a boring consultant—"

"Hey!" he interrupts.

"—and he hates it, but it pays a lot."

"Godzilla doesn't need my life story.

She continues. "Mom and I need him to stop complaining and go back to what he loves. Downside is that it means he will live here longer. Upside is that he will bring us free food."

"Food? You're quitting your office job and doing food?" I'm confused. Lise had told me that Ben works for a 'Big Four' firm. Those are amazing jobs that start with solid paychecks and can lead to job security. People work for years to get those jobs. I'd consider it if I wasn't going to be an appraiser.

He moves over to Lise to help with the detangling. "I miss it, but I'm twenty-seven."

"Do what makes you happy and stop talking so we can watch our show," Lise says. She pulls a plastic bobbin out of his hands and uses both her feet to push him away. He flops on the floor, and Halsted sits on his legs.

"I'd go away, but Halsted won't let me. He says I smell better than you."

"Want a trick for making hard decisions?" I ask.

"Does it involve stomping?" How can I teach Cliff to tease me more? I like the warm, tingly feeling I get when Ben sasses me and the corners of his eyes crinkle up. Cliff and I are good at Serious Conversation, but we don't do silly and goofy.

"I'll say two statements, and you tell us which one feels better. Okay?" Lise nods, while Ben concentrates on rubbing Halsted's ear. "Number one. You are staying in your job and will stop looking at culinary work." I pause, hoping I made number one sound good. How does someone give up a salaried position with benefits? "Number two. You will quit your job after you find a culinary position."

Lise and I both look at him. "Number two," he says while still focusing on Halsted.

"See?" Lise says.

I want to ask why their mom is in support of him leaving his job, but that's intrusive. And judgy, I guess. My buzzing phone distracts me. "Oh, Cliff's here! Crap, it's late. Lise, you can meet him. What's your apartment number again?"

I text Cliff to come around and get me here. I go down their stairwell to let him in and bring him up to meet Lise. Maybe I can convince her to join us for trivia at Collett's in case there's any hard questions about embroidery or dogs.

It can be awkward when friends meet for the first time, but Cliff is in a rush, so it's especially weird.

"This is Lise," I say, bringing him inside. "And her brother Ben."

"Hey."

The men grunt at each other with a nod while Lise turns pinkish and inches backward.

Too soon to get her to join us.

"We gotta go, Z." Cliff puts his arm around my waist to direct me away, but since I'm short, it's more like boob level. I can't tell if he's being possessive and marking his territory in front of Ben or just inconsiderate about my body.

We walk down their stairs, and my rage flares up from its current home under the surface.

I have to cool it so we can have a nice time. It's not his fault I'm short. And I always get irritated when I'm late.

"Stomp, stomp, little monster!" Ben calls after us.

Chapter Nineteen

Trivia's fine. I suck at it, but my ego isn't tied up in being right all the time. It's the first time I've ever been on a team, and camaraderie feels good.

Despite our late start, we get there before the rest of our team and have time to chill in our booth.

I read the menu though I know my options here by heart: fries, tots, chicken strips. Tonight, I kill time by reading descriptions of the "pub burgers" with all sorts of bizarre-sounding combinations. Do people want food topped with roasted red peppers, goat cheese and a cherry-balsamic reduction?

"Would it be easier to go places with me if I ate more stuff?" I ask Cliff.

"Don't change for me, Z." He concentrates on balancing a saltshaker on a pile of salt he's dumped on the table. I need to remember to tip extra tonight in silent apology for his mess.

"Eleanor says if I ate a few more things, it could make me healthier. Like to help with my anemia." He concentrates on his project and ignores me, so I say, "Maybe I'd get my period more often." I like goading him sometimes.

"Gross," he says while scooching lower in the booth to get a better visual perspective on the balance.

"It's not normal to be twenty-three and not have a cycle."

"You get it once in a while." The shaker seems to magnetically shift into place and holds its position. "Yessss." He gets out his phone to take a picture. While he gazes at his work, he says, "We've talked about this already. Infertility is a gift. Think about overpopulation."

I knock down the saltshaker and clean up what I can with a wet napkin.

"I worked hard at that," he sulks.

We don't get into a real fight, though, because Jerzei and another of Cliff's work friends arrive. I go to the bathroom to play on my phone and try to get into a better mindset. Cliff will change his mind about having kids when he's older and we're more settled. It's one of the bigger areas we disagree on, along with where we want to live eventually, how much we want to be involved with our families, and whether religion is important. But we can compromise on those things.

Most of the time we get along fine, especially if it's doing things we liked together as teenagers, like our old shows and video games. It just gets rough when we pursue new terrain.

The rest of the evening is okay, and both of us let our tiff slide off our backs.

On my way back home, my super social Sunday rounds out with a text from Lise. "LMK when you're home. I have a present for you."

I send a thumbs up. She replies with, "Don't get excited. It's not anything you'll like."

I respond, "A present I'll hate? PERFECT!"

We meet downstairs at the bottom of her stairwell, and she hands over a can of chickpeas topped with a red ribbon bow decoration. It's the kind that has two-sided tape under a cardboard square to make it easy to attach to presents. Lise has re-used it by turning a piece of scotch tape into an inside-out tube to reattach it to the beans where it bobs and sways on its throne of tape.

"Here," she says.

"Thanks?" I ask like a question.

"It's not to eat. It's in case you want to look at it for motivation or for exposure. I'm doing it too."

"For hummus?" I ask.

"Yeah. Ben's gonna help me with an exposure to the ingredients. This is like an invitation to join me for it. If you want! You don't have to eat anything. Maybe be there as a coach?"

"Um—"

She starts her fast-talking trick. "I don't want to pressure you. I don't know. This seemed funnier at home." She backs up her stairs. "Am I pushing you too much?"

Yes.

I get that Lise is ready to face her hummus fear, but I'm fine going my whole life without that mess in my mouth.

But I don't want her to feel bad. "I've been thinking a little about a food exposure. Like the other day, I touched a cantaloupe. I guess I could help. Maybe." I turn the can around in my hands. "The ribbon's a nice touch."

"Enjoy!" she says. "You can re-gift it next Christmas!"

I head to my place, shaking the can to watch the ribbon bounce around.

I love this goofy girl.

"What's that?" Paula asks when I set the can down on the kitchen island. She's sitting at the table eating cereal and milk.

"Can of beans," I say and turn it so the label faces her. "Or our new centerpiece. Are chickpeas the same thing as garbanzo beans?"

"We don't want that. Put it on the landing and I'll give it to someone at work."

"No, it's mine." I'm instantly irritated at Paula. "It's a gift."

"You won't eat those." Her voice grows louder. "It's a waste to keep them."

"They're not for eating. They're for looking at," I say, as Paula cleans up from her meal.

"That's ridiculous." She uses more force than necessary as she turns on and off the faucet and puts the cereal bowl and her water glass in the dishwasher. The spoon clatters against its neighbors as she drops it in a flatware slot on the bottom rack.

"Why are you mad?" I ask. She slams the dishwasher door closed and selects a sponge to clean the table. "Did I do something?"

"Zillah, this is outside of enough!" She puts the sponge back in its holder and grabs the disinfectant and paper towel roll. "Just get rid of it."

This is not worth arguing about.

I give the beans a home on my dresser. My heart rate is up, and my insides are finger-painty like when I'm scared.

Am I scared?

No. This it's about being scolded, not from fear of looking at beans.

The beans can't hurt me.

And the ribbon really is a nice touch.

Chapter Twenty

On Monday after class I get the email I've been waiting for: an invitation for my first interview. It feels important for Cliff to be the first to celebrate with me. An adult would tell her partner before her mother, so I pop by the campus IT office where he does tech support to tell him in person and say hi to Jerzei.

When he sees me, Cliff says, "I can take a quick break. Come with me while I smoke." I hate the smoke, but I'll take what Cliff time I can get. We sit next to each other on a freezing bench the requisite fifteen feet from the door of the low-slung brick building.

"So," I say in a Lise-style upturned voice. "I got accepted for my first internship interview!"

"I knew you would!"

"And it's at Conway & Cranos, the one I really, really want."

"Nice," he says and peeks at his phone. I lean against him for warmth and he puts his arm around me.

He doesn't seem to understand how monumental this is. I say, "It's a big deal. But I need at least three or four more. And I'm so nervous about the interview."

"It's gonna be fine. Sleep over tonight and we can practice interview questions."

"I can't. I have to—"

"Please sleep over? We don't have to have sex."

"I promised Paula I'd do the light fixtures and the crown molding." In truth, Paula would let me delay my chores for a day if it means being with Cliff. But I hate sleeping over there on school nights. I don't get solid rest, and I'm thrown off for a couple of days.

His voice turns whiny. "But I have to make sure I get up tomorrow, so I don't miss my make-up shift, and if you're there, you'll make sure I get up." Cliff has the habit of pressing 'snooze' on his phone repeatedly so he can enjoy the pleasure of falling back asleep.

There are two unfortunate side effects.

The first is that his alarm no longer wakes him up. He's trained his brain to ignore it, and he often sleeps through it or keeps tapping 'snooze' past when he means to get out of bed.

The worse side effect is that sharing a bed with him is torture. Every ten minutes when his alarm goes off, I want to stab him or cut off body parts. I've tried to get him to quit the snooze habit on nights we share a bed, but he's not interested.

Just *thinking* about it makes me feel stabby. This is another thing we need to fix before we move in together. I should probably make a list.

"If you don't stay over, can you come to my place tomorrow to make sure I'm up?" he asks.

"I'll see if I can borrow Paula's car."

"Good. Good! I start at 8:00 a.m. so we need to go at 7:30. Can you come over at 6:00?"

"6:00 a.m. in the *morning*?" I spit out "Fine," to convey it is *not* fine. Fuck.

For a second, I imagine the thrill of saying no.

Red terror follows.

What if he breaks up with me?

We're not breaking up over a stupid alarm.

Cliff is thoughtful and generous. We've been through adolescence together, his mom's cancer, COVID lockdown, and we have a future planned out. He loves me despite all the weirdness. Even my dad can't put up with my restrictions. But Cliff has signed up for life.

I can't imagine having to find another partner who *accepts* me but also *loves* me. Find another dude who is okay with no tongue kissing? Okay with the food thing? Okay with Paula?

And he's the only guy I've ever met that Paula likes, too. He's my ticket to an adult life.

My pulse increases, and my stomach tightens.

I take a few deep breaths and focus on the pedestrians making their way to Little Italy or Greek Town. How many of them are partnered? How many are single? Are they happy? Isn't it better to be somewhat mismatched, but have a partner who loves me?

Cliff puts his hand on my thigh and says, "Thank you. I'll be your servant tomorrow for the rest of the day, okay? I'll do anything you want." He gives my thigh a squeeze. "*Anything*," he says in a deeper voice, as though trying to convey all my wildest sexual fantasies.

What *is* my anything, I wonder. A gentle back rub followed by vanilla ice cream, in a setting where there's no yuck food around so I can relax. Or a nap on clean sheets. Or a block of two or three hours in the maker space. Or browsing in my favorite art supply store.

I'm an idiot. My dreams are achievable. Just do them.

I'm on my way to being a rich appraiser. I'll have spare cash to do fun things on the weekends. My life will be filled with happiness if I allow it.

"That's my girl!" Cliff says when he sees my face relax.

Chapter Twenty-One

After I finish housework and have dinner with Paula, I text Lise to see if she and Halsted want to go for a short walk. I try a new thing where I go outside and breathe if I have a few minutes (and if it's not raining). I'm noticing tension in my chest and the breathing outside helps. Plus, I don't get any exercise, so walking with Lise is a way to appease the Gods of cardio.

Lise looks concerned, with her eyebrows drawn together when she and Halsted join me outside, and I see that Ben exits with them.

She walks over to me with her head bent down to be at my ear level. "Is this okay?" She asks in a low voice.

"Ben? Yeah. Sure," I say. I'm trying for an indifferent tone, but I'm a little sparkly inside. Why does he hold eye contact so long with me?

Louder, she says, "Ben's going to walk with us so we can talk about my hummus plan. Zillah, I told him you might come over when we do the exposure." She gets in my bubble again and whispers, "I didn't tell him about all your, um—"

"How I'm a picky eater?"

"Yeah." Lise would be the worst spy.

Just what I want to promote relaxation: talking about Yuck Food on a dog walk with Lise and her hot, weird brother.

We walk a couple of blocks on Wellington toward the lake, but Ben insists we go south a block so Halsted can pee on a specific tree stump.

"You're ridiculous," Lise tells him.

"No, he knows it's his stump. Watch." Sure enough, despite peeing as soon as he came outside, Halstead lets out special reserves of urine. "It might take hundreds of years, but Halsted is going to erode that entire thing."

"You live vicariously through him," I say. "I bet part of you wishes you could also piss in public."

"How do you know I don't?" He says with a smile. He seems to light up when I taunt him. "Maybe Halsted and I come out here in the middle of the night to make sure all the dogs know this is *our* tree stump."

Lise makes a noise between "blurg" and "ugh."

"Plus," he continues, "think of all the potential fires we prevent by keeping it moist."

"So, hummus," I say to introduce the topic at hand.

"Lise says you've been coming up with exposure methods based on..." He trails off with a questioning lilt.

I think for a bit. "Mostly based on anger."

"Not surprising," he says and does that staring thing again.

"I'm a picky eater," I say. "Like, really picky." We slowly make our way in the general direction of the park and then veer west back toward home while we talk about Lise's plan to look at and smell hummus ingredients. Kind of like I tried with the strawberry, but hopefully with less panic.

"Whaddya both think?" She asks us. "Want to try looking at hummus ingredients? And maybe getting near the final product? I won't eat it, but I'll at least get up close."

Ben says, "Yeah, I'll do whatever you want. That's easy." Then, with a stern tone, he says, "But maybe check with a professional first? And not—" he turns to me, "What are you studying again?"

Lise jumps in before I can come up with a scathing reply. "It'll be fun. I'm supposed to lean into fear. This is leaning in."

"When?" He asks. "I have two shifts at Jason's this week, so it'll be busy."

"Did you quit your job?" I ask.

Lise answers for him. "This is a trial to see if he likes it as much as he remembers." I guess being excitable about stuff is a little sister thing.

"What about Saturday, like in the morning? Morning-ish? Like before lunch and I'll be hungry. Does that work for you, Zillah?"

Crap.

Do I have to be there? Everything I ate today is forming a lead rock in my stomach as I consider being there and seeing hummus up close.

Both of them are looking at me hopefully while Halsted sniffs a pile of old gray snow that refuses to melt.

"Can I be a 'maybe'?"

It would be good practice for being near others in the lunchroom at my someday-office building. Another good step to help me become an adult with a full-time job. To prove I can move out.

And I have a few days to prepare. Today's only Monday. Saturday feels a world away. By then I'll have heard from other firms. Maybe I'll have other interviews lined up.

I'll be a different Zillah.

Chapter Twenty-Two

It's Thursday afternoon and I'm a mess. I haven't gotten any more notifications from firms and there's only a couple more hours in the workday.

Real estate students who went through this last year say a lot of the firms don't message students until Wednesday or Thursday, so it's not over yet. But it seems like almost everyone I've talked to already has a few interviews lined up. Having just one is a bad sign. What if I mess it up?

I toy with the idea of writing to the two other firms I'm interested in. I go to ChatGPT to help me try to phrase a statement that communicates, "I'm still interested if you are. Don't forget about me! But also, you'd be lucky to have me and I'm not desperate."

None of the AI results work, and I'm too wound up to write my own.

I'm also in a heightened state because I realize how much my other schoolwork has slipped while I've focused on internships.

This week I've had stress dreams every night about being late for final exams or showing up for an exam and realizing I'd never attended the class. And I've been suffering through the usual playlist of nightmares about being forced to eat disgusting things or about accidentally falling asleep by myself in the apartment with no one else here.

After my class, I don't want to relax at home since I'm trying to be good three weeks in a row and not eavesdrop on Lise for her Thursday therapy appointment. I need something to distract me for these final two hours of waiting for interview offers, so I hang out in the school library. I binge reality TV on my phone to kill time until 5:00 p.m., and then I finally check my school email account to see which firms reached out.

None.

I didn't get any more requests for interviews.

Fuck.

I stare at my account for a few seconds and refresh a couple times just in case.

Nothing.

Fuck.

It's all I can think about on the bus home. I try calling Cliff for some sympathy, but I get his voicemail.

My cover letter must be too focused on appraisal. I should have made it sound like I'm a wide-eyed ingénue, willing to do any sort of work whatsoever.

Now my one interview needs to be amazing. Everything's riding on it.

I got a good feeling when I called to schedule the interview, but what happens if they don't pick me? I'll need to change my concentration from real estate to some boring aspect of business. Paula will be pissed at me for failing. She'll say it's my fault for not taking this seriously. She won't give me the money from Dad so I can move in with Cliff.

Am I going to be living with Paula for the rest of my life?

A woman sits next to me, and I'm crushed between her moist wool coat and the bus window.

It's hot in here. I imagine red sharpie all over my skin and inside my organs.

My backpack is on my lap and crushes my lungs every time the bus hits a pothole.

Can I get out of my seat and stand in the aisle? It's too crowded to move and the water I drank is swishing around and threatening to come back up. My ears pound and it's like all the liquids in my body are fighting to get out at the same time. I'm all Jackson Pollock inside.

We're at least eight blocks south of where I need to be, but I've got to get out of here before I puke or die or whatever is happening here.

I'm too short to reach the pull cord from my seat, but someone else must need to get off because I hear the ding, and the bus jerks to the right and to a stop.

"I need to get off," I say to the woman next to me. She doesn't move fast enough or expects me to climb over her. I hate that. "I need to get off," I try again, more shrilly. This time she shifts her knees to the left so I can slide out.

Fucker.

I get out and direct all my anger at the stranger on the bus.

"Mother fucker," I mutter and walk north. "Fucking fucker." I'm not creative when I'm dying.

I had expected to vomit, but I'm better now that I'm outside.

My heart rate slows and I'm in good boots, so I trudge the rest of the way home.

I pass the McDonald's where Lise says Halsted always drags her when they're this far south in Lincoln Park because he once found a handful of french fries dropped on the sidewalk.

I think about the texture of his fur, and how it feels under my hand.

Breathe, Zillah.

You still have an interview with the best firm.

You are an amazing candidate.

They'd be lucky to have you.

When I get home, I try to walk sneakily through our apartment, so I don't have to give Paula an update in person.

I get to my room and continue my pep talk.

It's going to be okay.

Even if I take longer, Paula's not going to kick me out.

I'm lucky to have this home.

I look around my room, and that's when I notice my dresser.

My can of beans and its jaunty red bow?

It's gone.

Chapter Twenty-Three

P aula claims she threw out my can of beans because we had "agreed it was garbage." She's also convinced that the rat problem in the back alley is getting worse.

She's mentioned it on and off in person, by text, and by email as though we're in a constant conversation that is top priority above everything else going on.

This morning, she traps me in conversation while I eat breakfast. "Did you see anything moving when you took out the trash?" She asks.

"Nope."

"You didn't notice any dead ones, right?"

"No dead-rat talk while I'm eating, please." I have my earbuds in, but that doesn't deter her. Paula has amazing volume when she's motivated.

"Do you think one of the zoology professors at UIC knows about rat deterrent? Maybe there's a new tool out there that Alexi doesn't even know about."

This last conversational ploy gets me to react. "Mom, I don't know if we even have a zoology department."

"Will you find out? Make a few calls?"

"I'll google it later," I say. "But today I'm helping Lise with a project, so I'll be pretty busy."

That's how I find myself with Lise in her kitchen looking at Ben's preparations while we wait for him to finish a call. Their kitchen island has six porcelain bowls in a row, each containing an ingredient. There's also a menacing food processor plugged in at the end of the counter.

Lise moves around the kitchen awkwardly, looks in the bowls, opens and closes the fridge, sits on a stool, and stands up again. "I'm nervous. Are you nervous?" She asks.

"I don't think so?" Nervous isn't what I feel. It's not the restless energy Lise exudes, either. I'm too exhausted from my week to panic today.

Ben announces, "Ready!" as he comes in the kitchen then he sees me "Oh. Zillah's here."

"Nice to see you too."

"It's fine, but I only set up for one person, so you'll have to share," he says. He's less frisky than usual. Ben's all business. Is this what he's like at work?

"Not participating. Just a cheerleader." He hands us both napkins.

I don't need a napkin. Nothing is going in my mouth. I don't have to do anything I don't want to do; I remind myself.

"Okay," he says. "We'll start with Step One, 'Look'." He points at each of the small bowls and tells us about each ingredient, including some of the history. I'm familiar with them all in theory, other than the tahini. It's like a pale and shiny peanut butter.

The background is interesting, and Ben doesn't intersperse it with jokes and sarcasm like he does everything else.

I join Lise for Step Two, 'Touching and Smelling.'

"Pretend we're in a botany class and investigate each ingredient like it's a specimen," he directs us.

Knowing I don't need to eat any of the food helps me approach it, smell it, and even touch it. "Play with it," Ben says. "Crush the salt in your fingers. Squeeze a lemon slice. Dip your fingers in the liquids."

I start with the salt, since I've touched it many times. It doesn't smell like anything in particular, but it's fun to rub between my fingers and crush. It's the big flakey kosher salt instead of regular table salt.

I touch a lemon slice next, which is no big deal. I like lemon flavor, and the smell is nice. Clean. Comforting.

I let a garbanzo bean roll around on my hand. It's like a deformed marble and not soft like I expected.

The garlic is separated into little papery packages and I pick one up, unsure if it would be solid or mushy.

"You can take off the paper by twisting it like this," Ben says, showing me his technique.

"No, thank you." I didn't realize he'd been watching me and I put my little garlic parcel back in the bowl next to his now naked one. Until now, I hadn't experienced any real anxiety. Even smelling the ingredients wasn't grossing me out, and I had been working up to sticking my finger in the olive oil and even the tahini.

So, why am I nervous?

Because I don't want Ben to know I'm weird.

Ben, who comes from the weirdest and most welcoming family. Ben, who set up this freak show for Lise.

I sit with the thought "Ben thinks I'm weird" and in less than a minute it wears off and I get to that feeling Lise talks about. That "Meh. Fuck it." feeling. I need a tattoo of that somewhere.

Lise and I both touch the oil and the tahini. She's bouncing around, ramped up. I'm still surprised that this doesn't bother me. Maybe knowing that eating is off the table makes the difference?

Does Paula eat hummus when she's at work? We never talk about what she likes when she's not home. Maybe that's my next food step — getting more comfortable with *Paula* eating Yuck Food around me. There's really no reason she can't eat what she wants at our apartment. I see Cliff eat gross stuff all the time, even though I usually turn away if I can. It's just an old habit she's kept up out of kindness for me.

Paula's odd, but she's loving. She turns her whole life upside down just to make me feel safe and comfortable at home. I need to chew on this more. There must be some way to show her I'm growing, and also to thank her for all the things she's done for me and my pickiness for the last 23 years.

After Step Two, I wash my hands and say, "I'm in cheerleader mode for the rest." I've done enough new things for one day.

"You may change your mind for Step Four, *Mystery!*" Ben says, with the final word in a non-specific European accent. "How are you holding up, Lise?"

"Fine," she says in a small voice. "Let's get on with it."

For Step Three, 'Tasting', she licks the solids and uses a teaspoon to taste the liquids.

For each item, she holds a napkin in case she wants to spit anything out. The only one she hesitates on is tahini.

But she does it. I'm impressed with this girl.

"Still breathing?" Ben asks.

"Yeah," she says without elaborating. After finishing the tasting, she drinks water and announces she's ready for Mystery. "But can we speed this up?"

"What's your number?" he asked.

"I'm at, like, a five."

It takes me a moment to realize she means five out of ten on anxiety. Not too bad.

No one asks me, but I'm at about a three. Fine, but on guard.

"On to Step Four, the game of Mystery! You'll wear a blindfold and I'm going to put an item in your hand. You have to tell me what the mystery item is to get a point, and you can touch and smell it." Ben is pleased with himself, but Lise rubs her temples. "You can do this," he says.

I don't want the momentum to fade. If it's only touching and smelling, I guess I could survive. "I'll do it too, okay?"

"Fine," she says, the closest to snippy I've ever heard from her.

Ben gives me a small smile, but it reaches his eyes. Not his teasing look. Gratitude.

"Lovely," he says. "You are the kindest monster neighbor in Chicago." Ben hands Lise the sleep mask and goes to his room and comes back with a bandana for me. "Sorry, we only have one mask."

I give the bandana a sniff, wondering if it will have that musky smell of Ben's, but it's clean. Lise seems cheerier while she helps tie it on me.

The Mystery Game is simple, stupid, and fun.

Ben puts an item in our hands, and whoever guesses the item first gets a point. I assumed it would be the hummus ingredients, but he has a bunch of different things prepped. Some of them I recognize (chickpeas, salt, a whole apple), but most are baffling (celery and quinoa) and a few are ridiculous (lip balm, dice, Halsted's kibble).

I lose the game 5-22, and I realize I've revealed more of myself than I intended. I guess most people can recognize mustard by smell.

While Ben gets Lise to help him blend all the hummus ingredients, he asks me, "You've never cooked?" They put all the ingredients in the food processor and use the pulse feature to mash everything up, one second at a time.

After the noisy part, I say, "I make dinner for my mom and me most nights. But we eat pretty much the same thing all the time. Like I said, I'm picky." Lise looks up at me and I'm sure she's curious about how much I'll share.

"Got it," he says. He uses a silicone scraper to scoop the blended hummus into a bowl. He smooths the surface, drizzles on more olive oil, and sprinkles the top with a red spice and more chunky salt. "You haven't been around food a lot?"

"Pretty much."

"Ever thought how at this moment in time we can eat like royalty? Better than even all the kings before. We can get any ingredient, spice, anything. We have the most options of any humans at any time in history."

Lise jumps in, "And maybe the *last* time in history if global warming continues."

"Depressing segue," Ben says as he gets out a bag of pita chips and pours some into a bowl. "Okay, children. Normally, I would let this sit in the fridge for a few hours to let the flavors blend, but I'm going to eat this now instead. Does anyone else want to try first?"

"I'll have a pita chip," I say. We get those once in a while if they're on sale. It's like if bread and potato chips had a delicious baby.

Ben tilts the bag toward me, and I grab a few. Normally when I'm around Yuck Food, my appetite disappears. But those chips look okay.

Lise's quiet again and says, "No, thank you." Ben tries the hummus with a thoughtful look as he chews. "I'm not getting much of the garlic, but maybe because we just made it. I'll eat more at dinner with sliced cucumber." He takes another bite and looks at the ceiling as though a mysterious recipe would reveal itself there. "Yup. Needs more time. But, nice work, team."

I'm absorbed in the way he tastes it and wraps the bowl with a reusable cover. So, it takes me a moment to notice that Lise looks odd. She makes a little noise in the back of her throat like a mouse is trying to escape.

"You okay?" I ask.

Ben stops cleaning up and says, "Lise?"

She shakes her head and rushes to the bathroom. Halsted follows and sits outside the door. We hear unmistakable noises of retching and vomiting. Do I know Lise well enough to go in and hold her hair? After the noises stop, I tap on the door and try to make my intrusion as quiet as possible. I say, "I'm here if I can help." She doesn't respond and must have turned on the ancient bathroom fan because a loud whirring starts up that prevents any conversation.

"Can I help clean up?" I ask Ben.

"I'm almost done." He looks and sounds defeated. I sit at a barstool by the counter and take another pita chip.

"It's a step, right?" I ask. "You did good, Ben."

"I shouldn't have pushed her." He leans over the counter on the other side, with a kitchen towel slung over his shoulder like a barkeeper. "She didn't want to disappoint me. I should have kept it simple."

"Well, you helped *me*," I say.

I mean it, too. Part of my brain is concerned for my friend, but the other part is going *Yay Zillah! You touched a chickpea!* "I won't ever try hummus, but I'd do the rest again."

While we chat, Lise comes out of the bathroom and walks toward us slowly, as though afraid we would jump on her with too many questions. I try to give her the same kind of warm smile Ben had given me earlier.

"I don't want to talk about it," she says. "I'm fine."

I hand her the water glass she was using. "Thanks, Ben. That's the closest I've ever gotten." Then, to me, she says, "You can't leave yet. Can you help Ben with a menu?"

"Lise," he says with an exhausted sigh, as though they've adjudicated this already.

"I don't know anything about food," I say.

"It's the design. Ben's making a menu for Jason's restaurant for Arts Walk weekend. Can you do the graphic design?"

"I can't pay you and Jason might not use it," he says. "So, if you like doing unappreciated work for free?"

"When would you need it, and what's the visual theme?" I ask.

"I need it next week, and the theme is 'Helvetica'." He pulls up images of the current menus, and I can see what he means. Design had been an afterthought. "No one cares what it looks like."

"Yeah, they do," I say.

I take notes on my phone while he tells me a bit more, and I already have a few ideas germinating. He emails me the content, and a warm pressure builds behind my breastbone. It's not anxiety. It's a feeling that sometimes happens when I'm excited about a project. It's like a thirst I can only quench with devoted creative time. I'm filled with blues and pinks and yellows.

Lise looks more like her usual self, and she walks me back to my place, apologizing for her panic.

"Yeah, how dare you vomit?" I tease. "What are you, a human with a gag reflex?"

"Do you want to touch more food? Do you think you'll want to try tasting?"

"Never gonna taste it," I say. "But I guess it's good to get more familiar. Especially if I ever have kids."

"Are you and Cliff planning that far?"

"We talk about it." I leave it there. It's too painful to discuss, even with a friend.

I love the thought of having my own children someday if my body ever gets in the spirit of having regular periods, but not if I can barely function like a normal human. And not until my partner demonstrates the desire to raise the children with me. I want to break the tradition of the women in my family picking up the pieces of the men who leave.

Chapter Twenty-Four

I t's a new week, a new Monday, and I'm on edge about the interview. I can't believe I still have a week to wait; my future decided in one week.

In the evening, I need to get work done. I allow myself a couple minutes of deliberate relaxation with a plan to get cracking on catching up with coursework and preparing for my interview.

But.

I see an Instagram post about leather made from cork.

I research the history of cork and how it's harvested.

I watch a series of TikToks about cork manufacturing.

Fuck.

I spent another hour scrolling on my phone.

There's no way to find my sense of discipline tonight, especially since Paula's working late.

I text Cliff, "You home yet? Can I come over and finish my paper?"

He responds with a thumbs up.

Normally I can't concentrate at his place, but it has to be better than this. Plus, he'll enjoy the story of Paula's freakout over the beans.

An hour later, Cliff lets me in with a quick peck on my forehead.

"Can I have a hug?" I ask as we walk toward his room.

We stand together in the hallway next to the bathroom and he lets me sink into him and rubs my back in the gentle, comforting way I like. Even the mildewy smell of wet towels doesn't bother me too much. "What's going on?" he asks.

I relax but tense up again as we walk into his bedroom and I smell the evidence of aged garbage, stale cigarette smoke, and sweat. It's cold, too, because he has the windows open with a fan blowing outward. Somehow, it seems colder inside than outside, maybe because I'm anticipating comfort and not getting it.

"I'm airing it out for a few minutes, but it'll warm up soon," he says. "Want a beer?"

"No. I need to finish my paper." I look around for a clean place where I can sit with my laptop and still reach an outlet. "Let's go in the living room while your room warms up."

"Stay here. Neil's annoying with all his chanting." I feel prickles of anger again.

"Cliff, your room looks like an encampment. How about you take ten minutes to do a quick clean while I work on the couch?" I look at a full ashtray, a closet that's vomiting up a pile of clothes onto the floor, a Subway sandwich paper holding crumbs and pickles on his desk, and several used plates and coffee mugs.

"It's fine. I'll light incense," he says while brushing his hand over the detritus on his sheets and adjusting his blanket.

"There's no way I can concentrate in here." My voice is shrill like Paula's, and this insight makes me even angrier.

"You're so picky. You can clean if you don't like it."

This isn't an empty offer.

I often tidy up for Cliff so I can feel comfortable in his space. I imagine him drinking his beer without any guilt at all, looking at his phone, knowing I'm grossed out and doing his housework. Tonight, though, I don't have the patience or mom-instincts or desperation that has allowed me to touch his filth and still be in love with him.

"I'm going to work at Waffle House. You can come with."

"But I want you to stay the night," he says in a pleading tone that verges on a whine. He slides his arm around my waist. "I'll take a shower first." He bends down to kiss my neck the way I usually like, but I'm brittle with the tension of unfinished tasks and can't relax into him.

"Maybe tomorrow."

"Don't go anywhere. Wait ten minutes while I shower."

I'm pissed at Cliff for ignoring what *I* want, but I'm even more pissed at myself for following his instructions and sitting on his dirty bed while I wait. I love this guy. I really do. But I don't love our time together. It's okay most of the time, but I'm not excited about it.

I struggle to think of the last time we really connected. On Halloween I remember laughing about something with him. Were we watching something together?

What do I get from this relationship?

Safety.

History.

Feeling needed.

Happy Paula.

Are these good reasons?

Cliff smokes cigarettes and doesn't bother brushing his teeth even when he knows I'm coming over. He doesn't take me seriously because he knows I'm terrified of being with anyone else. Why bother getting up to brush your teeth if your girlfriend will stick around no matter what? Why bother setting your alarm if your girlfriend will wake you? Why bother cleaning, graduating, using an alarm clock, adulting if your girlfriend will be your mother?

Will Paula let me leave home if it's not with Cliff?

I hear Bethany's voice in the back of my head saying, "You can leave anytime you want." I *do* want.

Well, fuck. The realization slaps me across the face: I want to leave. I want to be single and see what else is out there. Or just single and less irritated all the time.

But can I?

Can I really?

The knowledge that I want out of this relationship is a pebble in my shoe. My watch on the wrong wrist. My hair parted ear-to-ear instead of front-to-back. I need to fix it, and I need it now.

I draft a text to him, "`I'll love you forever, but I think I might want to break up.`" No, not direct enough. "`We are breaking up.`" Send.

I take my backpack, grab my 'University of Your Mom' hoodie from his closet, and I leave. I walk down his block and don't have to wait long for the train.

I get a window seat, but since it's dark outside and bright inside, it's like a mirror back. Seeing my face makes it real and somehow worse. I'm crying and my nose is running so much I can only breathe through my mouth. I use my mittens to try to absorb my excess fluids.

I'm a disgusting mess, full of brackish green splotches.

I'm breathless and nauseous, and like my heartbeat is coming out of my ears.

What did I just do?

What if I'm alone forever?

What else did I leave in his place?

What if no one else will give me dry kisses?

What if this sends Paula over the edge?

What if I have to stay home with Paula forever?

Is this what a heart attack feels like? Am I dying?

My panic lasts for a few minutes, but it feels like an hour. At the end, I'm exhausted and sticky with tears and snot and sweat and regret.

But also pride.

This feels wrong and right at the same time. More right than wrong, though.

When I'm on the walk home from the Fullerton stop, I replay the parts of our conversation that made me angry.

It helps keep me from being too sad.

I picture our future children that will never be and think about his assumption that I'd have no problem picking up the dirty tissues next to his bed.

I cycle through sadness, anger, rage, pride, and terror all the way home and gear up to ignore Cliff's texts and messages until tomorrow.

Once I get home, I throw myself into the one activity I know will distract me: playing with graphic design. Paula gets home soon after and

I'm nervous she'll somehow see right through me and know I've broken up with Cliff. But she's exhausted and bleary eyed. She slumps down on the couch next to me and watches me work on the draft logos I'm redesigning for Newell's, Ben's friend's restaurant.

I had sent Ben three options for the menu on Sunday morning. I wanted him to react with, "Holy crap. I can't believe I know such an amazing graphic designer! How can I ever repay you for sharing your craft? I don't deserve this!" Instead, he wrote, `Thanks, Zillah. I'll go with version B. You're good at this.`

My product was okay, but the Newell's logo is so amateurish that it's hard to work around. I like a challenge, so I thought I'd play with options Ben could bring to his friend. It's surprising how well I can focus considering I just broke up with Cliff. Shouldn't I be a hot mess, weeping on the floor?

Paula asks, "Is this for school?"

"No. For a—" Ben's not a friend yet. What is he? "—an acquaintance."

"Is that the pasta place over by where Tower Records used to be?" I know what she means, even though Tower Records went out of business before I was born. Native Chicagoans are annoying about things like this.

"No, it's for a newer place. I offered to design a special menu, but after I drafted that I thought I'd try potential redesigns of the logo. It looks flat, see?" I turn my laptop to her so she can see the before, and for a second, I forget who I'm talking to. I get excited to show her my variations, adding depth that looks good in color *or* black and white.

But Paula's eyes glaze over, and she doesn't focus on the screen. "Why are you wasting your time on this? Did you finish all your schoolwork?"

"Well—" She doesn't see my grades, so I'm prepared to lie. But she interrupts before I need to.

"If you have extra time to design *pasta* pictures," she says pasta as though it's a disreputable sex position, "you could have helped me at the office."

"I didn't even know you needed—"

"You better not do your little drawings in your internship, Zillah. What would people say? You don't want them to think you don't care about real work." Her voice gets louder as she lectures me. "They'll say you're lazy and they won't want to hire you."

This is *not* the argument I thought we'd have this evening.

"Are you stressed from work?" I ask.

"Of course I'm stressed from work! If it's not one thing, it's another. And the new printer!"

I tune out while she tells me about her printer woes.

I wish I could talk to her about Cliff.

But she's prickly and defensive now, and I can't bear a lecture about Cliff and what it might mean to lose his family.

And I certainly don't need her pointing at the break-up as evidence I'm not ready to leave.

While she walks around unpacking her tote bag and venting about her day, I imagine her saying softly, "Zillah, you look sad. What's wrong, sweetheart?" She'd brush my hair out of my eyes and let me lean into her. She'd give me a calm hug and say, "it's not your fault. There's lots of men out there. I'm proud of you, my brave girl."

Tears well up in my eyes, and I clear my throat a couple times to get rid of the lump that grew there.

Paula notices. "Why are *you* crying? I'm not upset with *you*; I'm upset at technology." She slams a cabinet shut. "You're too sensitive, Zillah."

I am.

"Go to bed," she orders.

I do.

Chapter Twenty-Five

I wake before my alarm with a heaviness on my chest. It takes less than a second to remember that Cliff is gone.

Well, over in Logan Square.

But gone-ish.

My dumping was impulsive, but now that I'm clear headed I do an accounting. What are the things he brings to my life?

Familiarity.

Company.

His family.

A way to leave Paula.

These are not the foundations of partnership.

I want someone who listens well. Someone who cares about what I want. Who has adequate, or even amazing, hygiene. Who makes me laugh. Who is curious about me instead of thinking they know me better than I know myself. Someone who challenges me to grow. To Cliff, I'm convenient and safe. He knows I like the way he looks and won't fulfill his fear of rejecting him due to his appearance. I fit into the future he has planned, even though it doesn't always sound so good to me. I'm his sidekick.

"It's better to be alone than with someone you resent," I whisper out loud to myself. "You're brave to make a change like this."

I pick up my phone to face the text messages. He didn't send a bunch like I was expecting, and there's no voicemail. Just, "`Can we talk?`"

He may not realize it now, but he'll be better off with someone else, too. A woman he sees as an adult instead of as a girl who grew up with him. Picturing him with another woman raises my jealousy hackles, but that's not a reason to stay together. I just want her to be uglier than me.

It's early, but I text Lise. "`Cliff and I broke up yesterday. Not ready to talk about it yet.`"

There. At least someone else knows.

I'll get her response in a couple of hours when she wakes up.

I crawl out of bed to brush my teeth and take vitamins. I count the remaining B-12 gummies when a realization stabs me. Paula could find out about our break-up any minute.

She loves texting and calling Cliff's mom to try to eke out a closer intimacy than naturally exists. I've picked up hints that Cliff's mom reciprocates enough to be cordial for my benefit, but that spending time with Paula is too irritating.

Urgh. I need to break the news to Paula before she hears it from anyone else.

In the shower, I practice all sorts of ways to tell her. Do I wait until tonight to sit her down in person? Call her this morning while she's at work?

That heaviness in my chest returns. I get a stabbing cramp behind my left breast. Is this a heart attack?

It's gone.

But what if it comes back? Is this cancer?

Now I have a dull ache and, oh crap, focusing on it is making it worse.

I cut my shower short. After all, I don't have to shave anything today. No one's touching this and I kind of like my body hair when it's past the stubble stage. It's like a little pet that lives in my armpits. Maybe I'll grow it out to piss off Paula.

Paula.

Fuck.

I chicken out.

Instead of speaking to her, I send her an email with the subject line, "Please read when you have a minute." In the email I say that Cliff and I have broken up and that I'm devastated and don't want to talk about it yet.

I don't lie, *exactly*.

I mean, I'm a *little* devastated. Not about losing Cliff as a partner, but about losing his friendship and all the ancillary benefits. Feeling like a normal adult in a relationship. Having a future roommate. Pleasing Paula.

Does this email imply that he dumped me?

Yes.

Maybe she'll do the proper mothering thing and support me instead of thinking about what this means for her.

Hopefully she'll be up for talking about other ways I can move out. Cliff isn't the only human in the world who needs a roommate. Maybe Lise. We could devote a whole room to art and craft supplies. Ben would bring us artisan french fries. Vivian would do her supportive mom-ing over any little design choice. Halsted fur would get on everything.

I might be willing to risk it.

Chapter Twenty-Six

Paula responds better than I expected.

Around mid-morning, while I'm in class, she leaves me a voicemail, and I listen to it right after. "Oh, my doll! He'll realize what a mistake he made and even if you stay broken up, you'll meet another boy soon. My poor girl. I can't believe Cliff could do this." She pauses and clears her throat. "I'll get the groceries today and give you a break, so let me know if there's anything special you want. My girl." She sounds more devastated than I feel. I listen to her message a few times for the blanket of compassion she's wrapping around me.

When Paula gets home, she even surprises me with a half pint of ice cream.

When she brings up the break-up and whether there's a chance we could "patch things up" I look down at my lap as though I'm too hurt to speak.

I know it looks pathetic and sad, because I practiced it in front of my mirror for this purpose.

I have thought about reconciliation and what Cliff could do differently to make things better, but I don't want that. He's a good guy. We just aren't a good match. He'd have to change his whole personality.

We eat our cups of ice cream together after dinner, and it's a nice moment. I like when she's thoughtful like this. I take a mental picture to pull out when I'm angry at her again.

"Shall we practice for your interview?" she asks while I scrape my spoon against the mug to get out every last drop of ice cream. We always eat it in cups instead of bowls so that it feels like more. But it never works for me. I often go back for another mug-ful when she's not watching.

"I'm all set. It might make me more nervous." I still have a couple of days before the interview and I'm trying to stay positive. Not my strongest skill.

"I know you don't want to talk about Cliffy—"

I give her a stern look, but she continues. "—But one good thing is that Conway & Cranos is so close to us. Now you don't have to worry about finding an apartment with Cliff that's in Lakeview. You weren't going to find anything good enough in your price range, anyway. Now you can take the 36 and you can walk on nice days." She pauses to inspect her empty mug. I try to interject, but I'm not quick enough. "And it's on the way to Rogers Park, so I can take you in or pick you up when the timing's right. Do you know anything about your schedule? What it would look like? Maybe that's something you can bring up in your interview. Oh! That reminds me. I found a terrific, an absolutely terrific, blog post with interview techniques. It's written for Generation Z."

I get up and motion that I'll take her mug.

"So, what do you think about that one?" She asks.

"The blog post?"

"No, the 36 bus and—"

"Mom, I still need to interview." I give the cups a quick rinse and put them and the spoons in their assigned spots in the dishwasher. "And I'll find another roommate. Maybe Lise?"

"Lise!" She spits out the name like it's hot.

I sanitize the table and the counter while Paula says, "I assumed, I guess I was wrong to assume, you know what they say. Nonetheless, I always assumed that you would live here until you move in with your fiancé. And that you and Cliff would get engaged or even be married before you moved in with him. And that until then, I assumed—I know, I know, we shouldn't assume—you would stay here where you're *safe*."

"I'm done talking about this now." I give my hands a quick wash to get off any stray sanitizer mist, and head for my room. But Paula follows.

"I'm glad *you're* done talking about this, but I'm *not*. How are you going to pay for all the moving costs without me?"

I try to remember all the tips for maintaining boundaries that I saw on a TikTok. I watched a really good one a few times to try to memorize the lines, but they're gone now. The main point, though, was that it takes two to argue.

I gather my backpack and laptop even though I don't have anywhere I need to be. I pop in my ear buds and put on my motivational playlist. Paula's saying more things, but I try not to listen even though snippets break through like "how dare" and "infestation".

I kind of wonder whether she's talking about rats again, but I can't get lured in.

I say "Love you. Bye." as though nothing is wrong and go out in our stairwell. Once I'm by myself and I'm sure she's not following me, I text Lise to see if I can come over. She replies with a thumbs up.

I'm grateful. Especially when I realize I left my coat and wallet inside.

Chapter
Twenty-Seven

We sprawl out in Lise's living room and settle in with our laptops and an ambient music stream. Halsted does that circle-walk thing dogs do around his bed and then lays down in it as though he hasn't slept in years and has found the most comfortable surface in the universe.

He looks like he's sleeping, but one ear sticks straight up. I ask Lise about it.

"Yeah, he's monitoring everything," she says. "Watch this." She rubs her fingers together to make a small rustling sound and moves her hand all around. His ear follows like eyeballs in a cutout painting in Scooby-Doo cartoons.

I could be a good dog. I don't mind eating the same thing every day. I like my designated poop and pee spots. I don't bite. How freeing to not have the constant flow of worries like lava under the surface.

Halsted's head pops up a few minutes later, and he runs to the door to greet Vivian. "Hello, sweet woofer!" we hear her say from their front door. "Did you dream about squirrels today?" She greets Lise and me and puts her things down on the kitchen table.

I like that she doesn't make a big deal about me being here, like offering me food or asking lots of questions. Some parents are overly solicitous, but she treats me like another human in her pack. "Is Ben home yet?" she asks us.

"No," Lise says while looking at her screen. She resembles Halsted picking up an interesting sound and perks up with attention to her mom. "Wait! Is today his staging?"

"Yup!"

"Staging?" I ask.

"It's like a day-long test in a new kitchen. You don't get paid, but you can learn stuff from the chefs there and see if you're a fit."

"Didn't he do that already?"

"No, he's done grunt work so far. Today is like a chef internship."

Halsted repeats his performance of perking up and running to the door when Ben gets home, too.

Ben is all smiles, but warns his family, "Don't touch me. I stink like cooking oil." He heads for his room.

"Just tell us if it was good or bad!" Vivian shouts through the door.

"Good! I'll tell you about it after my shower."

Vivian shares a happy look with Lise before she sighs contentedly and sinks into a comfy chair to look at her phone. She crosses her legs, and one foot does a little jiggle while we wait.

I try to focus on my presentation for my econ project while I hear distant shower sounds and singing. By the time I add content to three slides, Ben comes out in fresh clothes with wet hair. He looks like he ran his fingers through it and I wonder what it feels like. He's dressed more casually than I've ever seen him, in joggers and a worn band t-shirt that clings to him slightly. It looks good, and I feel guilty for a second, thinking of Cliff. I shouldn't be noticing another man's body yet. Ben rummages through their refrigerator and says, "Okay! Ask any and all questions my dear lady folk. And dog folk. And neighbor folk."

They take his instructions literally.

"How is dating going?" Vivian asks.

"Did you take my Draculaura doll while I was at camp in eighth grade?" Lise asks.

They go on like this for a while, as Ben pours himself sparkling water, and settles on the floor next to Halsted to give deep ear rubs.

"When are you going to cut your hair? Aren't you sick of it flopping in front of your beautiful eyes?"

"What are you gonna get me for my birthday?"

Halsted emits a loud groan and leans his head into Ben's open palm. "I'll entertain questions about my shift."

"How was it?" I pipe in. It's not my place, but I'm curious, and this family doesn't ever get to the point if they can make each other laugh instead. It's like they care more about goofing around than getting usable information.

"Good." Ben moves to Halsted's other ear and we are granted a groan that sounds like it originated from a much larger dog. "Jason let me decide on one of the sides for the special and it was cool to look through the ingredients on hand and be creative. I did a simple roasted Brussels sprouts with a light lemon reduction. I brought some home." Halsted stands up and moves his rear end into Ben's face. "You need butt scratches? I know how to give a dog butt scratches." After a moment, he continues. "It was a great team. Remember Ali? They're on prep."

"When are you going to do it again?" Vivian asks.

"I need to think about it." He gives Halsted gentle long strokes down his back. His voice is slower and more deliberate. "Jason said I could come on full-time since they are down a line chef. Coming in for a shift once a week isn't fair to them. I don't know. I keep coming up with menu ideas and things I want to run by him." He turns to Halsted, "No buddy, they don't want raw squirrel. They don't have good taste in food!"

Vivian adds her last bit of mom-wisdom before Ben can fall back into the ridiculous. "A full-time position as a line chef won't pay as much as what you're getting."

"About half as much."

"But what's the point of spending most of your waking hours doing something you don't like?" she asks.

I can think of lots of points. Savings. 401K. Emergency planning. Mortgage. Resume building. Family pride. Making use of a degree. It's like they're from a different planet where the point of life is fun and who cares if you don't have a retirement fund?

Vivian hoists herself up, gives both her kids kisses on their heads, and goes to her room to unwind. Lise and I re-orient ourselves to study while Ben moves over to the kitchen counter to prep something greenish. Lise changes the stream to Modern Pop and, as the first song begins, she warns Ben, "No ranting! We were here first."

He ignores her and rants anyway while washing and chopping the green thing. It looks like broccoli, but longer and thinner. "This music is garbage. What station is it?"

"It's 'go get your own apartment'," she says.

"It's so on the nose. This song has no subtext." He sings along with the popular song, but with his own lyrics to demonstrate. "Oh, baby. I am attracted to you. Let's have sex. I am good at the sex."

"Ben!"

He abandons his vegetables and comes over to mock serenade me. "I like sex with humans. Sex is good." I catch my breath and snort-laugh. I'm loving this attention and all the eye contact.

I like the spectacle of sibling conflict as well as Ben's antics. It's like the primate enclosure at the zoo. But Lise's eyes dart at me and she mouths "sorry" while turning red.

Ben sees the signs and stops the serenade. "What's your number?" he asks her.

Phone number?

"Eight or nine," she says.

Oh. Fear scale thing.

"Keep going," I say. "We can do an exposure right now." Ben and I both look at Lise. She nods.

Ben goes all out pop star. He gets on his knees and leans back, singing up toward the ceiling. "This is my cash grab. I write songs to pay for drugs." He gets closer to me, and during the musical bridge, looks me in the eyes. He asks, "Is this okay?"

He's close enough I can smell him. "Keep going."

So he does.

He sings me a chorus about how sex is a thing that humans do, and he is a human. And that sex makes babies, but condoms are good. The lyrics are inane, but he does have quite a good voice.

Toward the end of the verse, he looks me in the eyes and sings things like "anus," "mammary glands," and "kneecaps." My heart rate is up, but that makes sense. A dude is singing to me about ridiculous things. I feel the signs I sometimes get before a panic attack and I think *please don't freak out,* which makes it worse.

Vivian is right. He does have lovely eyes.

My hands are sweaty, and I rub them on my jeans.

This is arousal.

There is no danger.

You are turned on because a beautiful guy is singing to me.

He asks me again, "Is this okay?"

Is it?

I feel like I'm cheating on Cliff.

It's normal to be turned on by things.

By people.

I nod. "You're doing great." He sings a bit more but has exhausted his repertoire of faux-sexy lyrics and starts repeating himself.

Lise's color has returned to normalish, and she's able to make eye contact with me again. She leans over and says, "siblings are a mixed blessing." At the end of the song we applaud and Halsted jumps around Ben, clear that something exciting has happened.

"That was pathetic," Lise tells him. "You are the worst songwriter ever."

"What was your number at the end?" he asks.

"I got down to a four almost right away, but I didn't want to stop you before you were humiliated in front of Zillah."

Chapter Twenty-Eight

My stomach is tight from hunger when I leave Lise's place even though I had dinner a couple hours ago. Ben sent me home with a pretty bowl with a "tasting" of the side dish he brought back from the restaurant. I didn't have the heart to say no, and the little Brussels sprouts are actually adorable, although inedible.

So green.

But I might use them for a little exposure tomorrow if I get up the nerve. I could touch them. I kind of want to see what happens if I peel back the charred layers. I'll dissect them and throw them in the food waste without hurting anyone's feelings.

My hunger is a good sign. It means *carrying* the china bowl containing vegetables doesn't scare me so much that my fight-or-flight is up. If I were terrified, I wouldn't be hungry at all.

And if I were really devastated about Cliff, I wouldn't be hungry or horny.

I'm uncomfortable with the fear that I'm going to drop this bowl. Lise had said, "Mom is going to notice that missing," so I'm guessing it's valuable.

I consider my snack options while I walk up the stairs with a death grip on Vivian's bowl. I settle on a peanut butter sandwich, since that will be fast and filling.

But when I go to the fridge, I can't find any bread. I'll have to toast frozen bread. The peanut butter will get liquidy and messy, but not a big deal.

No bread in the freezer, either.

Weird, since Paula just picked up the groceries. Bread is on our standing order and generic white sandwich bread is so commonplace that Safeway has never been out of it.

"Hey, Mom." I say and knock on Paula's door. Is she still mad at me?

"Come on in, doll." That's one good thing about Paula. She gets over conflicts quickly.

I open her door and lean against the door frame. "Why didn't Safeway give us bread? Should I check the receipt to make sure we didn't get charged for it?"

She's at her desk, looking like she's in work-mode on her laptop. She closes the lid to her laptop and stretches while talking. "Oh, I meant to tell you. I took bread off our order."

"Why?" I come in and sit on her bed. This might take a while.

"Oh, you know about the insects, right? How they say that a single loaf of bread has about nine hundred insect parts in it? Or maybe it was nine hundred grams. Does that sound right? How much is a gram of insect parts?"

"Sounds like an urban legend."

"Yes, doesn't it? But it's true! I read it on the news site. Not the Post. The other one. Whatchamacallit. You know what I mean. The newer one."

My hunger pains have disappeared. Cold dread takes over. "Mom, you don't believe this, right? I mean, nine hundred grams is a lot. That's like half a loaf of bread or something."

"Maybe it was milligrams, but better safe than sorry until the FDA can figure it out. It's a crisis, Zillah! I can't believe you haven't read about this. What *do* you read?"

"I read lots of stuff." Is this a better argument than the bug thing? I'm exhausted all of a sudden. I almost don't have the energy to ask, "So, can I buy different bread?"

"No bread, Zillah." Her voice is gratingly loud. "Can't you live without bread for a few days? Maybe less carbs would be healthier for you anyway." Is she calling me fat?

"But I want—"

"Zillah, for goodness' sake. Relax!" I hate when she shouts "relax" as though that's ever worked to calm someone down. "It's only bread. You'll survive."

What's the best way to approach this? Logic? Emotion?

"Okay. 'Night."

Avoidance works.

Even though I got sleepy while talking to Paula about bread and bugs, now I've been lying in bed for almost an hour and I can't fall asleep. Every time I drift off, I jolt awake to think of another thing I need to do. I think about my interview tomorrow afternoon, jobs, Italian ice, Paula, texts I need to answer, a library book I need to return, climate change, and the weight of the world. I think about how long I'd have to work as a part-time anything until I'll have enough saved for a first month's rent payment, last month's rent payment, and a security deposit.

And I have a stab of regret about Cliff when I realize I can't text him to share this latest Paula quirk.

I think about Halsted and his ability to rest.

I think about Ben singing. Ben asking, "Is this okay?" Ben looking me in the eyes.

I touch myself.

I think about him singing and imagine him getting even closer.

"Is this okay?"

I imagine him cupping my cheek.

"Is this okay?"

I imagine him holding my hand.

"Is this okay?"

My heart beats faster and I roll on to my stomach. I imagine him moving my hair off my neck and giving me a dry kiss there.

"Is this okay?"

I imagine him running his fingertips along the side of my breasts.

After a couple of minutes, my mouth opens.

Am I drooling? Is drooling a normal masturbation stage?

I let my imagination keep going.

Based on what I've read, I'm positive that I've had little orgasms before. But this is the first one that comes on so strongly there's no doubt in my mind.

Afterwards, my heart keeps beating fast. My mouth is dry like I've been running.

Must have been from the drooling. My body slowly returns to normal, with a few residual throbs, and I consider the experience.

Fun.

Primal.

Not at all like female masturbation scenes in porn or in old movies like "Body Double." It wasn't artistic, or anything that would look sexy to someone else.

Is Ben touching himself and thinking about me?

I flip my pillow over, so the drool is toward my bedsheet.

Definitely not like in movies.

But something to try again.

Chapter Twenty-Nine

In the morning, Vivian's china bowl is washed and resting upside down on the drying rack. I peek in the garbage can and the food waste bin but can't find any remnants of Ben's Brussels sprouts.

Paula must have gone through extraordinary lengths to remove those little green guys from the premises. There's no way she could have eaten all of them.

It's kind, but weird how she keeps our home a safety zone for Zillah food. It must have been important to me as a little kid, farther back than I can remember. But the thought of her eating those sprouts, even in front of me, doesn't bother me. I really don't think I'd be grossed out.

And even if it does gross me out, I'd get over it.

Paula also left me a sweet note on the table, "I'll be thinking about you all afternoon during your interview! Break a leg!"

She does so much for me.

I'll figure out a way to get her to feel comfortable eating Yuck Food in front of me. After she does it once or twice and I don't freak out, her life will be so much easier. Maybe she'll be less grouchy if she's better fed. And no more circling the block when she's driving to get in that last bite of whatever.

That's a tomorrow puzzle. I bet Lise will have good suggestions for how to transition. I can ask her on our next walk.

Now I need to get through my morning and hope that my class is distracting enough to keep me from freaking out about the interview.

After class, Lise comes over to help me get ready for the interview. She sits on my bed and nods as I tuck my blouse into the skirt suit I've borrowed from Paula. I'm thicker around the middle, but magic with a safety pin fixes that.

"How conventional do you want to look?" Lise asks. "You're fine except for your legs."

I forgot about pantyhose (barf). But I guess my first real job interview is a reasonable time to bow down to the patriarchy. I go to Paula's room to take a pair of hers and return to find Lise going through my jewelry.

"Do you have anything that's less ironic?" she asks, holding up lime green translucent dinosaur earrings.

"My grandmother's pearls." I dig out the velvet bag from under my thief-deterring socks.

We dump the necklace and earring set onto my bedspread. "They're from my dad's mom. When my aunt gave them to me, she said not to wear the necklace until it's been re-strung, which is a thing rich people do?"

"It costs, like, a hundred dollars," Lise says as she prods the necklace with her finger. "But you could wear the earrings. They convey, 'I like to fit in!'"

When I'm ready, she takes pictures and walks me to the bus. I'm half paying attention to all her teasing now that this is getting real.

Chapter Thirty

Please don't sweat through the blouse, I beg my armpits.

I get there twenty minutes early, so I loiter around the corner outside a bank. I probably look suspicious while I pace back and forth in front of their entryway. At five till the hour, I return to Conway & Cranos Real Estate and check in with the admin at the front desk. She gives me a warm welcome and asks if I want anything to drink while I wait. I avoid the trap of spilling liquid on myself and try not to fidget on an upholstered chair in the lobby.

So far, I have a good feeling.

I like the sounds of staff laughing in the distance and that the art in the lobby isn't mass produced. I get up to look closer at the small business-card shaped plaque on the wall and see that all the paintings were purchased from a local high school on the south side that has free after-school programs devoted to fine arts. The plaque is showy in a virtue-signaling kind of way, but at least the firm spent money on a school rather than one of those companies that supplies art along with other decor as a total vanilla package.

Things change when the admin brings me back to see Mr. Seidel. She has me follow her to his office and gives me a little squeeze on my arm before she goes back to her desk.

Arm squeezes are odd. If she's related or a friend, *maybe* it's okay. What's she trying to convey? Maybe she's one of those touchy-feely extroverts. I'm little, so people assume I want hugs and touching. If they bring me on, I'll have to be assertive with her.

Mr. Seidel sits perpendicular to me, facing toward his wall and leaning far back in his leather upholstered chair behind a large desk, reading a stapled set of papers I recognize as my resume and cover letter. He doesn't acknowledge me beyond a quick look and nod of his head. He looks trapped in a u-shaped crescent of desk all around him, much too large for the space. Neat piles of papers and folders cover most of the desk surface, along with a computer docking system and two monitors on the far side.

I stand inside the doorway, waiting for him to invite me to sit down at one of the chairs in front of his desk. He finishes reading the first page of the stapled bundle, but instead of turning the page, he rips it from the other pieces and places it on one of the few empty spots on his desk. He reads through the next page, stops reading to sit up straight, puts the paper on his desk, and circles something with a red pen. He turns perpendicular again and continues to the end of the page. He repeats his performance of ripping it from the last piece of paper and returns to reading.

When he finishes, he rotates toward me and puts the remaining page on top of the other two.

Still no eye contact.

Mr. Seidel picks up the pages to tap them into alignment and sets them on top of a stack of other papers.

"*How* do you pronounce your first name?" He emphasizes the "how" as though he has been asking for several minutes without resolution.

"Zillah."

He picks up the set of papers again and frowns. He repeats "Zillah" to himself.

That's enough time on my feet. I enter the room and sit in a chair. What's he going to do — tell me to stand at attention? "And you're Mr. Seidel?" I ask to remind him I'm a conscious human being. He nods, without giving me permission to call him by his first name, so I guess we're Mr. Seidel and Zillah.

What a very normal dynamic.

He sets down my resume again and makes brief eye contact with me before he picks up a yellow legal pad, rotates again ninety degrees, and resumes his reclined position facing his wall.

"What do you know about our firm?" he asks.

Excellent! Dr. Duffie had warned us this would be a common question, and I'm prepared. I summarize the history of the firm.

"And what do you know about the internship experience here?"

Urgh. This one's harder, since the brief description I'd gotten from my prof is probably not what Mr. Seidel was looking for ("a bit of this, a bit of that. Learn the ropes and they'll see where you fit").

I regurgitate what I had seen on the Conway & Cranos Real Estate website under career opportunities, and add, "but I hope to learn from everyone here so I can contribute in a variety of ways." He turns and looks at me without saying anything.

At least he's looking at me.

Does this mean keep going?

I elaborate. "I'm especially interested in appraisal for residential and commercial real estate."

He turns back to my resume, placing it on top of his notepad.

"What is Northside Health?" he interrupts to ask.

"A family medicine clinic in Rogers Park." I describe the ways I have provided a variety of administrative services, without mentioning that my immediate supervisor is my mother and that I'm a work-from-home nepo baby.

The rest of the interview proceeds in the same way. Mr. Seidel asks me questions without looking at me ("Why are you taking so long to graduate?", "How will you prove yourself?" and "Why should we take you, instead of students with more experience?"), he occasionally makes brief eye contact, and he appears displeased the entire time. It's like he's auditioning for the role of "Dick Boss" in a stage play.

The interview prep advice I reviewed assured me I was interviewing the company as much as they were interviewing me.

Clearly, Mr. Seidel has not watched these same videos.

It lasts forever and then is over with a sudden finality like a book slamming closed on a bug.

I leave with the sense that I wasted his time and bored him.

On the bus back home, I think back to hints I had ignored from Dr. Duffie about this particular internship site. "A few of the older partners can be taciturn but have a tremendous amount of experience to share." I consider the arm squeeze lady, and how she had effusively said, "I'm *so* glad you are considering us!" It reminds me of how I'm often kind to others when I'm with Paula to compensate for her brusque manners.

Anger recedes with every bus stop and confused shock skips forward to take its place. Then devastation.

I bombed.

I bit the dust.

I failed.

I'm going to live at home forever.

How did I go wrong? It seemed like Mr. Seidel was set against me before I entered his office. Did I include an F-bomb in my application? Maybe he was forced to interview me. Maybe I'm a dead ringer for his ex-wife or there was some other coincidence I couldn't have helped.

Or maybe my resume isn't strong enough. I don't have any prestigious experiences. No academic awards. No years of admin experience in real estate. I've had to turn down opportunities like day-long shadowing because I wasn't sure about the bathroom situations. I didn't go to the out-of-town summits and conferences because I didn't know how I could manage to eat my foods and seem normal while everyone else was eating theirs in restaurants and wherever.

Paula always says that I'll know when it's right to travel for the first time because it will *feel* right. That hasn't happened yet. She says if I feel nervous about travelling, then it's "too much too soon" and that I need to trust my gut about danger.

Maybe I would have gotten used to it, though. Why do I always listen to her? Have I screwed myself by staying safe?

By the time I get off the bus, dread has joined the other feelings at the party in my brain. What the hell am I going to do next? None of my other applications produced leads. I counted my dinosaur eggs before they hatched.

I'm at Wellington Avenue, but I don't want to go home. What if Paula's there? She's texted for updates, but I don't know how to respond.

She'll be supportive, maybe, but she'll also hint that it's all my fault. She'll ask, "Did you say something to put him off?" My anger flares up at her, even though this is an imaginary conversation.

It's not too cold out, and the sun hasn't set, so I walk down Oakdale until I get to a short stone wall around a courtyard garden where I can sit and be.

Normally I'd freeze in this temperature, especially in my dress flats and a skirt. But I'm artificially warm today thanks to the adrenaline and red crayon still pumping around my scared and angry self.

Thinking back to a mindfulness app I tried and quit, I inhale all the peace around me and try to exhale the tension.

I try again.

Again.

I'm sitting in a beautiful neighborhood in the best city in the world. I have enough to eat, a safe place to sleep. I have friends and family that love me.

It's not enough.

I want more.

When I get back to our place, Paula's there. She must have been waiting for the sound of my key in the lock, because she's at the door waiting for me.

"That bad?" she asks after one look at me.

"I don't want to talk about it." Her face drops. I'm not being fair. "I'm going to eat on my own tonight."

"Just tell me if you think you have a chance?"

"We can talk about it tomorrow." I kick off my flats, grab them, and head for my room.

"Zillah—"

"It sucked, Mom. Okay? I'll give you details tomorrow." I go to my space, crank up my music, and pretend I can't hear Paula still asking questions outside my door. I wish she'd leave so I could drown my sorrows in potato chips and spoonfuls of sugar.

In the morning, I get an email from Dr. Duffie congratulating me on what he heard was a solid interview. About an hour later, I receive an official offer for an internship spot with Conway & Cranos. A dark and itchy dread fills me. I'll be working under the tutelage of Mr. Seidel.

Chapter Thirty-One

Paula makes us a celebratory breakfast in honor of my internship notification. She sings an extemporaneous song about being "over the moon" as she hands me dishes and flatware to put on the table. She even brings over our glass pitcher for ice water, so we don't have to get up for refills. This is peak Scriven fanciness.

But it all feels fake, like we are acting out a movie scene of "Happy Mother and Daughter". Even the frozen waffles taste carboardy when they come out of the toaster. I say, "Aren't you gluten-free now? Because of the bugs?"

"Waffles aren't bread," she sings. She reverts to her normal speaking voice to add, "I've only seen articles about insect parts in loaves of bread. Other flour-based products must have higher standards."

I scoop peanut butter into a mug, plug in the microwave and heat it for thirty seconds, then unplug the microwave and return to the table with my homemade waffle dip. Normally Paula would object, but I've got to take advantage of being the golden child while it lasts.

Adding a tablespoon of sugar would make this epic, but I don't have the energy to get up again.

I eat and attempt to tune out Paula's speech about the new copy machine at her office. Her voice is extra loud, but this may be due to my mood rather than an actual Paula volume issue. I can pretend to listen by nodding and saying "uh-huh" enough to keep her satisfied. But this morning, soundbites break through my thoughts. I hear, "—always runs warmer than our old machine" and "—just impossible to speak with a person, a real live person, on the customer service line."

I can't concentrate since I'm stuck on a worry loop about how to survive my internship.

On one hand I'm lucky I even *have* an internship. And it's only for a summer. But there's an expectation that we end up working for our internship site after graduation unless things go terribly. And I could barely stand Mr. Seidel for 20 minutes.

I'm caught red-handed when she asks, "So, what do you think about that one?"

"Um."

"What would you do about the printer?"

"I thought it was a copier?"

"Whatever. Printer. Copier. Scanner." She waves her hand around as she talks. "I can't turn it off at night because the start-up time is so long. I was coming in early to start it up so Jennifer wouldn't keep complaining, but you know how *that* went. I don't care how many bags of avocados she brings into the office. It doesn't make up for being sloppy with fire safety."

I finish chewing my bite and say, "If it's malfunctioning, have a repair tech come assess it. You guys just bought it, so I bet it's covered."

"Oh, my brilliant daughter! That firm is lucky they hired you."

"It's only an internship."

"Whatever you call it. It's a step in the right direction. They'll love you and hire you!"

"I don't know. The guy I'm working with is—" I struggle for a polite word for dick hole. "—unpleasant," I settle on. "I'm going to hate it."

"Nonsense."

"It's going to suck."

"I don't like that word."

"I don't like my life." I grab my plate and the empty serving dish and start cleaning up.

"What, are you twelve?" She joins me at the sink with her plate. "No one likes work. You're too picky."

"I know."

"You can't get through life drawing pictures on your computer. It's time you—"

"I know."

"Let me finish. It's time you get more serious about—"

"Mom, I *know*." My voice is so loud it's like I can hear it in my bones. I leave for my room and pretend I don't hear her trying to continue the argument. It takes two.

I stay in my room until I hear her leave and then I take an extra long, wasteful hot shower.

After I've used every possible product, I look for another excuse to stay under the hot water.

I need something positive to look forward to.

This is when Cliff would be helpful. He's always up for helping me kill time with something unproductive. We would watch a show or an old favorite movie and not need to talk.

Is this why people have dogs? I'll stop by Lise's and see if she wants help walking Halsted. It's becoming a Thursday morning tradition. And maybe she'd have ideas about turning my apartment into a more food-welcoming environment.

Showing Paula she can eat Yuck— no, *regular* food around me in addition to having an internship will be great evidence of my adulthood and my ticket out of this freak show.

Chapter Thirty-Two

B en answers the door. His eyes widen when he sees me. I'm conscious of my shitty bun and my lack of make-up.

"Godzilla," he says as a statement. Halsted is going nuts behind him, trying to get out of the door. "You okay with him?" he asks me.

"Yeah." I crouch down and Halsted comes out to sniff me and wag so much that his tail beats a rhythm on the wall. Doesn't that hurt him?

I like that once he's free of the doorway, he doesn't race down the stairs and away to freedom. He must like this weird, loud family.

"Just stopping by to see if I can help Lise walk him." I straighten up and Halsted leans against me doing that thing where he puts his snout under my hand no matter where I try to hide it until I end up petting him.

"She's not here. Dentist." Ben opens the door wider. "But I'll go with you so we can talk about the logo stuff you sent."

"I should have texted first," I say. This sounds uncomfortable, but maybe better than being alone. "You sure you have time?"

"I'm playing hooky this week."

"Hooky?" I squeeze by him to come in while he gets ready. He doesn't bother getting out of the way, but instead lets me get in his personal space.

"I gave my notice at work, but I want to use up my sick leave since I won't get reimbursed for it."

"Wow. You really did it." I'm impressed and also worried for him.

I find Halsted's leash and check the roll of poop bags in the plastic bone-shaped container to make sure we have at least three. Lise and I learned that lesson the hard way. I also grab a bag of treats in case we need an on-site intervention.

"Look at you. You're a Halsted expert," he says when he sees me with all the correct accouterments. "Halstexpert?" I shake my head at the stupid portmanteaux.

"Dogician," I say. "Dog magician."

"Terrible. You need to workshop that one."

We walk down the stairs. Halsted races ahead and waits at the bottom for us to leash him up.

"I got it," I say and hook him in. What the hell are we going to talk about?

"I need to give you that bowl back. From the Brussel sprouts."

"Brussels sprouts."

"What?"

"There's an 's' after Brussel. Brussels."

"Like 'Attorneys General?'"

"But tastier. Did you try them?"

My first instinct is to lie, but I say, "My mom cleaned out the bowl before I got a chance. They looked interesting." We're quiet for a bit while we watch Halsted sniff an oncoming golden retriever. "I'm not experienced with food."

"That was my impression."

"But I want to get more comfortable."

Halsted pulls when he realizes we're walking toward the park. We use the treats to try (and fail) to make him wait at a crosswalk.

"We should go grocery shopping together sometime."

"Maybe." Hell no. Not much embarrasses me, but that would be awkward. I'm not ready for Ben to know how truly strange I am. I want him to be impressed with me and not flabbergasted by my toddler-like diet.

"I'll stop by later to get the bowl," he says.

"No, I should drop it off. You were doing me the favor. The polite thing is to fill it with something homemade, but I'm not sure if chicken nuggets count?"

"I like a nugget once in a while." Then he adds, "You're extra pleasant today."

"I'm saving up all my grievances for a good rant."

"Perfect," he says. We walk for a bit and he says, "So. Business. Jason likes your designs. He gave me notes on paper and I'll bring them over."

This warms me all over. I want the notes so I can make revisions. Is it weird to ask to turn around? Patience, Zillah.

"I can do more. I'm happy to revise. That's the point of giving him something black and white to start so he doesn't get caught up in colors yet. Do you remember which version he liked the best? I also had other ideas in case none of those fit his vision."

"You light up when you talk about design. It's almost like you're not thinking about murder."

"Perceptive, Benjamin."

That earns me a smile. The same one I picture when I've been thinking about him in bed.

"You should start a Fiverr," he says.

"What do you mean?" I ask while teasing Halsted with a stick, trying to get him to chomp it. He gives it a little sniff and ignores it. If we hold up one he approves of, he'll carry it a few blocks and lift his snout high in the air to display his prize. He gets sassy when another dog is in the vicinity. The trick is finding one that he likes.

Ben says, "He won't take that one. You need to take off the leaves first. Gimme." I hand it over to him to prepare. As Ben predicted, Halsted reconsiders the offering and accepts it with satisfaction.

Ben gets back to the open conversational tab. "You could do menu designs for other restaurants, too. That package you made for Newell's was good. Really good. I couldn't believe one little reptile monster could be so talented."

"For five dollars?"

"The gig sites let you pick whatever you want. But you could re-package what you did for us as a template. If you price it low now, you can raise the cost later when you have a history of high ratings." He's talking with his hands, which I've learned is Ben's tell for excitement. He likes to play cool, but his hands don't lie. "Hold the leash and I'll show you."

I look over his shoulder while he searches on Fiverr for "restaraunt menu." Fiverr corrects his spelling. He hands me his phone.

"These all look the same," I say as I scroll through the results. "That one's pretty good. *Shit*. Thirty dollars?"

"Is thirty dollars good or bad?"

"Right now, it would be great," I say. "I need a lucrative hobby." Before I hand his phone back, I let him and Halsted get ahead of me and open his phone to the camera. I take a selfie featuring my middle finger and my best angle.

He's lucky I don't have time to snoop.

"I improved your photo roll," I say as I hand back his phone.

"I owe you for all the Big Management Energy you're giving me at the restaurant."

"Don't try to talk like the youth."

Our walk home from the park is too fast and I try to keep the conversation going even as we enter the courtyard.

"Ben, you might be able to help *me* with something. I want to surprise my mom. With food."

"Okay?" We're in front of his doorway, but he leans against the glass relaxed.

"Like, is there a food you can make that looks really boring but actually has something interesting in it?" I'm developing my plan while I talk.

"Is 'interesting' your code word for poison?" He gets me.

"I was thinking something that looks like a sugar cookie, but it has fruit in it? Is that a thing?"

"Lemme think. I'm making madeleines soon and I could pipe a little strawberry preserve in the middle. That would go well with the lemon zest. Is that the kind of thing you mean?"

"I think so."

"Want to come over and help? Do you bake? I could put out eggs tonight and we could do it tomorrow morning if you could be ready by eight."

"Um."

"Lise would like it. Let me check and make sure I have everything I need, okay?"

"Yeah. Thanks."

"Good walk, Zillah. You managed to keep up on those little legs."

"Good walk, Ben. You pick up poop like a pro." I walk toward my own stairwell and call, "Adding your pathetic short jokes to my rant!"

I like the sound of his laugh. It starts deep in his throat, and I resist turning around to see if he's looking at me. I may be in a messy bun and no make-up, but instead of my parka I'm in a short jacket. He can get a view of my butt, my most attractive feature.

When I get inside, I spend time on the Fiverr site to scope out the competition. Some designers look experienced and others are hacks. I'd have to start cheap if I make a storefront. But like Ben said, I could sell the template package I already designed.

I get a little flutter of vibrant yellows and orange. Is this what happy feels like? I can goof off during my lecture today and set up the Fiverr during class. The plan motivates me to get my amazing butt ready to get to campus. No small feat.

It wouldn't hurt to try a gig site, and it would give me something else to focus on aside from my upcoming summer of torture and the business classes I've come to resent. I love a delicious distraction. For the last forty-five minutes, I only thought about my internship and my insect-fearing mother a few times.

Chapter Thirty-Three

For the first time in weeks, I get out of bed with a bit of energy. The baking date with Lise and Ben will be interesting and I'm excited to follow through with my idea to give Paula a non-Zillah food.

Aunt Bethany's coming over for our postponed dinner tonight. I get the sense that she wants to see Paula with her own eyes to determine whether she needs to be sent to one of the programs she showed me or committed to an insane asylum. Bethany overreacting and getting all pearl-clutchy isn't helping anyone. Tonight, she'll see that Paula is just being Paula. Quirky, but fine overall.

Bethany will be reassured about both of us.

Paula's still happy about my internship placement, despite my lack of enthusiasm. Also, I'm coping with my break-up okay. Better than I expected. If my cookie plan with Ben goes well, I can show *both* of them how much I've grown, even without Cliff in my life.

Paula's also happy that I've promised to go with her to her office after the dinner when no one's around so I can see some sort of issue she's having with her new printer/copier. Almost all the work I do for her clinic is paperwork I can do here and there from home, but it's nice to go there in person once in a while.

Lise texts me at half past seven, "Come over at 8 and we can go together."

I send back question marks and she texts, "To Jason's. It's close, but we can drive if you want."

This is getting more complicated.

When I go downstairs at 7:55, Ben is coming up to the courtyard with Halsted. We exchange "hey"s and I give the four-legged boy an undersnout pet the way he likes. I follow Ben up their stairwell and ask about the plan.

"So, we're going to your boss's? Maybe I should stay here. I can figure something out on my own."

"No, please come. Lise won't go if you don't."

Men and their guilt trips. I get a bit too close for polite COVID-era distance on the way up the stairs and I can smell his cologne. Or Ben pheromones? Whatever. The guy smells amazing and he can't tell I'm lurking, I hope.

I could never breathe in deeply with Cliff due to the stench of cigarette smoke that has pervaded all of his pores. I don't even know what he really smells like under the acrid, stale sweetness.

When we get to their apartment, Ben hands Lise and me bags of ingredients and supplies to carry. Lise tries to ask about how I'm doing with my internship disappointment, but Ben cuts us off.

"You can do girly chitchatting on the way. Vamos!"

We follow Ben and I answer her, "The summer's going to suck, but at least I *got* an internship spot. And I'll be working on finding a place to move and stuff, so I'll just focus on that. I can survive one crappy summer."

"That's the spirit," Lise says.

Ben adds, "Suffer now and enjoy your heavenly rewards later."

We go to a brick townhouse. "Been here before?" I ask Lise while Ben and Jason give each other a manly grunting, back-slapping hug.

"No." She's in quiet mode.

Ben introduces us and leads us to a modern kitchen where we plop our bags on the center island. Everything is marble countertop, grey wood drawers and shelves, and chrome. There aren't even cabinets — open shelves with organized plates and glassware. I take mental notes to add to my wish list for future kitchen design.

"The deal is I can use Jason's kitchen if I leave him some of whatever I make." He points to the oven. "Convection," he says, as though that seals the deal on why the schlep makes sense.

Two children run in, dark-skinned and curly haired like Jason. Both are in pajamas, and I'm thinking age six and eight if my radar's correct.

Ben groans. "The only downside is dealing with children." He turns to them and uses a stern voice. "If you get in our way, there will be serious consequences."

The fuck?

Oh, he's teasing them.

He keeps talking to Lise and me with his usual voice, except the larger child somehow made it onto his back, and the younger is tucked like a floppy ragdoll under his arm.

"Let's lay out all our supplies and I'll go through Jason's stuff. I'll use his flour and some other basics." He pauses. "Does anyone else smell something weird? Like disgusting little gremlins? Where did those kids go?"

He dumps the giggling children on the floor and gets serious. We transform the kitchen into a madeleine factory. Ben shows me how to zest lemons and weigh things with the tiniest scale I've ever seen. Lise is using a metal thingy to sift flour. It makes a satisfying noise but is hard to do for long stretches so I take a turn.

"Your hands big enough for that, GZ?" Ben asks me.

"That better stand for Great Zillah."

Lise asks, "Is Jason leaving? And his family?" Her voice is tinged with whine and worry.

"Yeah. We'll have the whole place in a bit."

Ben tells us facts about madeleines and how whipping the eggs is the key to making them airy. And something about ribbons.

I nod, half paying attention. He's at his best when he's doing the things he's passionate about. It reminds me of his intensity when he explained all those hummus ingredients.

Jason's kids are now fully dressed, and their dad is trying to get them to button up their coats while the oldest tells Ben about their plans.

"We're meeting Mom at the market and we're all gonna look at bicycles, but we're just looking. We're not buying anything today, even if we see something really good."

"I don't need a bike. I have a pony," Ben says with an exaggerated yawn.

"No, you don't!"

The younger shouts, "You got a Halsted Doggy!"

Ben double checks my measurements and says, "He turns into a pony at night."

I could watch this all day.

But Jason urges them to use the bathroom before leaving and asks us, "Oh! Who likes pears? I made the best poached pear gelato. Ben, you gotta try." He pulls a shallow glass container from their gigantic freezer and lifts off the cover. He takes three spoons from a drawer and hands one to each of us.

Ben and Lise both take a spoonful. Ben moans in compliment before turning back to his project of whipping eggs. I say "no thanks" when Jason pushes the container toward me.

"I insist," Jason says. "You haven't lived until you've tried this."

"I already ate."

"No need to be polite. Just a small bite. I'll be offended if you don't."

He's smiling. I try to de-escalate my rising black and red scribbles, so I don't make it weird. But when I say, "I don't want to," I'm nearly shouting and I can hear the panic in my voice.

"*Okay*, then," he says with a slow emphasis on the "okay" and glances at Ben.

"Bathroom?" My voice is still so loud. Jason directs me and I hear Ben ask Lise, "What happened?"

The powder room is all dark vintage paper and gold tone fixtures. I watch myself cry in the ornate mirror, mentally chastising, "Stupid. Idiot. Child."

After a couple of minutes, I calm my inner paint splotches, and I'm just left with the exhaustion and embarrassment of acting out in front of other humans.

Lise texts, "`Jason gone. Safe to come out.`"

I clean my face as best I can. I make my way back toward the kitchen and peek around the corner.

They've put on music, and both look busy. But when they see me, Ben says, "Confession time."

"Me?" I ask.

"Me. I prefer an audience to active participants. What about you and Lise just hang out and help keep me company?"

"Sounds good to me," Lise says. She fills her water bottle and sits on a stool at the kitchen island. I join her to watch the Ben Show.

He lifts a whisk in the air, letting eggs drizzle in the bowl. He says, "Good. I'll bake, Lise can be supportive, and Zillah can tell us why gelato makes her lose her shit."

"She doesn't have to talk about anything," Lise defends me. "Ignore him."

"It's okay," I say. And it is, I'm kinda shocked to recognize. I guess I trust him. And I like that he's curious. It's so different to be with people who don't know everything about me already. "I have a weird history with food," I begin. "In my whole life, like since starting solid food, I've only eaten a few things."

"Okay?" He sounds like Lise, adding a question to his statement.

"Yeah. And my mom has been amazing about it, even though it's probably been hard for her." He continues baking, folding ingredients gently into others, and seems to be concentrating more on the madeleines than me. Except he raises his eyes often and does a lot of nodding. "Like she won't let any of the food I don't like in our apartment, and she only eats the way I eat when she's around me. She wants me to feel safe." He and Lise share a quick glance and a silent communication. "It's not like Lise's fears," I insist with some heat. "She's not accommodating me. I really can't eat anything else. I mean, you saw, right? Things like the gelato really get in the way. It's fine that I don't eat a lot of options, right? But I wish I was more comfortable around food."

"I get that," Ben says while buttering the madeleine pans. "Food is so communal and pulls at group culture. It would be hard to be on the outside of that."

"I guess." I've never thought about it in that way. "But that's the point of the strawberry filling. I want to surprise Paula and give her something in our home that she hasn't been eating. Like to show I'm maturing. It won't just be strawberry things. I'm ready to have her eat anything she wants at home."

Lise asks, "Have you ever seen her eat other food?"

"Not that I remember. Maybe she snuck it when I was little? But I don't think it'll gross me out. I try to picture it and I don't feel nervous or gross about it. It's just a habit we've gotten into. Her life will be so much easier, and she'll be more convinced I'm ready to move out. Right now, she thinks everything will be like the gelato incident."

Ben pipes batter into the molds and lightly taps a filled pan on the counter.

"Banging things looks fun. Can I help?" I ask.

"No. I don't trust your propensity for violence. We'd have batter everywhere."

Lise asks, "What if Zillah tries the gelato? Could she bang some pans as a prize."

Oh, Lise. "Don't push," I say.

"Every fear you avoid just gets stronger," she says. She goes to the freezer and pulls out the container. She gets a clean spoon and hands it to me.

I'm filled with red pointy rage at her. Here I am being all vulnerable and shit, and she has to play therapist with me? Love the girl, but at this moment, fuck her.

But.

Also.

Maybe?

She and Ben are having some sort of unspoken argument with their eyebrows, and I go over and look at the gelato.

I give it a sniff. I guess it's sort of like an apple smell.

I use the spoon to scoop out a small portion.

I can put this in my mouth and then immediately drink water. I'd only suffer for half a second.

But.

Also.

The gelato doesn't look like food. I've stared at it for so long that it's starting to melt on the spoon and get jiggly. It's sluglike. And maybe there's tiny chunks of sluglike pears in it. They'd get in my teeth. And maybe the taste would stay in mouth even after the water. And what if I hurl all over this nice kitchen?

I walk the spoon over to the sink and wash it off.

"Maybe next time," Ben says.

"Yeah. Maybe."

After two panfuls of regular madeleines, Ben makes a batch with strawberry jam piped in the middle. Then we go back to regular.

Lise and I get to dust the finished madeleines with powdered sugar. It's messy and my favorite step of the enterprise.

In all, we've spent about three hours making these little cakes. It's bizarre but oddly satisfying to create something ephemeral. I always hope my pieces will last decades, if not forever. It's strange to spend hours making something that people will destroy in thirty seconds and literally turn to shit.

While we clean up, Ben makes me a little to-go pastry box with the strawberry madeleines. "Keep the box open so steam can escape. They won't be fully cooled for another couple of hours."

"Okay."

"Don't close the box."

"Yeah, yeah. I heard you, Mr. Bossytrousers."

We pack up and leave two dozen madeleines on the cooling rack for Jason's family. The remainder go in a much larger container Ben had brought with him.

"Don't close that," I warn him. He gives me the finger. Our communication is coming along nicely.

Back at Lise and Ben's apartment, Ben makes us coffee with fresh ground beans even though it takes longer. "This is part of the madeleine process. They go with hot drinks."

"Ben's a coffee snob," Lise says. "Pretend it's normal so we can finally have a madeleine."

"I'll just have water," I say.

We talk about Lise's spring break plans while he measures water to the exact gram. Hers is a week before mine, and she might go back to Indianapolis to visit. I'll miss her, I realize. It feels good to know that I'm becoming attached to a new person.

"You sure this is one of the plain ones," I ask Ben when he finally serves us madeleines and gives Lise her coffee.

"Positive."

I take a bite. It's by far the best thing I have ever eaten in my life.

"Ben, you are a genius. An annoying and bossy genius." I want to hug him for feeding me something so delicious, but I settle for a salute.

Paula is going to have kittens when I serve the strawberry ones tonight.

Chapter Thirty-Four

This dinner is going to make me feel more normal. Sometimes I crave that sense of "I come from a regular family."

I pre-heat the oven and get the table looking nice. I dig out fabric napkins instead of paper, and I briefly consider a tablecloth. Nah. Placemats will seem more naturally glamorous. Like, we're just people who have others over to dinner all the time.

No big deal.

I cut an apple into extra thin slices and try to arrange them in a circular fan display while our chicken strips and waffle fries bake. I even got Bethany packets of ketchup from McDonalds on Broadway in a show of gracious hostessing.

Bethany texts when she's outside the gate to our building. I buzz her into the courtyard and go downstairs to let her into our stairwell and up to our place.

There's a moment of awkwardness when Paula reminds Bethany to take off her shoes "because Zillah and I like to keep everything nice and clean." Bethany doesn't seem bothered by the implication that at *her* home, people deliberately dump dirt on the floor.

"Dinner will be ready in just a few minutes, but there's apple slices on the table if you're starving," I say to both of them as I check on things in the oven.

"Nobody's starving, Zillah," Paula scolds as she sits at the table.

"How's the cast?" Bethany asks, joining her. She picks up an apple slice and nibbles it.

Paula pointedly unfolds her napkin and tucks it on her lap. "It comes off next week, and I can't wait for the brace. I don't even want to *think* about the kind of bacteria growing in here." We all stare at her cast for a moment, as though waiting for maggots and worms to crawl from the openings.

"Is it itchy?" Bethany asks, unfolding her own napkin before selecting another apple slice.

"Only when someone reminds me about it."

"How are the preparations for your internship going?" she tries again with me.

"Ugh. It's going to be the worst summer of my life." Be positive, Zillah! "But at least it's only for three months."

Despite the inauspicious start, dinner goes okay. I get an odd look from Paula as I put out more food than normal. Dinner is edible, which is a relief. With this old oven, I sometimes have to sacrifice a bit of frozen food to the Gods of the Raw and a bit to Gods of the Burnt. This time I paid attention, used parchment paper, and I didn't microwave anything in advance to speed along the cooking time.

It's while we're eating that we notice Paula's new habit. Bethany sees it first and I follow her frequent glances to how Paula touches her fork.

Tap tap — pick up the fork and use it.

Put the fork down — *Tap tap*.

It's a quick movement, like she's double-clicking a mouse. Maybe this is one of those mindful strategies to slow down how fast she's eating.

Once I notice it, it's all I can pay attention to. How long has she been doing this? This has to be the first time, right?

Tap tap — pick up the fork and use it.

Put the fork down — *Tap tap*.

Under normal conditions, I'd ask about it, but I don't want to embarrass her. Bethany looks at me and we make uncomfortably long eye contact.

Paula fills the awkward silence. "How's your sourdough bread and things?" she asks Bethany.

"I haven't made bread for a couple of months."

"But you were so into it. Everything had to be sourdough or sour-dough discard!"

"It's on ice until I'm in the mood again. Do you miss all those discard crackers I used to make you?"

"I can't believe you gave up on it," Paula says. "Why start something you're just going to give up?"

"What was your starter's name?" I ask. "Fro-dough?"

This time, my intervention fails. Either Bethany doesn't see the land-mines or she's tired of playing nice.

"I didn't give up," she says as she sets down the waffle fry she just dipped in ketchup.

"You always quit." Paula's perkier now that someone is engaging her in conflict. "The stained glass. Portuguese. All that garbage with coding workshops." She taps her fork twice and selects another waffle fry.

"It's not *giving up* to try new things. I love making sourdough. I love those other things. I'm richer for it."

"Ha!" Paula says. "How much money do you spend on all your hob-bies every year?"

I focus on the waffle fry Bethany set down on her plate. It touched an-other couple of items on her plate, and they're all stained with ketchup.

"I do fine financially." Bethany uses an overly patient tone as though she's explaining a concept to a child. This won't end well. "I'm able to spend on things that bring me joy. Do you do anything that brings you joy?"

Fuck.

Paula has a full mouth, so can't respond.

I jump in the fray. "I have a surprise for you both and I was gonna wait until after dinner, but let me get it now, okay?"

I don't wait for a response. Instead, I get the pastry box I've hidden in my room.

When I come back, I announce, "Look what I helped make this morn-ing!" I'm excited like a little kid, but the sisters seem delighted and Paula has dropped whatever retort she'd been thinking up.

"Those are beautiful!" Paula says.

"Madeleines? Wow." Bethany adds.

I put the box on the table and they each take one, even though they haven't finished their main course. "My friend Ben did most of the work, but I weighed stuff. And I did some other things."

Bethany takes a bite and sighs and after chewing. "Bliss! Can I have the recipe?"

"Yeah, sure! I don't actually know it, but I'll get it from Ben."

"And who is this Ben?" she asks in a teasing voice while Paula starts eating her madeleine. I'm warm all of a sudden. If I could blush like Lise, I'm sure I'd be all red.

"He's just a friend, but—"

"What's in this?" Paula interrupts. "It's red inside! What is it?" She's loud and must be worried I'll freak out.

"It's okay, Mom! That's the other part of my surprise. I wanted to announce that I'm okay with other food in our house and I was thinking for now on—"

But Paula is spitting into her napkin. She takes her glass of water to the sink. She swishes and spits several times like she's at the dentist.

She shouts, "What is it? What did I just eat?"

"Paula, it's just strawberry," Bethany says. We get up to join Paula by the sink.

"Yeah, Mom. It's got strawberry jam in the middle. To show you—"

"You fed me strawberry. You tricked me into eating strawberry!" she gets louder and louder. She slams her glass into the sink, shattering it. "Look what you made me do! Now we'll have glass shards in the disposal."

"I got it," Bethany says while gently moving Paula aside. "Zillah, help bring up the dinner plates."

But the words and anger and inconsistencies in the conversation are shifting and blurring. Like a puzzle I've been looking at all wrong.

"Mom," I ask. "Why don't you recognize the taste of strawberry?"

Chapter Thirty-Five

"'T'his isn't about me," Paula scolds in a clipped voice. "This is about you forcing me to eat a Yuck Food in our safe place."

"I'm sorry. I'm sorry! I just—" What? Why is Paula upset? "I thought it would make you happy."

"Well, obviously it doesn't. Zillah, you *know* we don't eat strawberries!" She's slurping water like her tongue is burnt.

"I thought— Mom, don't you eat strawberries when you're not around me?"

"Of course not."

"But you eat other food, right? Like at work and when you're driving around?" I open a cabinet and pull out saltines.

"Zillah, your mom's always been picky." Bethany uses a calm, school-teacher voice.

"Yeah," I say. "But how much *do* you eat, Mom?" I'm so confused, and I get louder. "Bethany, you've seen Paula eat fruit and vegetables and sauces and everything, right?" I sound shrill, like Paula. "You've seen her eat normal, right?"

"Oh, for goodness' sake." Paula grabs the saltines and puts them away.

Bethany continues to use her soothing voice. "Zillah, I don't understand why you're so upset. It's always been this way, right?"

"No. Right, Mom? You used to eat normal, but I made you stop, right?"

"Never mind that," Paula says after swishing and spitting again. "Let's talk about how you just violated my safe space."

"*My* safe space," I say.

"Exactly! And after all this time, for you to waltz in here—"

"Mom, is it—" I'm having trouble forming my question. "Is it my fault or not? The ten foods?"

"Zillah, this is too much nonsense. You've always hated new food, and I've always loved you so much that I did what I could — well, I still do everything I can do — I did what I could to make you comfortable in every situation! I did all of that for *years* for you!"

"I need a minute," I mumble and go to my room.

My earliest memory is reaching for something pink, and Paula slapping my hand away. She wasn't a frequent hitter, so this always stuck out for me. When I've thought about this in the past, it made sense. She was afraid that if I took a mouthful of whatever it was, I'd have a mega-tantrum. She was helping me since I was such a hellion about the ten foods.

But what if that's not the full story? Did Paula help me feel safe or prevent me from trying new things?

I text Dad that I need to talk ASAP. Bethany wasn't around when I was a baby and a toddler, but he was.

While I wait, I pull up one of the links Eleanor the nutritionist had sent, but words like undernourishment and restriction float by me without sinking in.

Dad calls me back, finally, and starts in with a panicky voice. "You okay? Your mom's okay?"

"Yeah. I didn't mean to worry you," I say. Our calls are always scheduled. "It's been a weird night."

"Okay." He sounds more normal, except he might be chewing something, "Tell me all about it." Finally, a parent is going to listen to me, I sit on my bed and fluff up my pillow for back support.

Paula knocks on my door and shouts, "You're still coming with me to the office, right? To look at the printer-copier-thing?"

"Hold on, Dad," I say and speak to Paula through the door. "Call tech support, Mom. Or call the salesperson who sold you the machine." I hear a muffled "for goodness' sake" but she leaves me alone.

I tell him, "I made cookies today with some friends—"

"Friends? That's great!" Embarrassing how excited he is that I have friends, but whatever.

"Yeah, and I gave Mom one with strawberry jam in it."

"Woah. Really?"

"Yes! And she flipped out!" He's silent, so I go on. "I don't get it."

"Zillah, you know how she is. Did she know there was fruit in it?"

"No! But she *likes* fruit, right?"

Nothing.

"Right?" I try again.

"But you know all this, Zillah."

"I know I used to have, like, massive tantrums if I was near Yuck Food," I say. "Mom made the apartment safe for us. But was there ever a time I ate other stuff? Or her? She used to eat normally, right? I thought she still does when I'm not around, but now I don't know. Tell it to me from the beginning, Dad."

So, he does, but it takes me a couple of tellings to reconcile my own understanding.

Once upon a time there lived a young woman named Paula Scriven. Paula learned to control her environment and feel safe with strict rules and safety practices. She was also a very picky eater. When things got stressful, she developed more rules and more food restrictions.

Nothing was quite as stressful as an unplanned pregnancy and then having a baby with her boyfriend, Mark Dewison.

During this time, Paula became more demanding about cleanliness, good luck rituals, travel, and especially about the food that was allowed to be in their apartment and around the baby.

Paula insisted that all the Yuck Food be out of the house. When she came in contact with any of it, she gagged and sometimes vomited. Mark was allowed (allowed? what the fuck!) to eat what he wanted, but couldn't do it at home and needed to brush his teeth before interacting with Paula or the baby.

Paula had done okay-ish at letting mess take over for a while and dealing with baby ooze. But, to compensate, she gained a sense of control in the one realm she had any agency: food.

Blah, blah, blah. It got worse and worse.

And no one fucking thought about saying, "Hey lady, maybe let that baby eat vegetables or something."

Mark, the one adult who knew best what was going on, decided to leave and just send money, since money *totally* replaces having a father around. He didn't even make Paula sign a parenting plan or anything that would give him partial custody.

The baby got older and became a small child. Paula homeschooled her and taught her how to be just like her mother. In fact, Paula let the child think that *she* had initiated the household food rules, and that it was all her fucking fault that she ate like a freak.

"Weren't you worried about me? Remember how I used to get sick all the time? That could have been from undernourishment. And my anemia! You knew what was happening."

"I used to ask you, Zillah!" Dad insists when I blubber recriminations at him. "'Let me know if you're tired of this.' 'Let me know if you want to eat differently, and you can come with me'."

But I had thought he meant, "You're allowed to come with me when you're no longer so problematic and picky." *Don't leave the parenting decisions up to the kid, assholes.*

It's easier to be angry with him than with Paula tonight, although usually it's the other way around.

"You could have demanded that she, I don't know, like, take me to a special doctor or something. You could have made sure she was at least giving *me* real food. Then maybe I'd like it now. You could have been here and made sure I had regular food when I was with *you* at least." He doesn't have any answers for me. "You could have told me it wasn't my fault." After about an hour of this, I have to get off the phone. I'm exhausted from all the rage and dehydrated from crying and snotting so much.

But my brain won't turn off.

What would my life have been like with a more assertive father? Yeah, Paula is a pain to deal with when crossed, but I'm *his* kid, too. I needed him.

I know he's always standing by in the wings if I ever need money or if there's an emergency. But what would life have been like growing up with him instead?

I'm suffocating in my room. Looking around, everything I see introduces more questions. My height chart on the wall (would I have been taller if I'd eaten normally as a toddler, at least?). The emergency supply of granola bars in my backpack (would I have liked other food if Paula and Dad had encouraged it?). My thin hairs filling my hairbrush (do I always shed from some deficiency?).

I walk out of the apartment and hear Paula shout "Zillah!" in the dissonant tone that means she's extra upset. And Bethany saying something softly, probably about letting me be alone.

Outside, I realize I have idiotically left without my phone. What will distract me now? No way I'm going back in.

I go up Lise's stairwell and knock on her door.

Ben comes to the door.

"Don't tell me you're back for more? Greedy much?" His jolliness shifts to concern as he looks at me closely. "What's wrong? What's happened?" I can't get words out. What do I even say? "Lise!" He shouts for reinforcements.

Vivian and Lise come to the door, and Vivian pulls me inside and holds my hand.

"I'm okay." I say, approximating normal Zillah. What would it have been like to grow up with a Vivian?

My heart is breaking.

I can't be around this family right now. They're too warm. Too connected. I'm jealous and angry and ready to strike.

And I need to wrap my head around the — the everything — before I'm ready to talk.

"I'm okay," I say again. "Sorry. I'm sorry. It's been a strange night."

I back towards the door. Lise follows me and gives my arm a squeeze as I leave. I think of the arm squeeze lady at Conway & Cranos, my internship site. *This* is an appropriate time for an arm squeeze. I try to communicate my appreciation through a look and a brief, "I'll see you tomorrow."

When I'm almost to the bottom of their stairwell, I hear fast and loud footsteps and Ben calling, "Zillah, wait."

What is it about conversations on our apartment stairwells? I'm plagued by stairs these days.

He catches up with me and moves a step below me so we're almost at eye level. "What can I do?" he asks.

I'm still venom and lava and all the angry things, but he's strong enough for it.

"Do you— do you want a hug?" he asks.

I kinda want someone to hold me right now. I could put my arms around him and lean into a fierce hug. He would hug me back, petting my hair while I sob. He'd say, "It's okay, Zillah. I've got you. You're gonna be okay."

I tuck that fantasy away for later and clear my throat. I'm not ready for comfort. "I'm fine. I'm fine." I scoot around him and give a fake smile at the door. "I'll get Vivian's fancy bowl back to you tomorrow."

He still looks concerned and so, so un-Benly serious. But I part with an un-Zillah "Bye!" and make my escape.

Chapter Thirty-Six

I haven't spoken to Paula since I got home last night. I came home after going to Lise's apartment and stayed in my room except for brief bathroom breaks. Paula kept trying to talk to me about little things like our grocery order and a problem with the electricity to the washing machines in the basement. But I can't pretend we're back to normal until we've discussed the ten foods.

After she left for work this morning, I tried to relax. But I keep getting stabbed by little slivers of ragey confusion. It's no longer below the surface. It *is* the surface.

I can't believe I've felt guilty about the food rules for years. Years and years. As long as I can remember. And I'm pissed at myself for not questioning things sooner.

Like when I go through all our vitamins to check our supply and see what we need to reorder... Usually, this is a satisfying task. It only takes a few minutes and feels productive.

But now as I look at our huge array of pills, I wonder if we need these. Do other families take this many vitamins instead of eating healthy food? If I ate broccoli and fish and gross stuff as a kid, would I like it now?

And *why* did she pretend the food choices were my fault? I would have still loved her if it was something she made us do for her. The way she always talks about the food rules is like she believes her story. It's not a lie for her: she believes she's doing this for me. I'll never really know if Paula made our apartment a 10-food-zone to help *me* or to help *herself*.

Bethany and I talk on the phone after Paula leaves for the office.

"You feeling better, Sweet Z?" she asks.

"I'm confused."

"Those madeleines were really something!"

I give a disbelieving snort ("Mh!") and say, "Dad told me it all started with her. That I was only picky because she wouldn't let me eat anything other than the ten foods."

"She wouldn't let you?"

"Well, she didn't encourage it, at least. What do you remember about how she ate from when you two were little?"

"Oh, Z, by the time Paula came along, I was already a teenager. We only saw each other at holidays once in a while, and I wasn't interested in squirmy little kids until I met you." I hear the smile in her voice. "I remember she ate like a bird, but it wasn't something I recall talking about."

"What do you remember about me?"

"Oh, lots of things!" she says warmly.

"I mean about eating."

"Well, I didn't really spend time with you until I moved here. And then you were eight, right? Or nine?"

"Eight."

"I just knew that you had some extreme food aversions and that Paula was working wonders to help keep you well-fed despite—" She trails off.

"Despite what?"

"Despite your quirks." She's quiet and then, "I should have asked more questions, Zillah. I felt like it wasn't my place, you know? But now, looking back—"

"Yeah, I know."

We finish up our call, and the thoughts keep swirling and taking shape.

Not only did Paula keep me from trying food, but she also got sympathy for it. Poor Paula putting up with such a brat.

My class isn't until 1:30, so I fill my time getting ahead on some administrative bullshit paperwork for the clinic. It doesn't take much concentration, so it's a good task for a day I'm angry. Well, angrier than normal. Good for days I dread my internship and curse my plan.

I'll go to campus early and walk around. Maybe I can throw rocks at a wall or something. Shout curse words in the echoey parking garage. Rip up papers in the recycling bin in a computer lab.

I need to destroy something.

But I'm not fated to get to campus today, after all.

Instead, Paula texts me to meet her at the Addison Street Police Station at three o'clock, when she expects she will be released from police custody.

Chapter Thirty-Seven

Paula doesn't respond to my texts or voicemails asking for clarification. I wish I did inane fork tapping that could reduce *my* tension. All I have is worry and walking in circles around our apartment.

I text her co-worker Jennifer, "Did something odd happen today? Something about the printer, maybe?" I've collected packages and watered plants for Jennifer when she's gone out of town, so we have a relationship that won't make this *too* weird.

But all I get back is "Your mom left to go to the equipment supplier, but then she called and said she had an emergency and needs the rest of the day off. I don't know the story, but I can find out. Do you want avocados? I have extra! They're huge. I can send them home with your mom tomorrow."

If Jennifer is texting me about avocados, things can't be too off kilter.

I bet Ben would like free avocados.

I can't believe I'm thinking about a stupid boy.

Man.

A stupid man-boy.

While my mother is in jail.

And thinking about a man-boy so soon after Cliff.

Am I a bad person?

I reach out to Bethany, who knows nothing and insists I call her "the instant" I find out what's going on.

There's nothing I can do for Paula yet, so I clean the kitchen and do half the windows to put my nervous energy to use.

I'm remarkably ineffective. I've done these tasks hundreds of times before, but my thoughts are whizzing by at 90 miles an hour and I spill the bucket twice. Twice! Fuck.

I get to the station at two o'clock in the hopes that Paula is out earlier than expected. I take the bus and walk around the block to use up the adrenaline flooding my nervous system.

Yay me. Even though I haven't eavesdropped for weeks now, I still remember some of the therapist's lessons.

I'm almost back to the front when Paula calls. "Are you on your way?"

"I'm walking to the entrance now." What kind of tone do I use when I see her?

She's waiting for me out front when I get there, and I'm a little disappointed. I've never been inside a police station before, and I wonder if it's like Brooklyn 99.

As soon as she sees me, her words come out with forcefulness like a balloon has popped inside her and must push out all her words.

"You'll never believe how rude they are here," she says as she leans in for a hug that I give automatically. "I need to write a letter tonight, or an email I mean. Although, knowing our district, I bet they have one of those artificial intelligence helpbots and no real humans to help. What nonsense!"

"What happened?" It's hard to reconcile my anger at her and the reality of her. It's like seeing an actor in two different movies and parsing out what kind of feelings I'm supposed to have. Worry? Love? Protection? Fury?

"Order an Uber for us to go to my clinic. I'd do it, but I bet my fingers are shaking from everything I've dealt with today."

"Don't you want to go home? Or a lawyer's office?"

"No, they dropped the charges. I need you to come with me because you *get it*." What do I get? She continues, "Doll, I need your help. And look at this!" She thrusts a bottom corner of her trench coat at me while I search for her clinic in the app to order our ride.

"Nice," I say, while trying to verify the type of ride we want.

"Not nice! Look at this tear. See?"

Oh, I'm supposed to be appalled at this damage. "Oh no. Your nice coat!"

That placates her while I finish ordering the ride. She reminds me where she bought her coat, how much it was, and how even a stranger on the street once stopped her to compliment it.

I practice deep breathing while we wait for the car. The theme for today now shifts to de-escalation. The food stuff can wait. My needs can wait.

Inside the ride, I trace a little pattern in the fogged-up window as we drive the few miles to her office in Rogers Park. I won't be able to get any important details until she vents about the judicial process and an irrelevant anecdote about another woman's son. My efforts at redirecting her are pointless, so I let her get it out of her system.

After she threatens our Uber driver that he won't get a tip if he keeps taking the turns so fast, she gives me her version of today's events. She tells me in dramatic tones how she had installed a new printer last week. It functioned well, but it was warm to the touch.

"Yeah, your new copier. You told me."

"Listen!" she scolds and tells me all about it again. Then, "I need you to go in and touch it, but only if you feel safe. See, I followed your advice and went to whatchamacallit, where I bought the printer to talk to the salesman. Yusef, or whatever he calls himself, refused to come to the clinic to assess the printer. And I didn't hit him with the clipboard. I grabbed it back to cross off my signature because I wasn't satisfied, and I had signed it under false pretenses thinking he was still going to *do something* instead of leaving us all to burn to death from a printer fire!"

"Who's Yusef?"

"Pay attention, Zillah. And that would have been *fraud!* Also, I didn't smack him. He wouldn't let me have the clipboard and it slipped and must have hit him by accident on his face because he wouldn't let go. When I let go, bam! This whole shenanigan is a mountain out of a molehill. People are too dramatic." She nods in agreement with herself. "And then he slammed the door to his office while I was still holding it, and can you believe the police said *I* could be charged with assault and battery? Me, with my ruined coat."

"You were arrested for holding a door?"

"Yusef claims the cut on his head is my fault because he says I threw the stapler, but I had nothing to do with that. That was all an accident."

"Oh, Mom."

The Uber lets us out in front of her clinic entrance, a glass door that leads up a staircase to the second floor of the brick building.

"Let's talk inside," I say. "I'm a popsicle."

"No, doll. It might not be safe." For the first time since meeting her at the station, she looks fearful. We stand outside an empty storefront on the bottom floor of the building. "Let's be very careful when we go in so we can sniff for burning and touch the machine to see if it's too hot. Tell me what you think."

We head toward the door, and she pulls on my arm to impart one last warning. "No one knows about the arrest, so pretend everything's normal." Pretend Everything's Normal would be the name of my memoir. "I know you get it," she says as we enter the building and walk up the stairs. "You'll tell me if I need to call the *real* fire department."

Paula ushers me past the admin on duty, who says, "Oh, you came back in! You feeling better?"

"Much better," Paula says without stopping and, "Come on, Zillah," when I try to say "hi". She leads me to the file room. It's empty of people and I touch the copier.

"This is how the industrial printer-copiers at school feel. You're fine."

Sid, one of the two doctors and also her boss, joins us. "Paula, I didn't think you'd be back today. Nice to see you, Zillah. Paula, do you have a sec?"

"I'll drive Zillah home and then come back to finish up a few things," she says.

"Mom, I can stay and help."

"Absolutely not."

"Well, don't drive me. I'll catch the 36. Just get home soon, okay?" I make my way through her maze of an office, past the admin, and through the lobby without any more conversations. There's so much unresolved between us, but she wants to keep up the illusion that everything's normal at work, and I certainly don't want to ruin that for her. I'm glad no one in the clinic knows what happened. Paula has an excellent reputation to maintain. She's great with "attention to detail" and she puts in plenty of unpaid overtime. Granted, the overtime is for doing tasks no one needs, but still.

And Sid always seems fond of Paula. He and his partner are supportive of both of us in the form of holiday gifts, remembering our birthdays, and invitations to visit their lake house in Wisconsin (which we always decline). He must know that Paula's worth it. But I worry that this latest fight is a sign that things are getting worse. That she's — what's the word — decompensating. It feels like every time I take a step toward independence, she falls backwards into some tarpit that we both get stuck in.

I'll feel better once I earn a salary, just in case.

That would be our motto if we had a family crest. Whatever the Latin is for Just in Case. Maybe under an eagle carrying hand sanitizer in one claw and paper towels in the other.

I'm on the bus home when I get her text. "Sid fired me."

Chapter Thirty-Eight

At home, I look around. I'm antsy with tension and red polka dots. What can I do to make things better?

Food.

I'm not hungry, but Paula will be. And if she's not, at least dinner will give us something to do while she tells me what happened.

I use the quickie method on the fries and chicken nuggets. Forty-five seconds in the microwave for the fries before I put them in the oven. Two minutes on the chicken strips before I add them to the fries.

It's ironic that I spend so much time feeding her.

Was there ever a moment when she considered giving me "yuck" food? Did I ever eat that stuff as a baby? Like creamed spinach or whatever babies eat?

My palms hurt from digging my nails into my fists. My heart rate is still flipping around, and I have nothing to do while I wait.

I need distraction.

In my room, I search for my favorite comedians on Instagram to see if they've posted anything new. I'm soaked in the bliss of avoidance until our smoke detector goes off.

Fuck.

Forgot to set a timer.

I rush to the kitchen. The noise feels like a wall and all I smell is smoke.

I deal with the food first before I attack the alarm.

I pull out the cookie sheet.

The meal's three-fourths blackened.

I throw the baking tray into the sink and run water on it.

Big mistake. Huge.

Smoke billows up and I'm in a stinky grey fog.

Fuck.

The alarm is quieter now. I guess I'm deafened.

I grab a kitchen chair and stand on it to get on the counter and reach the smoke detector. It unscrews and I pop the large battery out and fling it across the floor.

I'm going to regret that later.

At least the noise has stopped, although the echoes still ring in my veins somehow.

This gray smoke is going to stick to everything.

I open windows and prop open the front door to our stairwell to help with the air flow. I shove a potholder under the heavy door to keep it wide open. I need to remember to shut this before Paula gets home – she'll say an open front door is an invitation to intruders.

I make sure Paula's bedroom door is closed and I close the door to the bathroom, too. No need to get these rooms all gross.

It might be my imagination, but after a few minutes, the air looks less hazy.

I go in my room. The air's freshest in here. I open the window, and prop my door open, too, for the cross flow of air.

I want to sit, but not on the bed — I might be sooty and I don't have energy to change. I'll sit here at my desk for a bit while the apartment clears up, and then I'll go clean.

I check my texts.

Nothing from Paula, but Ben texted earlier asking, `Can I drop by for my mom's bowl? I can bring you more plain madeleines.` I send him a thumbs up and `Sure—whenever`.

I also have texts from Lise. `Is your apartment next to ours through the wall? We hear smoke detector. Do you hear, too? How are you doing? Worried about you.`

"My bad cooking = next Great Chicago Fire,"
I text back. "Sorry about smoke alarm. Dinner died,
but I'm fine."

I'm anything but fine.

I miss her and want to be vulnerable a bit, too. "It's been a
bad couple of days," I text next. "Walk and talk when
things calm down? I'm having Lise-withdrawal."

I wish I could talk to Lise about Paula and the strawberry cookies and
the arrest now, but I need to wrap my brain around what everything
means before I can process it with anyone else.

Did Paula hurt that salesman on purpose? Did she think the building
would burn down or was she making a point? It's hard to tell what's real
with her. Sometimes if other people minimize her fears, she exaggerates
them, so everyone takes her seriously.

I wish she could be a normal mom who works, comes home, and
watches shows.

A normal mom who wants her child to be healthier than she is. She
should have acknowledged her own pickiness and encouraged me to eat
regular food, even if she didn't want to.

I wish she'd try to get me to move out.

I wish she'd ask about my art. Or design. Or anything that I'm interested in.

Maybe I'll get hit by a car. I'll have an excuse to drop out and spend
a few months drawing and watching shows while my broken legs heal.
Even Paula would feel bad for me and let me take a break from our plan.
I could get out of that internship.

Or maybe I'll die in the accident. Death sounds peaceful.

"Is this better?" I hear through the wall.

"Loud and clear," Lise says.

Oh, shit.

I look at the clock.

Lise's therapy.

I should leave.

I've been so good about not listening. It's been weeks.

"I'll start with an update on my new friend. Zillah."

I grab my electric blanket and settle in.

But I get bored.

Lise's therapy session isn't as fun as I remember.

Even the part about me is quick and nothing surprising. "We're getting closer. She's the first friend I can really lean on in as long as I can remember," I hear her say. Then she's on to other topics.

It's good that I'm bored.

This will be my last time eavesdropping, and I'll know I'm not missing anything.

I'll be a good, non-snoopy friend.

A good friend to Lise. And maybe something like a friend to Ben. Maybe something more.

But first I want to hear Lise and her therapist imitate cartoon characters to repeat some of the words she has difficulty saying. I'll miss this when I'm a better person.

Lise's voice is hard to hear during the activity. She must be facing the other way or she's embarrassed. I rarely have to use the glass-to-the-wall trick, but I've got a Darth Vader pint glass here for this purpose.

Better. I shrug my shoulder into my other ear so I can focus on the wall.

"What are you doing?" Ben asks.

Ben.

Ben is in the doorway to my room.

Chapter Thirty-Nine

Ben is in the doorway to my room, looking at me.

"What are *you* doing?" I ask. I slide the glass under a fold of my blanket. Maybe he didn't see it. "Did you break in?" I get up and face him.

Try not to look guilty, Zillah.

He backs up a little. "Your front door is propped open and you texted me to come for the bowl—"

"Vomit."

"Vomit."

"Vomit."

"Vomit."

The therapist and Lise, in terrible fake British accents, take turns shouting the word.

Ben comes toward me and the wall. "Is that Lise?"

Of course they have to shout *now*.

"Vomit."

"Vomit."

He leans toward me and whispers, "You're listening? Is this part of her exposure?"

"No." I push him out of my room into the hallway. "I wasn't. It's an accident." I close my door. At least he isn't in there, knocking on the wall.

"You accidentally held a glass up to the wall?" He looks at me like I have snot coming out of my nose and dripping into my mouth. "What the hell?"

He looks around, like he's trying to find other examples of my perversion.

I can't get any words out. My eyes well up and I manage a few guttural sounds around the lump in my throat.

"You're sad because you got caught," he says. "She likes you, Zillah." He runs his hand through his hair and walks to the door. "Damn."

On TV, when people have big interactions, there's long conversations explaining everything and a hug to close things out.

How do I make that happen?

I follow Ben down the stairs and wait for genius inspiration.

At the bottom of our stairwell I whisper, "I'm sorry."

"Fuck off." The door is extra loud as it slams behind him.

Chapter Forty

When I was ten, I dropped Paula's phone in the toilet while trying to take a video of flushing. That feeling of my stomach dropping into my bladder. Wanting to curl up into a ball. That's what this feels like.

I need to *do* something.

There's nothing I can do.

I lock the apartment door behind me when I get back inside. It still stinks in here, but not as bad as before.

Shit.

My teeth clench, but this isn't the time to relax my jaw.

I try to compose a perfect text to Lise.

My hand is so sweaty I need a death grip on my phone.

I need to talk to her before Ben does, but what can I say? `"Ignore your brother until I make up an excuse"`? That duck won't quack.

I want to blame this on Paula, too, but I can't. This latest fuck-up is all me.

I can tell Lise is still in her session, but my brain is too loud to hear what's going on there. Doesn't sound like Ben's barging in to stop the proceedings.

I go to the kitchen to see what I can do about cleaning up my mess from earlier. I swoop a finger along the white tile backsplash, and I leave a trail in the light gray soot.

Buzzing phone.

My nerves are tuned in. The vibration sounds loud.

"How dare you? Don't leave. We need to TALK."
There it is. I feel better for knowing the truth is out.
Wait.
This isn't from Lise.
It's Paula.
"My privacy is impotent." And then "*IMPORTANT!"
I check her location and see she's almost home. I shoot a quick text to Bethany, "Hey — call when you have a minute," and start on the kitchen backsplash since it's the most obvious. I'll go from top to bottom and finish with the floors.

I'm wiping down the front of the oven when Paula gets in.

"Zillah!" she calls in that dissonant tone I hate. It's somewhere between a sharp and a flat and brings to mind every time I've ever been in trouble.

"In here," I call and get up. "Don't freak out. Give me fifteen minutes and I'll have it all cleaned up."

She makes the usual noises of taking off her shoes and coat and sanitizing by the door. But somehow everything sounds stompier.

"I don't *freak out*, Zillah. I don't care about a *mess*," she says as she gets to the kitchen and looks around. "I'm not *obsessive*. I can handle a mess as long as you clean up after yourself." She rubs her hand on the counter and sniffs her fingers. "What did you do?"

"Burned food." I kneel on the floor to get a good angle into the oven. I've got a bucket of warm water and a wet soapy rag that should get the job done. I need it clean enough that it won't smoke next time we use it.

"When will you learn to be more careful? Can you use your brain for once? For someone who puts everyone else down, you could at least pay attention when you use serious implements like the oven." It's a standard lecture, but her words are coming out fast, like each thought is in a race.

I stop cleaning and look at her to try to gauge her mood.

"Don't put that on the floor!" she screeches, startling me and I hit my head on the countertop jutting out above me and I kick over the bucket of water.

"Shit," I whisper and rub the top of my head. It hurts so much I'm sure there will be blood.

There's not.

Damn. If I was bleeding, I bet Paula would be kinder.

"Clumsy, clumsy!"

"It's only water. I'll get the mop." I say this quietly, hoping she'll match my volume.

"Well, get it already! The water's getting under the oven. Are you stuck in a tar pit? *Honestly*, Zillah." She slams open the pantry, grabs the mop, and drops it at my feet.

"Thanks," I say. I have a lot more I'd *like* to say and shout, but I can't tell why she's pissed. Maybe an emotional hangover from her brief incarceration.

"And when you're finished here, you can explain why you texted Jennifer and cost me my job!"

Oh.

That.

"Mom, you're the one who went to—"

"Nobody knew, Zillah! They thought it was a sick day until you told Jennifer to investigate—"

"I didn't!"

She opens and slams cabinets while scolding to punctuate her anger. "—And Ms. Jennifer-Nancy-Drew called the store and heard *their* version, not at all accurate, I assume, and now thanks to you, I'm on administrative leave for six weeks and fired after that."

"So, you're *not* actually fired yet?" I ask.

I should have kept my mouth shut.

"You selfish, self-absorbed girl! Are you listening to me or not?"

She continues her rant while I finish cleaning up. I still have a gross, slimy green sensation in my stomach. It's urging me to figure out my next step with Lise. And Ben.

But it's impossible to plot while Paula shrieks and scolds.

"Mom, let's talk after I take a shower." I need a few minutes of something soothing.

I should have locked the door. She follows me in, sits on the toilet, and keeps talking to me.

At me.

"And I have Bethany telling me I should urge you to skip your internship. *Urge* you. What does she know about it? What nonsense. Let me read you her text. Where is it? Here we go. Oh, wait. No. Um. Okay, I can't find it, but the long and short of it was that you told her you're scared of your new supervisor and that I, as your mother, should make sure you know you have options and don't have to work with him. As though I hadn't already said almost exactly that! And more! If you didn't like him, of course you shouldn't work with him. You're not a slave."

Don't respond.

Don't respond.

I can't help it. I say over the sound of the shower, "I told you I didn't like him."

"You had a bad first impression. He liked you, so he must be at least intelligent."

"No, remember? It was the worst—"

"Don't exaggerate with your stories. I *told* you that you could find another internship. And for Bethany to talk to me like I'm an evil villain. Was she born in a pickle jar?"

She leaves with a slammed door, and I rest my forehead on the ancient, acrylic interior of our shower. The warm water is so, so good. I push in the knob to make the flow weaker. Maybe that will help it stay warm longer.

Paula comes back and I peek out of the curtain to see her go through our toiletries and throw things in a plastic grocery bag.

"What are you doing?"

"I'm taking time to clean out this storage. A very *motherly* activity. You have so much trash in here. What's a wax pen?"

"Leave it alone. I'll do it later. I promise."

She slams the door for a second time, and I turn the water all the way off so I can hear her mutters and slamming of cabinets and doors in her wake.

I dry off the most important bits as fast as I can and wrap my towel around me toga style.

The bag she filled is on the floor, with the handles tied like bunny ears at the top. "Mom?"

She's in my room with the kitchen trash can propped open, going through my sock drawer and tossing singlets in the garbage.

"So many of these are mismatched. I haven't noticed how worn down the heels are," she says.

"Enough, Mom." I grab the trash can and move it back to its home in the kitchen. "I wear the mismatched ones under boots. It's fine."

I go back in my room and see she's emptied out my other dresser drawers onto my bed. "So much garbage in here," she mutters, and picks up thong underwear like it's an alien specimen.

"Mom, I promise I'll clean out my dresser this weekend. Please leave my room." I use my most gentle voice, like I'm trying not to startle a toddler. "It's been such a long day."

"*You've* had a long day, Zillah?"

"No, I mean—"

"You have it bad? Living here rent-free, doing your doodles and whatsit and ignoring your responsibilities?" She picks up my jelly jar full of drafting pencils. "Who paid for all of this?"

Those are the ones Cliff gave me last Valentine's Day, but now isn't the time to make that point.

"Mom." I hear the whine in my voice and know it makes me sound like the little kid she's describing. She's much better at steering an argument than I am. *I'm* the injured party here. It's not my fault she's on leave for violence *she* caused.

"It's time to get serious, Zillah." She picks up three pencils and tries to break them in half for effect, but they're strong. She throws them down instead and they lie inertly on the ground. She throws the jelly jar against the wall, and it bounces. Those canning jars are sturdy, and this one doesn't give her the satisfaction of breaking.

"Mom. I get it. But we—"

"You don't. You don't get *anything*. You don't know how difficult you make everything! I want to keep us safe!" She's shouting and looking around my room as though searching for more evidence of my malfeasance.

I try to pretend she's calm and I sift through the pile of clothes on my bed to find underwear and leggings.

"I'm sorry I texted Jennifer. Can we please talk about this tomorrow?"

"No. You need to grow up and face reality."

I think she's falling, but no. It's a deliberate lunge.

To my desk.

My laptop.

"Mom!"

She slams the lid. Yanks out the power cord and USB extender.

"That's enough, Mom. Put it down."

"Too much screen time, Zillah!" She tips the laptop on its side and slams it like a sheaf of papers she's trying to straighten.

"No! Give it back, Mom." I'm shouting, too, but she ignores me.

Slam.

"Too much art!" she shouts.

Slam.

"Get out of my room!" I try.

She does, but she takes my laptop with her.

I follow her to the kitchen. "Mom, no!" She turns on the kitchen sink faucet and washes the laptop. She adds dish soap and keeps going while I shout nonsense.

Fuck me. There's no saving it. I rush back to my room to finish putting on clothes.

No. Wait. I've got to text Bethany. My last one wasn't urgent enough. "Mom needs you. ASAP. 911 level weirdness."

I hear rattling drawers of cutlery. Is she throwing out silverware again?

I've got to get out of here. I can call Bethany from outside.

I grab my backpack and purse. Water bottle. Check for keys. My phone's in my pocket. Charger.

"Mom?" I try one more time.

"Get away from me!"

I do.

Chapter Forty-One

Outside our front door, standing on the landing.

The stairs look extra steep this evening. Man, I'm tired.

My phone vibrates. Lise's calling. Decline. I can think about that mess later.

Once I figure out where I'm sleeping tonight. The green rolling grossness in my stomach is spikey and metallic.

Lise texts, "Come over? Do you have a minute?" What does this even mean? I wish texts came with a mood reading like, "This person wants to strangle you because her brother told her what a butthole you are."

I wish I was someone who could sleep alone and it's no big deal. I should have started with that fear instead of stairs and strawberries.

Do I go to Bethany's?

No, she's on her way here and will stay the night, probably. That means I'd be alone at Bethany's, too.

Lise calling again. Decline.

Maybe Paula will calm down soon. I could come back in an hour?

I hold my ear to the front door in time to hear a crash. Sounds like a kid playing the drums on pots and pans.

Nope. Nope. Nope.

Dad! Why didn't I think of him first? I sit down on the top step and text, "Sorry about this. Need to talk ASAP again. I want to get away for a few days. Mom having meltdown. Can I come stay with you? Could you send me $ for car rental or train or bus fare?"

I'm not afraid of travel, really. It's all the associated details like bad food, unfamiliar toilets, and the possibility of being alone. He's offered me money for tickets before, but I've never taken him up on it. Hell, I've never even been further than an hour outside the city. If he *gets* this in time, I bet he'll jump at the chance to be "Hero Dad".

Maybe I can hang out in an all-night diner tonight and take tons of caffeine until morning.

My stomach turns at the thought of caffeinating myself like that. I need sleep. In a safe place. Near other humans.

I wish I had more friends.

Bethany texts, `Be there within the hour. Calling in ten.` Well, that's Paula taken care of.

I call dad while I walk down the stairs. No answer. Voicemail. "Hey Dad. Hope my text didn't alarm you too much. Can you call me?"

Goddamn Paula.

I'm half a flight down the stairs when I hear the door at the bottom of the stairwell open and close. I don't want to deal with neighbors right now. But I can't go back inside.

Look normal, Zillah. I wipe my eyes and nose on my sleeve and pretend I'm a normal person having a normal day.

But it's Lise. We meet on the stairs between the first and second floors.

"Zillah! I've been calling."

Fuck me. All the worry about her and Ben floods up from where I've tried to contain it. I don't even have time to plan my apology speech or come up with justifications. I've got nothing.

"I'm so sorry, Lise. I wanted to come over and talk right after Ben left."

"What's going on? What the heck?" She doesn't look mad. Concerned. Eyebrows almost comically tent shaped like a cartoon.

Anger would have been better. Her sympathy makes me start crying all over again.

"I'm sorry, Lise. It's that the walls are so thin.

"Yeah, I know. That's how I—"

"And the first time I heard you, I didn't know you, you know? And like, I didn't think of it like eavesdropping because I was just *there*."

"What?" she asks.

"And I did it again a few more times, but I stopped when we got close. I promise. And today was a fluke because—"

"Zillah. What are you talking about?"

But I can't stop now that I'm confessing.

"And I know it makes me a bad person. I *am* a bad person. I'm the worst friend. But I will do whatever to make it up to you."

She stares at me, so I keep talking.

"It made me feel less alone, you know? And your therapist is nice. And that's how I knew to go meet you outside that time. You know?" I stop to wipe my nose on my sleeve again. "I knew you needed to go meet a neighbor, so I wanted to be that neighbor. And it ended okay! Right?"

She steps backwards, downwards a stair. "Zillah. Are— Are you saying you listened to my therapy?" Now her eyebrows are doing a different thing, and her face is all pink.

I'm confused. "Didn't Ben tell you?"

"Ben knew?"

"He came over today and—"

She interrupts, "I wanted to check on you when we heard your mom screaming." She turns around and walks down the stairs. "I thought you might want to come over. I thought you might be in danger."

Oh fuck.

"Lise—"

"No. Just— No, Zillah." She turns and walks quickly down the stairs.

Chapter Forty-Two

H as anyone ever screwed up this badly before?

I walk down the stairs carefully. Maybe Lise will rush back and insist we make up and I sleep on her couch.

On her dog's bed.

On the floor.

I'm not picky at the moment.

I walk through the courtyard waiting to hear, "Zillah! Stop!"

But there's only the sound of traffic over on Broadway.

Aunt Bethany calls from her car.

"Zillah, are you okay?"

"It's not me. It's Mom."

"Yes but first tell me are *you* okay?" she insists.

"I'm fine. I'm fine." I give her the barebones update using terms like "police misunderstanding" instead of "arrest." "Argument" instead of "bat-shit crazy."

Dad calls on the other line.

"I gotta go. Keep me posted, Aunt B!"

I click over to my dad.

"Hey Kiddo, what's the emergency?" His voice is such a relief. The red stabby bits of my fear settle down a notch.

"Oh, Dad." For a moment, I don't know where to start. "Can I come to you? I need to get out of the city."

"Of course. When are you thinking?"

"Like, now? Or I guess tomorrow morning?"

"Oh, Zillah." There's a muffled noise like he's scraping the phone against an unshaven cheek. "What about this summer? We could plan it out and even go to the beach." He knows I've always wanted to see the ocean.

"Yeah, sure, but also can I come now? Like both?"

"Oh." I hear the "no" in his voice.

I don't want to hear the excuse he's cooking up, so I give him one. "Is it a bad time?"

"Yeah, busy at work, and a bunch of stuff going on."

I'm quiet.

"And, Kiddo, I mean it about this summer. You'll like it out here. Maybe we can talk next week about dates?"

"Dad, I don't have a place to sleep tonight." It comes out like a whine and saying it out loud is devastating. "Please, can I come to you? I can put it on a credit card. I need to be with—" I almost say "an adult" but I'm one of those and look how far that's got me. "—family."

"Lemme Venmo you money for a hotel, okay? A cheap one near you? Or maybe an AirBnB? I bet you could find one under a hundred bucks."

It's clear that he doesn't know I've never spent a night by myself. How much *does* he know? Yeah, he knows I want to see the ocean, but that's just because I used to draw it all the time. Does he ever think about me? Is he a sperm donor who sends me a check for my birthday and Christmas?

"Mom broke the MacBook you gave me for graduation."

"Oh! I can help you troubleshoot whatever error it's giving you." His voice is peppier now that we're on familiar ground.

I picture my poor, sudsy laptop, probably still in the sink. Maybe in the drying rack now like it's a piece of our nice china. Maybe she was just giving it a pre-rinse before putting it through the dishwasher.

"Yeah, Dad. Sounds good."

"I'll send you money in a minute. Find a good hotel for the night. Love you Kiddo. Let's talk soon, okay?"

"Love you too."

I'm gutted. Dad's always been off in the wings like a safety net for me. But the first time I test him out, it's an illusion. It's like planning on eating delicious leftovers all day, only to open the fridge and find them gone.

Paula wasn't entirely wrong when she called him an empty vessel.

I have one last shot.

One last anchor to tether me.

I cross my fingers and hope I don't get voicemail as I click the contact in my phone.

"Cliff?"

Chapter Forty-Three

I flip up and back between texts, email, and WhatsApp, hoping for something from Lise until Cliff picks me up from outside Cafe Korzo.

"I'm a knight in shining armor," he says as I get in the passenger seat. He leans over in kissing position, but I go in for a hug, awkward due to the gearshift poking my stomach.

I breathe in his familiar smell and say, "Hero for sure. Thanks for letting me stay over."

The conversation is easy, and we fall back into our usual Zillah-Cliff rhythm. He tells me about his license and Rik's terrible poetry. I tell him about Paula.

"She'll have fun yelling at your aunt, and she'll feel better and pretend nothing happened."

"Maybe."

"And you can borrow my podcasting laptop. It's in the trunk. It won't keep a charge, but it's okay as long as it's plugged in."

Cliff's pilot podcast has been waiting for him to edit for months. He's probably glad to have another excuse not to finish it.

At a stoplight, he gives me a long look. "You look worn out," he says.

"Yeah."

"I didn't mean, like, ugly or anything. You're cute." He puts his hand on my upper thigh.

Ah.

He thinks this is romantic. Like we're getting back together.

For a moment I toy with letting this slide for the night. He'd be thrilled, I could avoid conflict, and—what? Would I be trading fake romance for a place to stay? Sex? No way.

I gently pick his hand up off my thigh and hold it my hand.

"I'm so glad to have a friend like you," I say. He's paying attention to traffic and a pesky jaywalking pedestrian. I can't tell if this sank in. "You think the guys will mind me sleeping on your couch tonight?"

That gets his attention. "You're not sleeping in my room?"

"Cliff—"

"Do you even *want* to get back together?" He asks.

"No, I—"

"So, you're just using me for a place to stay?"

"I need help and you're my friend," I try.

"We're not friends, Zillah." He spits his words with anger but starts crying at the same time. "You blocked me and haven't talked to me since we broke up. That's not friends."

"Cliff, please. You're still one of my best friends and you're helping me. You're giving me a safe place to stay tonight."

"Don't you still love me?" Ouch. That's a hard one.

"Let's not do this now."

"Zillah, you use people." He pulls into the Shell station at the three-way intersection mess of Diversey, Lincoln, and Racine and puts the car in park. He wipes his eyes and nose with his sleeves and takes a few deep breaths. "Let me read you an email you sent me last year." I stay quiet while he searches on his phone. He needs to get this out of his system, and we never really had a post-breakup debrief. After a moment, Cliff finds an old, loving note from me. I had written it after I got in trouble with the bursar because I misunderstood the school payment schedule and he loaned me $350 so I could register for class. I remember feeling grateful and cared for. Is it gross that I felt loving after he paid for stuff? "I will love you *forever*, and I'm glad you're my man. Love *always*, Zillah." He finishes reading it out loud, with an emphasis on the words 'forever' and 'always'.

He puts down his phone and asks, "So, was that a lie?"

My first instinct is to defend myself. I should come up with an explanation that allows all my statements to be true and for me to stay with him tonight. But I doom myself with, "You can't argue me into loving you like that."

"So, you don't love me." And now he's crying again.

I feel bad.

But not as bad as I should feel.

I guess he's right. I *am* mercenary and cold-hearted.

I imagine Lise on the other side of our shared wall. Revealing truths to her therapist. Convinced it's private. Getting help because her whole life she's feared people are watching and judging.

While I've been watching and judging.

What's she doing right now, in this moment? Is she crying? Does she think our friendship isn't real? Did I break her heart, too?

My nose tingles and tears well. I haven't had the chance to think about losing her.

But.

One thing at a time.

I can't stay with Cliff tonight.

"Cliff, I'm sorry," I say. I say it slowly and try for the depth of emotion he deserves. "You're one of the most important people in my life, and I think we can be friends again someday." I check my seat to make sure I have everything and get out of the car. "You're a good man, Cliff." He's just not the right fit to be *my* man, "Do you— do you want a hug before you go?"

"Yeah." We both get out and he gives me a bear hug in front of his headlights. "Um, can I still borrow your computer?" I can feel him shaking with deep sob-interrupted breaths. I think about the times he worried his mom might die. He's been through worse and come out okay, but it's not the time to remind him.

"Drive safe," I say, and go into the gas station to get out of the cold.

I walk around, browsing at the shelves for a bit to center myself, then approach the middle-aged woman in an eggshell blue hijab behind the counter. "What can I help you with?" she asks.

"Actually, um—" I pull out my phone and lean toward the counter. "I need to get a hotel room for the night, but I've never done it before. I googled 'hotel near me' but—" I show her my overwhelming search results.

"What about Airbnb? What's your budget?"

"I'm really wanting a hotel," I say. I want the safety of knowing I'm in an institution with vetted staff and not a creeper's apartment with cameras everywhere. I listen to enough true crime podcasts to know what's what. "I can spend, like, a hundred dollars. Or I guess a hundred and fifty. Is that enough? And it needs to be in walking distance if I can get one." Dad sent me two hundred dollars, but that seems insane to spend all at once.

"Booking at the last minute is good. Hotels have deals so the rooms aren't empty." She pulls up her own phone and just goes to Google Maps and types in hotel. We both look at the search results within a mile.

She's right. I have options.

"Oh!" she says. "You could get a room at The Willows. It's beautiful and in a good neighborhood."

"Do you think it's safe?"

She gives me a serious look. "Are you okay?" she asks. Her compassion brings all my emotions up and I feel my telltale nose prickles that always precede tears.

"Yeah, yeah. Thanks." I finish booking my first hotel room while she watches over my shoulder. Then I buy a toothbrush, as well as an overpriced package of crackers, applesauce, and plain salted potato chips for dinner. And probably breakfast.

Before I start my walk to the hotel, I text Lise. "I'm so sorry, Lise. I don't have a good explanation, but I'm so sorry. Can we talk?"

Chapter Forty-Four

The Willows Hotel is a snapshot of what I love about Chicago. It's modern and old and unapologetically fake at the same time. Like so much of the city, the edifice has limestone cornices and scrollwork to look like Parisian buildings from a slightly earlier time period, and both outside and inside there are still features reproducing the 1700s French Provincial style. The building says, "Yeah, yeah, Chicago burned down. But look! Now we're Paris!"

Even with my heart breaking, I can appreciate the details. The interior design highlights the marble work while still conveying warmth. Hard to do. The lobby feels like a respite from the windy darkness outside. There are ridiculous gilt-framed prints of animals in Victorian-era poses and clothes, antiqued black fixtures, and even a fireplace with faux animal skin-covered armchairs. I'm going to sit in those at some point while I'm here. The effect is "Welcome, you lucky duck!"

I take a couple of pictures in case there's anyone left in my life I can send them to.

I've watched enough media to know how to check into a hotel. I even have cash ready for a tip, but I don't have a suitcase for a bellhop to carry. I use my keycard to go into my room, and I almost start crying again. It's so bright and warm. I lock the deadbolt and pet the stark white bedspread. I inspect the bathroom (clean!), the floor under the bed (also clean!) and the closet (yup! Clean!). I won't use the free coffee pods or eat the complimentary cookies, but I appreciate the gifts. My body starts to relax, and I grab the binder on the bedside table and bring it to the bathroom to read on the toilet. It's like an instructional guide for how to use a hotel. I read every page for details and, after I finish washing up, I look at all the free toiletries. I do a quick sketch of a jeweled necklace on the The Willows Hotel pad of paper, and stick that in the safe for some confused cleaner to find tomorrow.

Tomorrow.

Paula will be calmer and we can talk things out. About her getting fired, but also about other topics we haven't gotten a chance to discuss. The strawberry jam. My eating. My school plans, moving out, and that internship I'm dreading.

Tonight, I'm going to pull my first all-nighter. If other college students do this all the time, I can too. I'm in an elegant room, I have thousands of hours of entertainment available, and I have caffeine pills in my backpack. An intruder can't surprise you if you're awake and binging 90s romcoms.

I flop on an armchair with the crackers and a cup of water. We don't eat on living room furniture at home, and this bit of rebellion is satisfying. I check all messaging options, but still nothing from Lise.

What would Paula think if she could see me? What's she doing right now? I have a text from Bethany saying, "`All okay. She's ready to make up when you come home.`" but no other details. Cliff was right. She got to spit venom about me and now regrets her actions. Hopefully she's regretful enough to buy me a new laptop and release those funds to me so I can move out.

If she doesn't, then fuck it. I'll fill out a FAFSA and get student loans. It'll suck to be in debt, but I'll have less debt than people who've used loans for four years.

Money.

How's she going to support herself? Maybe she exaggerated the getting-fired thing. Maybe it really is just a nice long vacation? If she's fired, am I fired, too? Sid wouldn't do that, but there's no way I could still work there.

I chew on a cracker slowly and let it dissolve in my mouth. I don't *feel* hungry, but I hear my stomach rumble. I need to eat to help me make any sort of decisions tonight.

My Universe, it's been a long day.

Nothing on Netflix looks good, so I try a show I've seen before. Maybe the comfort will help me kill time.

But even reality dating can't distract me from the little creaks around the hotel room.

I listen to the show with one ear bud so I can stay tuned for strange noises.

What does a murderer *sound* like? Real life should have a soundtrack, so you know when you should prepare for a jump scare or a heartwarming reunion.

I'm uncomfortable in my clothes and tense all over.

A shower! I can take a long shower without anyone complaining that I'm going to use up the hot water.

The shower starts fine, but it's not the rejuvenating experience I'd hoped for.

In an instant, I know something's wrong.

I sense an intruder right after applying the complimentary grapefruit facial cleanser.

My inner calm of light blue pastels shifts to ragged red acrylic.

With my eyes still closed because of the soap all over my face, I turn off the water. I hold my breath and listen for footsteps and other clues.

I hear nothing.

He must be a pro.

I use my upper arm to try to scrape the cleanser away from my eyes. I should have brought a towel closer. I can't turn on the water, because he'll know I'm here and vulnerable.

I open one eye a teeny sliver.

Mistake.

Ah fuck, this burns.

Fuckfuckfuck.

I turn on the water and give myself a ten second rinse and grab a towel and prepare for an onslaught. At least I'll be able to see during the attack.

I hear nothing.

I wait in a hunched over crouch.

After a few minutes, my muscles scream at me from the strain. I un-hunch my back and quickly towel off.

I sit on the bathmat. It's wet from my shower, but it's a better waiting spot than the toilet.

I'm cold. I'm wet. I close my left eye tight against the memory of the soap pain.

Fuck it. If this is how I go, then this is how I go.

I unfurl from my wet nest of bathmat and stand. My foot is asleep and I do a gentle dance on it to get out the pins and needles.

I open the bathroom door, and nothing happens. I check out the front door and see the ottoman I've moved in front of the door is still in place.

By the time I complete a thorough search of the empty hotel room, I'm exhausted. My adrenalin has receded, and I'm a parched, shallow husk.

I get back in the shower to rinse, and I even stay for a round of sea kelp conditioner.

With the water halfway pulled on, the shower is quieter and I listen for noises.

This is stupid. I can't hear anything.

When I was twelve or thirteen and developing breasts, Paula and I practiced how to wrap a towel around ourselves in an emergency, like in case a fire alarm goes off while we're in the shower. I had lifted my small breasts up and wrapped the towel around my torso tightly to make it look like I had cleavage. Paula had scolded, "No! That makes you look even bigger. What! You want to get raped by firefighters?"

What a world view. Poor Paula.

I can't live a life wrapped in fear.

I turn the water on high.

Now that my rainbow of anxiety has receded, there's only sadness.

Can I blame Paula for everything? She's responsible for not encouraging me to try food when I was little. She shares the blame for me not trying food now. Maybe some blame for my trouble shedding my anxiety. But not for this aching loneliness. The knowledge that I've hurt Lise.

That's all me.

Once I'm dried off, I put some of my clothes back on.

Have I ever been this tired in my life? I'm not even worrying about plantar warts from walking barefoot on the carpet. I sniff the sheets and crawl in the bed.

Wow.

I've slept in my bed, Paula's, and Cliff's. This one is crafted by angels. I need to remember to look at the mattress tag to see what brand it is. Wow.

I have one more moment of fear while I almost drift off and my feet do that falling-in-a-hole sensation. I hug one of the extra pillows and pretend it has magical powers that will protect me all night.

Chapter Forty-Five

When I wake up at five, I pull the sheet over my head so I'm alone in a little tent. "I did it," I say to the pillow. "I slept by myself all night."

I'm content until the flood of emotions and jumbled problems from the past eighteen hours wash over me. I logically know that my biggest challenge is Paula and her (our?) employment status, but the one that keeps floating to the surface is the image of Lise's face on the stairwell.

I consider going to class for a hot minute, but there's no way I could concentrate. And I want to get my money's worth (well, Dad's) by spending every possible minute at the hotel. My time will be better spent by checking out Cliff's laptop to make sure it's functional enough to install Adobe Creative Suite and download my backed-up files.

But first, Lise.

I didn't get any response from my text last night and it's too early in the morning to text again or call. Instead, I write her an email.

> *Lise,*
>
> *In the short time I've known you, you've become one of my closest friends. I can't believe I put that in jeopardy by being such a buttwipe. I'm so, fucking, incredibly sorry, and I don't blame you at all if you don't forgive me. Just please know that I'm hoping to talk soon and I'll do whatever it takes to show you I'm sorry.*

What *can* I do? Chop off my ears? Give her something? Let her listen to *my* therapy? No, but that gives me an idea.

I've signed up to start therapy so I can learn why I did what I did. I hope we can talk soon.
Love,
Zillah

It's repetitive and not my finest work, but done is better than perfect. But before I click 'send', I need to actually sign up for therapy, so it isn't a lie. I look online at my options. I pick a company that offers a free session, fill in my info with my spam email address, and within a minute I'm looking at a long list of online therapists across Illinois.

I pick the least normy-looking one. They have rainbow glasses and a cat in their profile picture and specialize in "family-of-origin" issues. I'm supposed to send a description of my "presenting issues". I google this term, and it means a list of what the hell is wrong with me.

I don't know how much detail to give, so I sit on the armchair and just write.

Zillah Presenting Issues, a.k.a. What the hell is wrong with me.

1. I lost a friend, and it's 1000% my fault.

2. My mom is overprotective, and I worry about her, too. Every time I try to be independent, it backfires.

3. I don't do new stuff. I've never been outside of Illinois and I really want to see more things and travel. I want to see the ocean. I live in a bubble and it will hurt my mom if I try to escape too soon. I don't know what's my choice and what's my mom's.

4. I'm interested in a guy (I think), but I've already messed it up.

5. I'm studying business and I hate it. I have to do an internship this summer that I'm dreading. I don't even want to be an appraiser. I want the $$. And I want my

mom to be happy with me.

I pause.

Is that right? Is that why I'm not doing design?

If Paula didn't care at all, or if she was whisked away by aliens, what would my major be?

I'm still chewing on this question and staring at a sepia print of a jaguar in a riding habit in my hotel room when my phone rings.

It's Lise.

"I was just emailing you!" I want to sound casual, but I'm breathless from the surprise.

"Zillah—"

"Did you call me by accident? Please don't hang up. I really want to apolo—"

"Zillah, you need to come home. It's your mom."

Chapter Forty-Six

My Uber drops me off and I add a tip of two dollars with money I don't have. That's another tomorrow problem. Today's problem screams at our building manager in the pavement and grass courtyard in the middle of our apartment horseshoe. She's dragging her suitcase, which is notable since neither of us has ever used it. It was a free gift when she signed up for her bank account, and it is so old it doesn't even have wheels.

A police officer tries to speak to her while another stands to the side talking to neighbors.

I take a moment to process what I'm seeing and hearing, in part because Lise's outside with Vivian. She turns beet red when she sees me.

"—and anything is better than this deathtrap, so don't even bother!" a shout from Paula sinks into my consciousness. "Just don't blame me when this place is up in flames. And *no-o-o*," she directs to the police officer using a singsong, sarcastic voice, "That's not a threat. Just look at the daisy-chain electrical plug in the basement!"

I move toward her like my feet are stuck in thick mud and bits of her speech snag in my ears. "Protection order." "Fire inspector." "My lawyer."

"Mom," I say when I reach her.

"That's fine," she tells me as though I've said something brilliant. "You'll drive me to Bethany's and I'll contact my *attorney,*" she pauses with a fierce look at Alexi, "from there. Zillah, go up and get my charging cord and a box of granola bars. I'll see you in the car." She grabs her suitcase and drags it toward the steps down to Wellington Ave.

What a reunion.

I look around to the rest of the cast of this bizarre play, wondering what I'm supposed to be doing. Alexi says, "Please take her from here. You and me, we will talk tomorrow. It is good?"

"Uh." What am I agreeing to?

Vivian parts from the spectators and asks, "Zillah, what can I do to help?"

"I don't understand what's happening." There are so many people here, even though it's not even seven o'clock in the morning. I'm overwhelmed like a lost kid in a mall. Vivian and I go upstairs toward my place.

"Your mom was banging on doors and shouting about fire." When we get inside the apartment, the smell is comforting. My body is like, "this is the place where you can relax," and I get the urge to poop.

But then I notice our belongings in disarray. Dining room chairs are piled on top of the couch. The microwave is pulled out from its hutch in the wall. There are bottles of industrial-strength cleaners all over the kitchen. My anus tightens up again and the animal inside me is like, "Nope. Not safe to let the guard down here. Pooping can wait."

I grab chargers and snacks. I slide my apartment key off my key ring and ask Vivian to hold it for me, just in case.

She gives me a solid hug before I leave. I feel like I'm going to drown in tears, but I have to choke them all back. What is it about true empathy that pulls all the sadness out?

Lise and Ben don't know how lucky they are.

I jog to Paula and find her almost at our parking spot.

"Mom," I say loudly to get her attention when I'm a few yards away.

She makes brief eye contact, but keeps walking with a curt, "Catch up." How is she so fast with that suitcase?

"I'll drive," I say when we make it to the parking lot and I help her load the suitcase in the trunk of her car. "Does Aunt Bethany know you're on the way?"

"You worry too much, Zillah." This, as she taps each of the car doors three times before getting in the passenger seat.

When we're on the road, I ask, "What was that all about? The stuff with Alexi and fires? Are we evicted?"

"Evicted," she repeats with a sarcastic "Ha!". "Can you relax, for once? You're the one who needs therapy. You always jump to the worst conclusions."

This stings since I'm sort of, almost, in therapy. It's not like a principal's office you go to when you're in trouble.

I stay quiet, but Paula continues while looking out the window. "You don't know how good you have it, Zillah. Everyone pitching in to help you. Your family letting you stay for free. You're going to have a career and be comfortable. But all you do is complain."

"What am I complaining about? That I never get to do anything? I've never been anywhere? I never learned how to eat like a normal human?" My hands are tight on the steering wheel.

"You've got a short-term memory problem, kid. Everything was for you. I kept you safe, and you *liked* it."

"Mom, my whole life has been in a bubble."

She gives another sarcastic "Hm!" and then "You could have eaten other food any time you wanted."

"It's not just food. I've never been outside Illinois. I've never seen the ocean."

"How dare you! You *know* my happiest times in my life were at Myrtle Beach. You *know* how much I wanted to go back. But we couldn't. Because of *you*."

"Bullshit."

"I don't like that," she responds automatically to my swear.

"How did I keep you from going?"

"How would you have slept by yourself if I went? And if I took you? Ha! How would you have eaten? Where would you have a bowel movement?"

"We could have gone any time! We could have packed our foods. And those disposable toilet guards. People travel, Mom. We would have been fine. Can you please just admit that you did something wrong? Just admit that you should have encouraged me to try food! Admit that it wasn't my fault that we eat this way? That our life could have been better!" Shouting feels good, but it doesn't seem to penetrate.

"There was never a good time to travel," she says, changing tactics. "Your schooling and me needing to work. A single mother doesn't get to fly to South Carolina."

At the Ashland and Fullerton stop light, I put the car in park, and open Google Maps to see how long the drive is. "Myrtle Beach is fifteen hours away. We could have driven in a day."

"It's fifteen hours without stops. You've never been on a road trip. You don't know about all the stops."

"That's my point! I never got the chance."

"You would have hated it."

I put the car in drive, and we sit in silence for a bit, each of us breathing heavily.

"Well, let's go," I say. "Let's do it now."

"Fat chance."

"You're not working. You have your toothbrush in that suitcase. I've been keeping you from traveling? Fine. Let's go."

"Zillah, you like to act tough, but we both know you can't travel yet."

I press "Start" on Google Maps and let the navigation begin.

And that's how I abduct my mother.

Chapter Forty-Seven

She doesn't get what's happening until we pass the ramp to Wacker Drive and she scolds, "You missed the turn. Take Randolph instead."

I ignore her. Shocking her with profanity felt good, but I like to concentrate when I drive. Especially when I'm taking a new route.

We pass Randolph and she says, "For goodness' sake, Zillah. Pay attention." I continue south on Lake Shore Drive. "So you go from a tantrumming toddler to a silent teen, is that it?"

When I merge on I-90, she tries again, "Is this supposed to convince me how grown up you are? Because let me tell you something, Kid, it isn't." She pulls out her phone and in my peripheral vision I see her navigating to Bethany's from our current location. She says, "I could call the police and say you're kidnapping me and holding me against my will."

I grab her phone despite her "Hey!" and tuck it under my ass.

"Not funny, Zillah! Give it back."

I keep driving.

Her final ploy is "How far do you think you're going to get before you get hungry, scared, or need to use a bathroom? Think, Zillah! Ignoring me still? Fine. I'm not the one who needs to stay close to home."

Now it's a game of chicken, with each of us feigning being relaxed and *totally* fine with a sudden car trip. I want to rub it in her face that *I'm* the flexible one. If I haven't seen the ocean, it's *her* fault.

But her comments sink in. Where *will* I poop? What if I freak out and get us in a wreck? What if I drive into oncoming traffic and kill us?

But I'm more thrilled than nervous. How far will we go? Could we get to Indiana or even Kentucky? Are grits really a food people eat? Maybe I could see those if we get south enough before we turn around.

Maybe we won't turn around. Maybe we could see the ocean.

Holy crap.

I might see the ocean.

I expel a cough-like laugh, like steam escaping from a pot. 'Look at what I did!' I want to shout to all the other drivers. 'Isn't this amazing? We're on a highway!'

On I-90 when we pass the state border, I can't help but break the silence when I exclaim, "We're in Indiana!" I sound like a delighted kid, but it cracks the ice.

"We used to go on road trips all the time," Paula says. Her tone is cold, but I'm lured in.

"What— you and me?"

"Your dad. Mark."

"Where?"

"Just small trips. All over the place. If there was an exhibition he wanted to see. Or an old friend. There used to be a program called One Tank Trips that gave us ideas."

"Did you— Did you like it?"

"Of course! I wouldn't waste all that gas otherwise. The money your dad was willing to burn on gas. You wouldn't believe it. But it was fine until I got pregnant. One time, I got sick all over myself on our way to Madison. We couldn't turn around because of traffic, and I had to lean out of the passenger seat window in stop-and-go-traffic, vomiting for all the world to see. Right on the side of the car! After that, I didn't want to take the risk. And I didn't want to be stuck in traffic with a baby. What if you had an emergency?" She narrows her eyes at the road with lips pursed, I assume imagining all the ways a baby might die on a road trip.

We're quiet again for a couple of miles.

"What about later?" I ask. "We could have taken a train or—"

Her voice is harsh again. "Zillah, you were the least flexible child ever. You threw a fit over the smallest thing."

"Maybe you were the fit thrower!" Great argument, me. I try again. "I could have adjusted."

"Turn around at exit 253."

"No. I want to see the ocean."

Six miles of silence. I put on the Lofi Girl station on Spotify and Paula shouts, "Keep your eyes on the road!" After a few miles, she complains, "This is putting me to sleep."

We keep to ourselves, but every once in a while, Paula offers more tidbits. I want to tell her to shutthefuckup since she still doesn't seem apologetic, but it's all new information, and that's a scarce commodity. Like when we pass Crown Point, she says, "There was a neat antique mall over there. I wonder if it's still there. Your dad saw a fake suit of armor and he wanted it, but there was no way we could fit it in our little Nissan." She sighs. "It was too expensive. Two hundred dollars! But the helmet opened up, and he wanted to put things in it."

"I wonder if I could find him something like that online. That could be a cool gift."

"Once you're an appraiser and earning a nice salary, that would be a lovely gift for him. But for now, save your money to buy professional clothes for internship."

"I'm not doing the internship."

"Zillah!"

"I don't even know where I'm living this summer."

"You'll come home—"

"And I can do an internship next summer with a different placement if I still want to." She tries to interrupt, but I keep talking. "I'm changing my major to Graphic Design, and I might even get a scholarship to the Fox Usability and Design Bootcamp."

"This is— This selfishness— This absolute selfishness." She's talking to herself more than me.

It hurts. I knew it was impossible, but I'd hoped for a more understanding reaction. I knew this would happen, but it still hurts.

"We can talk about it more when I know more."

"I forbid it."

"I'm an adult."

"I won't support you. No housing. No nothing."

"Okay."

"When I *think* of all the sacrifices I've made for you to achieve this. It was your dream!"

"Was it?"

She continues ranting, and I let her vent.

After another hour, I pull into a parklike rest stop so I can pee.

I reach out to Lise before I brave the bathroom. I text, "Long story, but I'm on my first road trip. Can we talk?" I hope this will lure her into *some* communication.

The toilets aren't horrific, but they look well-used. How many thousands of people have sat on these? I wipe down the seat with toilet paper, make a little barrier with more toilet paper, and sit.

My bladder is full, but I can only relax enough to go after telling myself, "If I catch a disease through my thigh skin in Lebanon, Indiana, it will be a great story." Peeing feels so good once I'm chillaxed enough. Immediate gratification for my bravery.

I smile at myself in the mirror while I wash my hands. I peed in a *very* public toilet!

I can celebrate more later. I've got to get back to Paula before she steals the car back to head home.

I can tell there's more people outside now.

Kids shrieking.

Engines revving.

Dogs barking.

So many dogs.

Or maybe just one loud one?

And a shouting Paula.

Fuck.

I rush outside. Paula's across the pavement plaza with her back to the vending machine and a fat, pug-sized dog standing in front of her barking. It's white, with a hot pink leash dragging on the ground.

"Whose dog is this? Whose dog!" she shouts.

"C'mere Daisy!" a little kid shouts, running up to her. He looks about eight and has the disheveled appearance of a child stuffed into a minivan for too many hours.

I jog toward them both in time to see the dog run away from the boy, lead him on a chase, and return to bark at Paula again.

She sees me and shouts, "Zillah, wait in the car!"

"It's okay, Mom." I say as I join her. I get down in a squat and use my best Halsted-wrangling voice to say, "Who's this good woofer? Are you being a silly and barking at my mom?" I continue in my singsong voice. "Would you like to sniff my hand? Oh, kisses, too? Why thank you!" I take hold of his leash and return him to the boy.

Paula's deflated but more relaxed as we head to the car. "You learn that from the neighbor girl? Lisa?"

"Lise. Yeah." My nose prickles a bit while I consider the term 'backsliding'.

"So, you like dogs now?"

"I like one. But I can tolerate the rest. Do you want to use the restroom before we go? It's not too terrible in there." She has a small shudder, and we both get back in the car.

After I navigate out the exit and merge on to the highway, she says, "Can you believe the nerve of some people! Why they need to bring dogs on a car trip? Ridiculous." A minute later, she continues, "What if he bit you? Don't play with strange dogs."

"Noted."

We're quiet for a while and then she says, "You're getting braver." I glance at her and return my eyes to the road. "The food. Dogs. This trip." She exhales in a sigh and then, "It's something. Good or bad, I don't know. But it's something."

Her admission changes something for me. Finally, a break in her facade of "everything is better my way."

"Mom, do you want to turn around? I've gotten to get out of Illinois."

She's quiet for a minute, then says, "We've come this far."

"Ok?"

"If you give me back my phone, you can keep abducting me for a while."

It's a temporary truce.

For now, I'm reveling in the fact that I'm a true explorer. I'm a multi-state traveler. This is the most time I've ever driven in one day, and of course the longest distance. Every mile I go is another high score I've beaten.

We navigate around Indianapolis, but we only get to see suburb stuff. When we get into Ohio (Ohio! My third state!), Bethany calls and I click the icon to let her connect through Bluetooth to our speakers.

"Hey Bethany! You'll never guess where we are!" I say.

"Just south of Dayton?"

Ironically, Paula's "take-a-photo-after-parking" scheme worked to help discover abduction after all. Last night, she asked Bethany to be her new checker. Paula hasn't checked in with a photo, wasn't answering her texts, and Bethany was alarmed when she checked Paula's location on our family tracking app.

We share our Myrtle Beach plan with Bethany.

Well, I share our plan.

Paula is silent and fidgety.

Bethany asks, "Paula, when's the last time you ate something? Do you have water?"

Paula grunts a bit and I realize I'm a selfish idiot. I've got snacks and I took a restroom break, but I believed Paula when she said, "I'm fine." We've been gone for over five hours, and I'm not the only one who doesn't like to pee and poop away from home.

"We're going to stop soon for provisions and, um, comfort," I promise them both. After we hang up, I find us a Target along our route. I buy supplies to clean one of the toilets myself so that Paula feels comfortable using it. I also get some basic toiletries, another t-shirt and some underwear for myself, our brand of granola bars, and sunscreen. Paula has all the things she packed for staying with Bethany, so I can raid her suitcase for anything else I need.

Then we drive for hours, with our trip punctuated by refueling the car and looking for our foods in gas stations. There's so much to see on the road and off it. With the rate we're going, we could get to Myrtle Beach by midnight or even earlier. We could get a hotel room (I'm an expert) and see the beach first thing in the morning.

It's dark now, so it's not as entertaining to look out the windows, and I get bored.

I sneak in my left earbud so I can listen to podcasts without Paula knowing.

After we pass Davidson College, I ask, "Should we go through Charlotte or around it?"

"Just go where she tells you," Paula says, referring to the Google Maps voice.

I glance at her to gauge her status. For the past hour, she's been closing her eyes. She's got fidgeting fingers, so she's not asleep. But, also, not responding.

"You okay?" I ask. "Mad at me? Sleepy? Hungry?"

"Nauseous," she says through clenched teeth, as though she'll be able to avoid puking by keeping her mouth shut. I should offer to pull over, but we're on such a strict schedule and we'll only have half a day at Myrtle Beach as it is.

She takes us on highway 77, which cuts over and through the city (sort of). Charlotte's shiny and new. At least the parts we drive past at 70 miles an hour are.

Paula still looks ill, but she's more alert when we get to Marion, South Carolina. "I'll drive for a while so you can rest," she says. "Let's fill up here so we don't have to pay Myrtle Beach prices."

Paula drives the next leg, and I study Google Maps to see our travel options. When we go home, I'll take us back up through Greenville and then Tennessee so we can see Dollywood. Even if we don't go inside, just driving by should be interesting. I bet the billboards are spectacular.

That means that by next week I will have visited a total of seven states. I should get a map and put pushpins everywhere I've been.

I doze off while Paula drives and I wake up to sense that something has changed.

Paula leans forward toward the steering wheel and stares at the road as though a deer is going to cross the highway at any moment. She looks ready to pounce, and her knuckles are white in her ten-and-two position.

"Mom? Where are we?" I ask. I sip from my water bottle and clear my throat.

"Almost to Conway. It'll be about an hour till we get there."

"Close! Want me to drive for a while?"

Her teeth work at the inside of her mouth like she's chewing her cud. "No. I'm less nauseous this way."

"After we see the ocean tomorrow, want to eat at someplace authentic?" I ask. She doesn't answer, but I'm too excited to shut up. "There's a gallery by the water I want to see, but I don't think we'll have time if we start back home tomorrow evening. It's called— um— I don't remember. I'll look it up again. Something like Franklin Chapin Boroughs. Maybe it's a museum. Does that sound familiar?" No answer. "Do you think everyone'll know we're tourists?"

That gets a noncommittal grunt from her.

"I can make a list of things we want to do," I say and open my notes app. "Any places you remember loving? Oh! Is there anyone we should visit? Like old friends? Do you know anyone down there?"

She makes a strangled noise and then, "Stop talking. I need to concentrate."

I read posts on the travel sub-Reddit.

"Hey Mom," I say, "Did you know people call it 'Dirty Myrtle'?" No response. "Is the boardwalk dangerous or can we check it out?"

"Dangerous."

"Maybe it's better nowadays?"

"Dangerous. And stay away from men."

"No men. Check."

"I'm serious, Zillah. Sometimes they come up to you and act nice. Or get you alone when you're swimming and touch you because you can't get away—"

"Oh my god! Mom—"

"Just stay away from them!"

"Okay. Jeez!"

I slip in my ear buds and close my eyes, but a minute later she shouts, "Zillah! Did you see?"

I pop out of my slouching position and look around stupidly while Paula fights traffic to pull over.

"Call 911," she says. "I hit someone."

Chapter Forty-Eight

I call 911 while she parks the car as far from traffic as she can without us rolling into the embankment. I hold my phone to my ear, but the call connects to the car's Bluetooth and speaker system.

"911. What is your emergency?"

"My mom hit a car," I say.

Paula shouts toward the microphone, "A pedestrian! I think it was a woman. Send an ambulance!" she shouts to the dispatcher. And then, to me, "Go look. Find her and see if you can help."

"I didn't see anything. What did she look like?" I ask.

"Zillah, look for a woman bleeding on the road, for goodness' sake. Just go! Go!"

Fuck.

She stays on the line with the dispatcher, and I get out and jog north against oncoming traffic. It's dark, and I'm half-blinded by the occasional headlights. But Paula's right. I've got to find her. I can at least give first aid while we wait for first responders.

The truth sinks in: this is my fault.

A woman is hurt. Maybe dying. Maybe dead. If I hadn't forced us to take this trip, none of this would have happened.

A black pickup pulls into the emergency lane in front of me. I jog up to the driver's side window, trying to keep far from the traffic, but also out of grabbing distance.

A young man in a red ball cap asks, "You okay, ma'am?"

"Someone got hit by a car. But I can't find them!"

He puts on his hazard lights and joins my search. Two other cars pull up, one full of people, and join the search, too. Now we're six searchers, plus Paula in our car down the road.

Traffic slows down, with looky-loos like we have in Chicago. I guess that's not a regional thing.

The searchers keep shouting questions at me ("What does she look like?" and "What was she doing in the road at night?"), but I'm the opposite of helpful and don't know what we're looking for.

Sirens in the distance. But I'm distracted when a red minivan rear-ends a Tesla between us and Paula. Another car hits the minivan, and spins dangerously close to our group. Two of our searchers go to the accident scene to see if anyone there needs help while the others keep looking for Paula's victim.

Traffic in the southbound lane is stopped behind us, with the collision blocking the road.

We can't find her.

The original searchers move their vehicles toward Paula to clear room for the fire truck, ambulance, and police cars coming closer. Or maybe Sheriff's cars. I'm not sure about the difference between police and sheriffs, and fuck why am I thinking about this? I don't know what emergency vehicles are coming, but it's a lot of lights and noise.

I head back to Paula.

She's still talking to the dispatcher through the car speakers. I hold her hand for a moment through the driver's side window. Her skin is papery thin in some spots and rough with calluses in others.

Traffic is moving slowly past us again, one vehicle coming at a time to gawp. Still no first responders, but they must be getting closer, especially with the jam clearing up.

My red cap friend drives his pickup truck over to us and parks right behind Paula. She gets out of the car and joins me outside so we can hear if he found a body. We stand side to side, and she holds my hand tight for support.

"We can't find her," he shouts as soon as we're close enough to hear.

Paula grabs her stomach and leans forward like she's been punched. "But she's out there somewhere. Bleeding!"

The professionals arrive, with most of them going to the three-car accident.

A cruiser drives to us, too, and we try to explain the events to the pair of officers.

The officer who's been interviewing us tells others on a radio that Paula had no "visual" on the victim. Paula interrupts, "But I *know*! I could *feel* it!" She turns to me, pleading.

"We'll find her, Mom! We're not giving up."

She lets out an anguished cry. "This isn't right! There's a dying woman and you don't care! None of you care!"

I try to hold her hand again. "Mom, we're going to keep looking."

"It's not in my head!" She pushes me away, and I fall toward traffic, trip, and land with a thud. A white car coming toward me swerves into the next lane and taps another white car.

"Fuck!" I crawl toward our car and sit there with my head between my knees. A strong arm takes me further away from traffic. Someone asks me something, but I can't talk. I just keep seeing that white car coming toward me.

I deserve to get hit by that car.

Someone hands me water. After a minute, I brush myself off, grateful that the traffic was slow enough to prevent me from getting run over. My heart is beating like it's going to pop out of my chest.

Our main police officer is over at the latest collision, and Red Cap asks me about a hundred questions to make sure I'm okay. He calms me down by telling me about his toddler. I like this guy. But I still keep picturing that white car.

When we return our attention to Paula, she's squatting on the ground on the other side of the car, away from traffic. "I can't breathe," she says. "I'm having a heart attack. I've got knives in my chest."

Red Cap summons one of the EMTs at the three-car pile-up.

I have to back away to let them treat her. The EMT tells me, "Looks like a panic attack, but we'll bring her in, just in case."

Our first officer asks, "Has this happened before? That she may have thought she hit someone?"

"What do you mean?"

"Tell me again what you remember," he says.

"I didn't see anything," I say. "If my mom hadn't said something, I wouldn't have known we hit anyone. I— I didn't feel any impact at all." I was listening to my music pretty loud, but I still have nerve endings.

But she couldn't have just imagined this.

"So— So you're saying she didn't hit anyone?" I ask.

"We'll canvas a little longer, but that's my theory. Does your mom have a history of mental illness?"

"I'm not going to State," Paula shouts, demonstrating both her powerful hearing and lung capacity. She's crying louder now, almost wailing. The locals exchange looks.

"What's State?"

"South Carolina State. Closed back in the nineties, maybe was the early 2000s. Was your mom ever hospitalized there?"

"I don't know."

"It used to be a mental hospital, but we have other facilities now." I chew on this and follow the ambulance to Conway Medical Center.

When I get to visitor parking, I stay in the car. I update Bethany and then google "think I hit someone with my car".

Holy fuck.

This is a thing.

It often happens when the driver is already stressed.

So, what makes more sense?

Theory One: Paula hit someone. No one noticed. There was no damage to the car, and no sign of any injured person.

Theory Two: Paula was stressed from a surprise road trip and when she hit a pothole or something (or nothing?), her brain put two and two together and came up with manslaughter.

I think back to those times I watched Paula circle a block on our tracking app. Was she checking to make sure she hadn't hit someone? She certainly wasn't chomping on Yuck Food.

Anxiety is a dick.

What the hell happened to her to make her like this?

And what's my responsibility?

An old lady with a stroller walks toward the SUV I'm parked next to. She's cooing to the baby, and her face is animated with joy. But when she moves the baby into the car, it's actually a little white dog, with curly-fluff hair like hers.

What if this sweet old lady was in the emergency room after having a panic attack? What if she was struggling with the misplaced guilt of hitting a nonexistent pedestrian?

I'd want to help her.

Well, if it's good enough for a stranger, I owe it to my mother.

I get out of the car and head toward the public entrance.

My mission: get Paula all checked out and then visit the ocean.

Chapter Forty-Nine

We once again have a mother-daughter reunion after triage, while she answers questions with a CNA in a cubicle.

Yes. Paula *was* hospitalized at South Carolina State Hospital.

Twice.

Once at age fourteen for a week, and again at sixteen for two months, Paula confirms.

When I ask, "What for?" she scolds, "You should be out there searching instead of wasting time with me in this COVID breeding ground. Put on a mask, for goodness' sake."

I try to suck down all her passive-aggressiveness. And the aggressive-aggressiveness ("I can't believe *I'm* the one with pending legal action after you dragged me on this cockamamie trip. We could be safe at home right now, but no! And to think there might be a woman dying on the road out there somewhere. Think, Zillah! Just think about what you did.").

At least my visions of that white car are getting less frequent. I'll look up PTSD later.

Paula's less twitchy after her insurance is verified. We aren't put in a private room, but we get a bed and a chair with curtains we can close around ourselves. It helps us pretend there's not a man in the next bed with testicular damage from an off-roading incident.

Her stabbing heart pain is gone. "It's just an echo of the pain now. Know what I mean?" she asks the white-haired physician when he finally gets to us around one in the morning. Paula perches at the end of a papered bed like she's waiting for a lollipop after being such a good patient. He grunts at the computer mounted on a little cart and I can't tell if he's listening. "I keep expecting it to start up again, but, so far, it's receding. My grandfather died of heart disease. On my father's side. Paternal." Then to me, "Zillah, ask Bethany to track down all of our relatives who had heart disease, and especially those that passed from it. You should know that anyway for your future care. Doctors always need to know. I wish I had one of those thingamajigs that keeps track of heart rate."

"Your Fitbit does that," I say.

"Doctor, is there a kind you'd recommend for someone with my condition? I wonder if insurance pays for it. Maybe if you put it in my chart as a medical recommendation?"

But the EKG and blood tests confirm no heart attack.

Likely, just a good old panic attack.

Paula rolls her eyes at me when the doctor returns and talks about therapy and medication.

"We're going to keep you for the rest of the night to monitor you just in case. Dr. Mayall will do her rounds around seven, and you'll be out of here lickety split if these readings stay in the normal range."

"They just want our insurance dollars," Paula says after a nurse helps me unfold a convertible chair into a cot. She gives me the most delicious heated blanket – the one advantage of my hospital accommodations over The Willows Hotel. Holy hell. Was that just last night?

We both doze on and off rather than sleep.

Dr. Mayall visits at six. "How much longer, do you think?" I ask the physician. I don't want to be insensitive, but Paula's clearly not dying and there's no dead woman in the road. No arrest for manslaughter, although I've been googling laws related to filing false reports.

Before the doctor can answer, Paula jumps in with, "Don't rush her, doll. She needs to make sure everything in the chart is complete so I can bring it to get a *second opinion* in Chicago." She emphasizes 'second opinion', and then says, "I want a paper copy of the results, too. Just in case your system isn't compatible with what we have up north." She's using her most urbane tone of voice now, like she wants to put this Podunk hack in her place.

"Nurse Jacqueline will be back with your prescription—"

"And the paperwork?" she interrupts.

"And the paperwork. And then we'll work on discharge. But social work is going to pop by first to talk about stress reduction and follow-up care. We're slammed out there, so it will be about ninety minutes. Maybe more. Sit tight, and Jacqueline will bring over the breakfast menu."

When she leaves to consult with hurt-balls-dude, Paula says, "Believe me, Zillah. You can't trust medical care here. I could tell you some stories."

"Mom, panic attacks—"

"Don't get me started. The EKG tech didn't know what he was doing."

"It's like you *want* it to be a heart attack."

"Calm down, Zillah. 'Like you want a heart attack'," she mocks me using a baby voice. "When you know as much as *I* do about medical care and myocardial infarctions, you can have an opinion." She returns her attention to her phone.

"What do you think about me taking a breather outside while you wait?"

"If Doctor Whats-her-face says two hours, you can bet it's more like three, right?"

"Do I have time to see the ocean? We're really close, right?" I know we're close. I've mapped out several options.

"Fine but find my charger before you go. I need to call Bethany anyway and you're in the way."

Chapter Fifty

It's about a thirty-minute drive to Myrtle Beach State Park from Conway Medical Center. If I drive a little fast and just see the ocean for a few minutes, I should be able to get back to the hospital before Paula's discharged.

It might be my only chance, so I go for it.

I'm actually going to see the ocean.

I get to the park entrance at half past seven and the gates don't open until eight, so I drive around on Kings Highway to see what I can. I pass campgrounds, hotels, and RV parks. I finally see a bit more of the Myrtle Beach I've been reading about on Reddit. There are two-story candy stores, beach supply shops advertising impossible deals, and miniature golf with dinosaurs and electric blue Gatorade water features. A couple more miles in, as I get closer to the Skywheel, glimpses of the ocean wink at me from between hotels and breakfast restaurants.

But I want the big reveal all at once, so I head back south toward the state park and pay the eight dollars to get in at eight o'clock. After a few short turns of foresty wilderness, I come to parking lots, pedestrians, and a wooden boardwalk.

And the ocean.

There's so much blue. I don't have the words for what I'm experiencing.

The pier is just a few steps from the parking lot, and I scramble out and walk to the end, until I'm standing over the ocean. Over this dangerous and beautiful beast. My heart is pumping fast, but I'm not scared. I can't describe the colors I'm feeling, but I like it. It's one of those mismatches the therapist talked about the time she made Lise breathe through a straw.

Lise would like this place. I'll check my phone again soon.

The wooden sides of the pier are perfect for leaning on and avoiding all my past mistakes. I don't need my phone to distract me. I stay still and look around until my skin prickles from the sun.

I walk back along the pier slowly and go down the path to the sand. I take off my boots and tuck my socks inside. I make a little knot to tie the laces to each boot together so I can wear them over my shoulder. It's my Chicago decoration.

I take pictures of everything, but I also close my eyes and try to study the smell.

I want to remember how warm the sand is on my feet. Nothing like the little pebbles at Lake Michigan.

I memorize the feel of waves pushing and pulling at my ankles.

I need to come back with a friend, so I don't feel this aching loneliness. I've got to make things right with Lise. We'll build sandcastles and go to the Skywheel. Maybe I'll even get on it. And we'll go to the store we passed with confederate flags in the window. I'll take a shit in their toilet and not flush.

Gods, I love this place.

I'm gutted when my thoughts turn to what's next.

What's odd is that when we were searching for the body and driving to the hospital, I didn't really get flashes of paint and fear. While I was in the midst of the danger, I was pretty okay. It's not that I was calm, especially. I don't know. I didn't pay attention to my colors and inner state. I just did the things.

But now I'm a roiling mess once again, and it's getting in the way of me enjoying my first beach day ever.

I don't understand what's happening with Paula, but it's getting worse and she's too much for me to manage alone.

I tear myself away from the beach and sit in the car to call Aunt Bethany.

"Guess where I am? One of the many places I've never been to because of my weird-ass upbringing."

"Zillah—"

"I got to see the ocean. Probably not a big deal to you, but—"

"Yes, it's a big deal to me." Her voice gets louder and sounds more like Paula. "Of *course*, you should have traveled and seen the ocean and eaten vegetables. I get it, Zillah. But I need you to be the adult. Bring Paula home and we can get her into that program for people who lead restricted lives. The IOP."

"The intensive therapy thing? She won't do it," I say.

Bethany says, "We use the ride home as leverage. Tell her— Tell her you're staying in Myrtle Beach unless she agrees." It's a stupid plan, but I've got nothing better.

I promise the ocean I'll be back, and I return to Conway and Paula.

Back in that curtained room we strike a deal with Bethany on speaker phone as moderator: I'll drive Paula home and she agrees to stay with Bethany for a week to try the intensive outpatient program, the IOP. The program is a month long, with follow-up therapy twice a week. The goal is to teach her how to lean into the things that scare her instead of avoidance. I snort my skepticism, but Paula agrees to try it. Perhaps a small part of her recognizes the need for help.

"But Zillah needs to be on her best behavior," Paula says darkly.

"What did I do?"

"All of this! You did all of this!"

"I'm not the one who—"

But Bethany cuts me off. "Not helpful. Zillah, do you promise to come directly to my home, with no other detours?"

"Yes, unless we need to go out of the way for Target or Paula's—"

"Fine. Good. Stay in a hotel when you get tired and I'll see you both by tomorrow night," Bethany says.

And so ends our beach vacation.

Chapter Fifty-One

We get on the road just after ten o'clock in the morning. I'm taking us on a more direct route so we can see different things and save time. Assuming we can get a room at a clean-looking hotel in Knoxville, we should have our heads on pillows by ten tonight. Tomorrow we'll finish our drive, I'll drop Paula off with Bethany (even if I need to tie her up to get her there), and then I'll go to...

Okay. I'll stay in our apartment by myself. For the first time. I can do this. It's not as pretty as The Willows Hotel, but it's familiar.

In the car, we revert to silent treatment. Paula scans the road carefully when we approach the section of the highway where she suspects she may have hit the woman, but she relaxes into her seat when we are well past the spot and there's no evidence of first responders or other indicators of calamity.

"Did you go to a restaurant like you wanted? When you left the hospital?" she asks.

"No." I consider leaving her hanging, but I don't want to be childish. "I walked on the beach. I saw the ocean."

"I hope you wiped your feet with a paper towel or something before you put on your socks or you'll be miserable."

She closes her eyes and I risk going ten miles over the speed limit since she's not watching.

It's quiet and I don't put on music since I don't want her to wake up. The downside is this gives me extra time to be alone with my thoughts.

I still haven't heard back from Lise.

When we stop for gas, I text both Lise and Ben, `"Sorry to both-er you. Can I have your mom's #? Or can you give her mine? Coming back to apt late tomorrow and will need the key. Just me, not my mom. Maybe your mom can put it someplace for me so I don't have to wake anyone."`

I don't really need the key (I could ask Paula for hers), but I want an excuse to reach out to them. Like dipping my toe in a pool to see how freezing the water is before I'm thrown in. Because if I stay at the apartment while Paula's with Bethany, I'm bound to see them. And I'm ready to talk. Like, really, really talk.

I can't help myself and I text Lise again. `"I miss you. So much has happened."`

The drive is easy with a bad-movie podcast distracting me, and after four episodes we're in Knoxville. I pick a hotel near the highway with a familiar brand name. I need to learn more about hotels and how they're different from motels. And do the star ratings really mean anything, or are they based on crowdsource reviews? Maybe I could get a design job eventually where I get to travel all around like Dad does.

We park and I wake up Paula. "Mom, want to come in while I check in or wait in the car?"

"Gimme a minute," she says. So, I leave her there while I register and pay. When I have the key and come back for her, she's alert but quiet. Fine with me.

We settle in for the night like we're both experienced travelers. No one spying through the gauzy curtains would guess we're constrained by a bizarre truce.

Before sleep, I get a text from a new number. `"Zillah, this is Vivian. I'm so glad to hear from you! Can you please wake me up tomorrow no matter what time you get in? I need your help."`

She needs more help screwing up her family? I'll see what I can do.

Chapter Fifty-Two

We leave in the morning without fanfare. I just need to survive this drive, drop Paula off, and then I'll be free of drama for a few days at least. We get on the road early, with me driving to start. "You want to drive some today?" I ask.

"We'll see."

She closes her eyes, so I go back to listening to podcasts through one ear and speeding. I'm still slower than other drivers and everyone has to pass me, but I feel like a rebel. Seventy-two in a sixty-five? Hell yeah.

After Louisville, I notice that Paula's awake and alert.

She takes a turn driving in the afternoon after we fill up, but she gets antsy quickly. "Talk to me about something interesting, so I don't fall asleep at the wheel."

"I can drive," I say.

"I didn't say I'm *going* to fall asleep. I just feel sleepy. It's too boring to do this two days in a row."

"What kind of trips did you do as a kid?" I ask. I don't expect a response; Paula doesn't like talking about her childhood. But she surprises me this time.

"We didn't travel a lot, except when I stayed with your grandfather."

"So you didn't do road trips until you met Dad?"

"I only remember one," she says. "I don't know if it counts as a road trip. It was when we moved to Minnesota."

"Wait. What?"

"I was only there for a week or two. Mother had the dream. She had this intense dream, or a vision, but I think it was just a dream, that there was a woman trapped in Minnesota and that God was sending her the message. She said it was so vivid, she could see the woman's face like God was etching it on her soul."

"Woah."

"Woah is right. Be careful with those apple slices! Anyway, Mother and I packed up what we could fit in the station wagon and moved to Minnesota."

"How old were you?"

"Well, it was during third grade. I remember I missed my test on the state capitals, and I was so upset about that. Isn't it funny how things like that can feel so important? And after Mother went to prison—"

"Prison!"

"—I lived with your grandfather for a bit, and he didn't enroll me in school since it was only for a month. I remember being so worried about the lady God needed us to save and that stupid test. Can you believe that one?"

"Did stuff like that happen a lot?" I'm pushing her, but these details are so rare I've got to get them while she's in a talking mood. Maybe it's something about both of us looking forward at the road that makes it easier for her to open up.

"No, no. Not too often. And, before you ask, *yes,* I know it was just a dream. I'm not crazy."

"It must have been hard."

"It was," she says. "She could be kind and loving once in a while, but we never knew what we were going to get. It was like God rolled the dice every time she got out of bed, and that was that."

"I never met her, right?" I ask.

"Oh, no. You never met any of my people."

"Why?"

"Zillah, this is enough history time."

"Why couldn't I even just *meet* them?"

"They weren't safe for us."

"Like how?"

"I left Galena when I was sixteen. And then a few years later, once I got pregnant, I knew I couldn't let them be near you. They were very 'spare the rod and spoil the child.'" She rubs her thighs while she says this like she's remembering old wounds.

"They, like, hit you?" I don't know the right questions to ask.

"They were horrible, Zillah. Mother was the worst, but I had aunts and uncles and cousins who were all of a piece. And when they found out I was knocked up without a ring on my finger? They had power and connections, and I needed to get out of there." She's quiet for a moment. "I thought I'd never see her again."

She concentrates on passing a slow-moving van and after, I ask, "But you did see her? Did she visit us?"

"No. I almost went home once. After Mark left, and we were alone in Chicago, I was scared. I was so scared. I never wanted to live in Chicago. It had been years, and I thought it might be better to go home. I called Mother, and she said she'd take us in, but only if she could adopt you."

"That doesn't make sense."

"You're spilling those all over the seat. For goodness' sake! Grab a wet wipe from my purse." She continues, "She wanted me to relinquish my parental rights to her. I could live there in the big house with her, but you would have been her child."

"Oh, Mom."

"I thought about it. There's money, you know. You would have had a real inheritance and a family. People know the Scrivens in Galena. We were popular at the church. It would have felt safe."

"But not *actually* safe."

"No."

"I wish you'd talk about this more often."

"Zillah, the past is the past. There's nothing good to come from digging into these old stories."

But that's not true. I need this context. I never realized how much she gave up. I'll never know what it was like in "the big house". How scared she must have been to be a single mother in Chicago without a high school diploma after Dad left.

She could have gone back. She'd have had community and wealth. She'd have the approval of her family.

She stayed for me.

So I could be safe.
Well, shit.

Chapter Fifty-Three

I drive the last few hours and Paula dozes. I'm so antsy to finish this trip that I even go ten miles an hour over the speed limit and set cruise control. We get to Bethany's at half-past nine, and she's extra chatty, wanting to hear about the trip back north.

"Ask Miss Adventurer, here," Paula says and heads for the bathroom.

"Aunt B, I need to get to sleep."

"Stay here! You can have the couch. I've got enough—"

"I want to be alone." Aside from those stolen moments on the beach, I've been surrounded by Scriven energy for days.

"Just tell me how she's doing," Bethany says in a low tone.

"Pissed. Good luck getting her to that intensive therapy IOP thing."

What a bad idea to ask Vivian for my key. If I'd just taken Paula's, I could be in my bed now instead of waiting on the landing by Lise's apartment, hoping Vivian wakes up soon and takes pity on me.

I texted her before I left Bethany's to give her the heads-up that I'd be back within the hour, but she didn't respond. I texted her again after parking, and I don't want to knock or call.

Maybe I could break into my place. Or I could call the emergency helpline for our rental management company. Urg. Which is worse - calling the mom of the people I've hurt or paying a fifty-dollar lock-out fee?

Money is money, so I make the dreaded call.

"Zillah? Oh good! I was waiting for your call. Oh, shoot. You texted me and I didn't see."

"It's okay. I'm at your door," I say.

"Can I have a minute, and I'll meet you at your place?"

"I can just grab my key from you."

"No, no. I'll see you over there in a few."

Maybe she doesn't want to risk her kids seeing me.

I don't have to wait long at my door. Vivian, dressed in pajama bottoms and a Rocket Crocodile hoodie, huffs coming up the last steps. "Zillah," she says, as though discovering me unexpectedly.

"Sorry to drag you out."

She hands me the key. "First, how's your mom?"

"She's fine. She's at my aunt's for a few days."

"Good. Good. I'll come in for a bit. I need to show you what I did before you settle in."

"You did something?" I ask and unlock the door.

She follows me in while I turn on lights and sniff. The air's different, more floral than usual. Maybe eucalyptus.

What happened here? There are half a dozen plastic bins on the floor, stacks of papers on the surfaces, and a few Amazon boxes repurposed to hold metal things I don't recognize. "You did this?"

Vivian blushes like Lise sometimes does. "Your mom did some of it. But, Zillah, remember when we came up to get some things for you to take with you? Did you notice all the chemicals?"

I sit down at the kitchen table, and she joins me. "There was a bunch of weird stuff, but I didn't have time—"

"Zillah, honey, your mom had some dangerous things up here. Looked like maybe she was making her own pesticide? Either that or she was starting a meth lab. Sorry, I shouldn't joke about it. The toluene is flammable, and I didn't want to leave it here, especially since I didn't know when you'd be back. So the kids and I—"

"Lise and Ben were in here?"

"I thought about calling the nonemergency police or Alexi to help, but I was thinking you might lose your apartment or get in more legal trouble."

I put my head down on my arms. Can I just press pause on this moment, take a nap, and then hear the rest?

"Ben took out the things that looked really dangerous, and Lise helped me sort some of the things that might have fallen by accident."

I'm guessing she means things Paula had thrown while in her rage. I hadn't taken a good look before we left – I just remember a sense of chaos.

"I didn't know it was this bad," I say. I picture Paula here by herself, trying to feel safe. "It's my fault." She starts to interrupt me and I continue, "No, I know it's not. But, like, it *feels* like it's my fault."

"When's she coming back?" Vivian asks quietly.

"I don't know. Maybe next week."

"Can we bring you some food while you're here? We must sound like the biggest busybodies, getting in your business."

"Vivian, that's— That's ridiculous. And ironic. Did they tell you what I did?" She nods, looks away for a moment, but returns her eye contact and sits down with me again. "And now you're all doing all this nice stuff for me? I don't deserve it."

"People make mistakes, Zillah. Humans are the worst." She takes one of my hands and holds it while gently stroking it with her other hand. It's such a small touch, but it reaches deep. "And to be honest, I need your help."

"Oh, yeah?" I forgot about that part.

"While you're here, could you walk Halsted in the evenings while Ben is working? Lise's on spring break and I want her to come to Indianapolis with me for a few days. But Halsted's been having some problems with peeing inside. With Ben's late nights, he'd be alone for too many hours, and she won't leave him with a stranger."

"Vivian, your kids don't want me in your place." Her pinched look tells me I'm right. "I bet another neighbor could do it."

"Please, Zillah. It doesn't need to be a long walk, and you can fit it around your schedule. We could pay you."

"It's not about money. I couldn't take money from you. It just— It seems wrong."

"But won't it help the kids and you get back together?"

"Is that why you're asking me? Why do you even want that?" I get up and pace around the kitchen, opening and closing cupboards to take inventory and see if there's anything else unexpected or dangerous.

"Lise's back to pre-Zillah. Before you, she wouldn't do any of her big exposures and then once she had you in her corner, she was up for it most of the time."

"That's just a coinci—"

"No, Zillah, it's not. It's *you*. You're her big motivation. And frankly, she would kill me for saying this, but you're her first real friend in-- maybe always. The first friend she could really talk to."

Me too. "But I screwed it — sorry — I messed it all up."

"It was screwed up before you. She and Ben aren't spending time together. He was always going with her on walks with Halsted in case you'd show up. Now it's just like it used to be, with both of them living here like roommates who barely acknowledge each other." She pauses. "What do you say? Will you take care of Halsted?"

"Do you think there's really a chance she could forgive me?"

"I can't promise that Zillah. But I hope so. I really do."

For the first time since Ben's discovery, I feel a small spark of yellow highlighter deep in my chest. There's hope.

Chapter Fifty-Four

The upside of exhaustion is that I don't have the energy to be scared of sleeping by myself. I lean into my isolation by narrating my actions. I can say, "Yup, these sheets smell okay," and "I wonder how Paula's sleeping" without someone barging into my room to ask, "What? Are you talking to me?"

When I wake up, I text with Bethany. She claims Paula's fine, but "taciturn" (which I have to look up), and that she'll call after she gets home from the mental health treatment center. Aunt Bethany has to stay for part of the first day to learn about the program and stuff she might need to do at home for Paula. I picture a padded room and a straitjacket, but I'm guessing it's more like the ways Ben and Vivian help Lise. Like asking, "What's your number out of ten?" and "What else can you tolerate?"

How the hell is Paula going to last more than ten minutes?

Not my problem. Bethany's got the ball.

If I keep repeating this, maybe it will sink in.

More good news is that I get to campus in time for my econ class and I even worked on my term paper for a solid forty minutes. Not my finest work, but good enough. Now that I'm set on switching majors, I'm okay with just a B or even a C. It's such a different perspective on how to succeed. During my funk, I missed some small assignments and a quiz, but as long as I kick the final's ass, I'll be okay.

I also have a good talk with Sid at the clinic. He assures me I still have a job if I want it, but that I should finish up a couple of tasks I have and take some time to help Paula "so she can get back on her feet and back to work." I don't know him well enough to tell if this is real, that she can still have her job, or just fabrication to make me feel better. But it's better than a closed door.

My first evening walk with Halsted is uneventful. There are no obvious potty accidents on the floor when I arrive, and it's gratifying how he scampers around me. At least I'm not a villain to *this* guy.

His leash isn't in the usual spot, so I hunt around for a few minutes while he prances in a circle and pokes my arm with his snout. He whines in a curiously human way. "I know, buddy. Keep your tail on." It's bittersweet to be here. I've had so many fulfilling moments in this apartment, and my body is more relaxed here than in my place. I fight the urge to lie down on the couch to rest, and instead I keep looking for the leash. I find it on a kitchen counter next to a composition notebook. It's one of the classic mottled black and white kinds, and the subject area says, "Ben."

I stare at it for a few seconds, and I don't touch it. I *want* to flip through it, and, miracle of miracles, I don't. He deserves to have his dumb Ben thoughts in private. Lise deserved her privacy, too. I wish I could time travel back to that first time I eavesdropped and just smack myself across the face.

Outside, while Halsted walks and sniffs, I wonder if Ben's written about me in there. Yeah, he's allowed his privacy, but I can wonder. If he *has* written about me, it's unlikely to satisfy me. Anything less than "I'm haunted by dreams of my alluring and tiny neighbor" would be disappointing. And if he *hasn't* written about me, I'd feel shitty. But it's probably not even a real journal. Maybe just recipe ideas. Or a honey trap with a note like, "Ha! Vivian was wrong and you suck now and forever. Go eat a shit sandwich and die alone." Or whatever that sentiment is in Ben language.

Now that I think about it, it's an obvious trap. Want to test your nosy neighbor who spied on your sister and broke her heart? Leave out a journal and put a hair or something between the pages to see if she disturbs it.

Amateur hour over here.

But I give myself a mental pat on the head for not looking. I'm not terrible today. "Yay, me," I say to Halsted.

Over the next two days, Halsted and I find a good rhythm. The weather is nicer and the days are longer. The trees are budding and some of the flowerpots reveal crocus buds peeking out. We'll have daffodils next if I remember correctly.

Movement after a day of classwork and sitting in front of my computer feels good. Bethany and I often talk while I walk, and she's patient with occasional dog sounds or when I need to concentrate on picking up poop.

On Wednesday night, she says that Paula may make it through the week at the IOP treatment, but it's hard to know whether she'll stay and keep going for the full month. "We're just thinking one day at a time," Bethany says.

"Isn't that an Alcoholics Anonymous saying?"

"Maybe there's crossover. Anyway, she seems to take it seriously, for the most part."

"But?"

"No buts! I mean, well, she's irritable about it and complains that I'm treating her like a naughty child. She just likes to blame someone, you know?"

"Like me?" I ask.

Bethany doesn't bother responding. That Paula hasn't texted me or called is answer enough. "She's doing her homework and talking about what she's learning, so that's something."

"You're doing a crap-ton of work for her."

"It's not just for her, Sweet Z. And not just for you. I want to pal around with my little sister again. I wish I had done something sooner."

I need another few blocks of walking after this call, so Halsted and I go exploring, and I let him pick all the directions.

We go farther than I intend, with Halsted leading me to the Mac-Donalds on Broadway, and we're both soaked from rain when we finally get back. I can tell Ben is home right away — all the lights are on and there's music over the speakers. Plus, there're cooking smells. Something smokey in a good way.

What's the etiquette here?

I call out from the doorway, "Don't want to surprise you, but—"

"Zillah?" Ben's expression is delighted for a fast moment and shifts to pained. He's beautiful in a rumpled band tee and flannel pants, holding a wooden spatula.

"I'll get out of your way in a sec," I say. "But I've got a wet dog." Ben returns to the kitchen where he's flipping something on the stovetop. I get Halsted's towel and attempt to dry him off while I keep talking. "Sorry. I thought you were working late. I'm really sorry."

"Zillah, calm down," he says with his back to me. "It's okay. I don't work late on Wednesdays."

"Oh." I squat down to get at Halsted's paws, and he takes advantage of my position to lick my face. "Come on, dude. I'm not your popsicle."

"You went on a trip?" Ben asks. He's turned toward me now and he doesn't look angry. Just Ben-ish. It's confusing.

"Yeah, my mom and I— What is *that*?" He's got a bizarre bowl with a cord that he's yanking on like when Alexi can't get his lawn-mower to start.

"Salad spinner. Wanna see?" He opens the lid so I can see salad greens inside a plastic mesh bowl within a bigger bowl. He pulls the mesh bowl out and there's a puddle of water on the bottom of the bigger one. "It's for washing greens. Uses centrifugal force."

"Can I try it?"

"I don't know if your puny arms are strong enough. Salad is a man's domain." But he re-assembles the spinner and shows me what to do.

"You have more experience yanking," I say. And like that, we're back to our regular schtick. Him teaching me about stuff and me making dumb jokes.

"What are you putting on the salad?"

"Red onion, walnuts, I think I have some gorgonzola cheese, prob-ably some pear slices if I have a fresh one. Vinaigrette." He points to the pan, "And I've got chicken there if you want some. Chicken's one of your foods, right?"

"I don't want to take your dinner."

"Shut it. You're drooling all over yourself."

So, we sit on opposite sides of their kitchen island and eat together. I'm nervous, but the simple chicken he made is amazing and I accidentally moan out loud. "You're a unique one, Godzilla."

The nickname brings my tears to the surface. I take a second to collect myself. "I'm so sorry, Ben."

"I know," he says. "She knows, too."

"I don't have a good enough excuse."

"Yeah, it was a big fuck up. Take more chicken."

"How can you stand to be around me?" I'd rather him yell at me and throw things than be so goddamned pleasant. I don't know the rules.

"The shock's worn off some. Also, Mom reminded me of— of some unpleasantness I caused a few years ago. And she said she'd done worse when she was young, but I don't want to know the details." He gets us both more water. "People do bad things, but it isn't who they are. We're more than that."

I can't meet his eyes, so I leave my seat and join Halsted on the floor. He leans his head into my hand to force me into ear scritches, which I dutifully provide. The boys in this family are so bossy.

"When you're done down there, make yourself useful and pack up some leftovers to take home."

"That is the second-best chicken I've ever had. After Chicken Hut."

"Yeah, I'm a food genius," he says and joins me on the floor to scratch Halstead's rump. "Where did you and your mom go?"

"Myrtle Beach."

"Wow. Wait. What? You *drove* there and back in three days?"

"Yeah, and I got to see the ocean," I say with reverence. Ben gives me another of his intense stares, like he's trying to see the beach through my memory.

Our hands briefly touch in the middle of the Halsted. I pull it back and shift my eye contact to the dog instead. My feelings are much safer with this mammal.

"Want to help me walk him tomorrow before my shift? Like ten-ish?"

The romantic in me wants to say, "it's a date." But the real Zillah says, "If you're picking up all the poop, I'm happy to tag along."

As I put on my coat, I ask him, "Think she'll talk to me when she gets back from Indianapolis?"

"She's got incentive. She loves you, and it's the last item on her fear hierarchy."

When I get home, I put away the chicken and pull up that old fear hierarchy Lise sent me so long ago. After "return food to a restaurant server" and "wear a t-shirt that says Birthday Girl" is the final item: "Disagree with a friend."

Chapter Fifty-Five

In the morning, none of my food looks good. I even go through the effort of making instant rice, but I can't get down more than a mouthful. It's not anxiety. Well, not most of it. My stomach is filled with ebru, that colorful Turkish paper marbling. There are orange bits of fear that Ben will be cold when we meet up for our walk, but also white and gray shades of excitement. And blue relief that he might still be a friend.

He and Halsted are already waiting for me outside at ten. Ben gives me a warm smile with eye crinkles while I squat to pet Halsted on the snout and remove his eye gunk with my sleeve. Paula would shudder at my deliberate grooming of this beast. We *are* different, I remind myself.

I rub my sleeve on Ben's and transfer the eye gunk to his hoodie. "Gift from Halsted," I say.

"That's a dangerous precedent, Godzilla." We follow Halsted, letting him pick our direction. "You never told me about your Madeleine project. You were really upset that night. What happened?"

I chew on my lip, trying to grab the right words. It feels so long ago.

He misunderstands my hesitation and sounds like Lise when he says, "You don't have to talk about it if you don't want to."

"It— It was terrible." I walk a pace or two ahead of him and Halsted while I tell the story so I don't have to make eye contact. "She flipped out when she got to the strawberry filling. You remember how I told you that I kind of forced her to follow my food rules? That I was, like, a total monster about it as a little kid? It turns out she actually ate that way first."

"Whadya mean?"

"She made the food rules, and she thought she was helping me by having me eat that way it, too. And she just never corrected me that I thought it was my fault, you know?"

"So, she gaslit you?"

"No! No, it wasn't like that." Was it? "She wasn't doing it on purpose. It started really gradually, I guess."

"So, she doesn't eat other food at all?"

"Yeah. Not since I was born. And I used to think she was eating other food at work or when she'd drive around and around in her car. But it turns out she was going in circles because she was afraid she'd hit someone and wanted to go back and check."

"Did she want you to eat other food? Or— I don't get it, I guess. Wouldn't you want your kid to be open to food?" His tone is tense and fierce.

"I would. I do."

I'm betraying Paula, but it's good to get this out. When I talked to Bethany and Dad, both were sad for me, but neither was angry on my behalf. We stop at Halsted's tree stump.

"So, what happens now?" he asks. "When she comes home? Are you going back to the usual stuff?"

"I have to."

"Bullshit."

"Ben, I can't eat other stuff. I don't *want* to eat other stuff. I wish I'd liked it from the beginning, but you can't force yourself to like something you don't like. It's like—" I hold Halsted's leash while Ben picks up poop. "It's like only seeing mannerism art your whole life and then standing in front of a Rothko mural."

"You've lost me. Those aren't real words."

I smack him on the arm. This is me flirting.

"So, you can be angry at me," he says, "but just fine with your mom?"

"I'm not angry at you. I'm happy at you. I like the fact that you're upset about the situation. It's validating. And I'm furious at my mom, but I'm more worried about her. And sad, I think. I'm holding on to the rage for a while, but I can't really express it yet. I'll paint with it eventually and that'll feel good."

"Catharsis."

"Exactly. Ready to head back?"

When we get back to the apartment, he keeps talking and doesn't say "bye", so I follow him up his stairs.

"Maybe you would have been just as picky if she had tried to get you to eat other things," Ben says.

"Maybe."

"You know what would be good revenge?"

That gets my attention "What?"

"Trying new food."

"Ugh."

"Zillah. What exactly are you afraid of when you have food in front of you?"

I think about that strawberry at Clark's on Belmont.

"A gross taste in my mouth. It's like deliberately making myself suffer. And then I might not get the taste out, and it could slide down my throat and choke me. And I'd just have that taste in there forever."

He finishes unleashing Halstead and putting the leash and poop bags away. "You know the difference between you and your mom?" He doesn't wait for an answer. "She messed up, but you have the choice to live differently."

I shouldn't have encouraged him. "I'm done talking about this," I say.

"Last question and I'll drop it. I promise. What was it like when we did that hummus thing and you touched and smelled the ingredients?"

"Oh, that was awesome," I say without hesitation.

"Why do you think it was okay for you? I mean, why didn't it gross you out?"

"I knew I wasn't going to eat any of it. It was like being at the food zoo. The food petting zoo. And that's what got me thinking I could be more open to Paula eating food around me."

"Can we do more of that? I've got so much food here."

"What, now?"

"Why not? I've got another half hour or so."

I've got the time, and I like being around Ben when he's high on food fumes.

"Do you promise on Halsted's life that you won't pressure me to eat anything?"

"Uncool, but yes."

I wash up in the bathroom, and when I return to the kitchen, I see he has lined up boxes and jars, as well as produce and plastic containers.

So much food for one family!

"You ready to explore my treasures?"

Ben puts on loud music, and I walk around his display, trying to decide if there's something I'm willing to start with.

I pick up a box of cheese-flavored crackers. I open it and look inside. There's a foil bag with impossibly orange-colored squares.

"Good choice," he says.

"I'll touch and smell these, but you have to tell me about them."

"Well, those are generic Cheez-Its since the real ones are expensive. They don't really taste like actual cheese, but they're good and salty." While he talks, I shake a few into my hand. "They go great in tomato soup. But even better is goldfish crackers, because they're like little swimming targets for your spoon. It makes you feel like a hunter. But we only get those when they're on sale."

"I've had the plain flavored goldfish crackers," I say.

"Salt flavored," he corrects me.

I sniff the crackers. I don't feel nervous. I knew these wouldn't be mushy or anything. I drop them in the compost bin and wash my hands.

"Can you do more?" he asks.

"You need to give me better food history. Remember how you did for the hummus ingredients?"

"Okay. The ancient grains used in Cheez-Its are known for their antibiotic nature and mosquito-repellent coloring."

I read the ingredients on a can of mixed nuts and then play with a walnut while Ben makes up more history. "In olden days, pioneer women kept a metal tin full of the dried-up body parts of their fallen foes. These cans of 'mixed nuts' were thought to ward off evil and could be pulverized to help fertilize crops during lean years. In modern times, we continue the tradition of mixing nuts together..." I tune him out and consider a pecan. I smell it and feel little surges of fear knowing that at any moment Ben could try to compel me to eat.

But he sticks to his promise so far. No pressure to eat, and he seems to be having fun. So I waste a shit-ton of his food by touching it, smelling it, and throwing it out when my mauling it renders it inedible.

Some are easy. The cucumber doesn't smell like anything. The sugar snap peas are fun to open. The bottle of barbeque sauce smells intriguing when we uncap it. I'm tempted to put a little on my finger. But it's too soon.

The rest of the food is overwhelming, like pickles (they have an alien tentacle quality) or tame (mayonnaise looks and smells like sandwich glue. I don't get it).

We finish investigating the ingredients on the counter and I wash my hands (again). I say, "One time I was here and smelled your sausage." I instantly want to crawl in a hole and die as I consider the double entendre, but he ignores it other than a quick glance my way. "I remember my mouth watered and I didn't understand why. But I got that same mouth-watering after I started eating the fresh madeleine the other day."

Ben digs through the freezer until he finds a resealable bag of vegetarian sausage patties. "These?"

I nod. "You microwaved it and ate it on toast. I don't want to waste, but could you cook one for me to smell?"

"Do you want toast, too?" he asks while selecting a plate.

"No, I'm an expert with toast already."

Ben takes the cooked patty out of the microwave and slides it onto a clean plate. "I'll even sacrifice another plate for your pleasure." He puts the plate on the kitchen counter next to me. "Don't worry about wasting. I'll have the sausage after you're done fondling it. You're the cleanest person I know."

The sausage patty has a bit of steam coming from it and somehow looks both wet and dry at the same time.

"We use the word 'moist' to describe that," he says while I tell him what I see and try to find the right words.

I run my finger along the top of the patty. It's warm and looks crumbly on top, but it holds together when I touch it. The smell is familiar from the breakfast plates Cliff often eats at Clarke's. Sausage doesn't have the same smell as other meats, and this one smells like Cliff's even though it's made from mysterious soy substances.

"Isn't it weird how many smells there are?" I ask.

"Yeah, *that's* what's weird in this situation."

The sausage is cooler after my investigation. I pick it up. I imagine tasting it and I don't feel as anxious as I expect. Maybe a three or four out of ten.

My tongue is thick with saliva and I'm swallowing a lot.

Is this going to be food number eleven?

My tongue darts out like a lizard to taste and retract.

"Reactions?" he asks.

"My tongue was too quick, and I didn't get a taste. Can I have a napkin?" He hands me a paper towel.

I take a tentative nibble and grasp the paper towel like a security blanket in case I need to spit. I take a small bite and chew.

The sausage is... weird. It's not as firm as a chicken strip and takes less chewing. It's not unpleasant. Is it good?

Do I like this?

My mouth waters, which I take as a signal for *yes,* and keep eating.

I ate an eleventh food. And it's staying down.

I ate an eleventh food. Holy mother of Dog!

After we've cleaned up and I go for a short walk to clear my head, I come back in time to see Ben eating a snack at the counter while looking at his phone. He's got out a small bowl of fruit and a larger bowl of those generic Cheez-Its.

I sit next to him and look at the bowl of strawberries and blueberries.

He pushes it toward me. "Ready for number twelve?" he asks.

"No."

"Sausages are way scarier than strawberries," he says. "And you can spit it out right away."

"I'll look at one, but that's it." I get a fork and use it to spear a small strawberry.

"Think how horrified your mom would be."

I imagine her leaning toward me like she did at Clarks on Belmont when she was scolding me for taking Cliff's berry.

Why didn't she tell me to try?

Fuck her.

I pull the strawberry off the fork and consider it. I clench a paper towel, ready to spit, and bite into the strawberry, almost up to the green top.

It isn't mushy. It doesn't pop and become goo. Instead, it's crisp and cold. It's not firm like an apple. It's sweet, but not like candy. It's vibrant and tangy. I know I can spit it out, but I don't want to.

It's good.

It's actually good.

I'll just chew until I want to spit it out.

But I don't want to spit. I chew it slowly and collect data. Before I know it, it's gone.

I just ate a strawberry.

Ben is delighted. "Yeah, Godzilla!" He moves the bowl toward me. "Want more?" I'm scared, but his enthusiasm is infectious. "Here, try this one. The little ones that are dark red like this are always the best."

I eat another strawberry.

Me, Zillah.

I freaking just ate two strawberries.

"Want more? Want to try something else? If you like the strawberry, try the blueberry."

"That's enough adventure for today," I say. He gives me a little side hug and pulls the bowl back to his place setting.

I ate twelve foods. I *eat* twelve foods. I'm a woman who can eat twelve different kinds of food.

That second strawberry — once I knew what to expect in terms of texture — it was like going to an art exhibition and standing inches from a mural so that the image fills all my peripheral vision. Overwhelming. But beautiful.

I did it.

Twelve.

I'm amazing.

I'm a food hero.

An adventurer.

I'm happy for a full five seconds.

"You did great. What's wrong?" Ben asks as tears fall out of me. "You should be happy. You're being so brave!"

"Why did she keep me from this?"

"I don't know, Zillah."

I gift him with a tidal wave of tears. So much sadness that has been hanging out near my vocal cords comes pouring out, and I don't know if it's the grief about years without strawberries and vegetarian sausages, or about losing Lise, realizing I suck, or the worried pit in my stomach about Paula.

He holds me and lets me cry. He doesn't try to make it stop. He's just there, and warm, and Ben.

The big question I consider afterwards while I'm trying to settle back in at home is this: What else am I missing out on?

Chapter Fifty-Six

The next day, Friday, increased noise from the other side of my wall heralds the return of Lise and Vivian. Vivian texts me, "Can you stop by tonight? Halsted has a thank you present for you! Any time between 7 and 9 is good."

It's obviously a Vivian plot to get me and Lise together. I wonder what Lise is feeling over there. "7:30 okay?" I send back.

After class I'm antsy and can't do the assignment I had scheduled for myself. I try some of Lise's therapist's quick tricks for disrupting panic. I suck on an ice cube for a bit and sniff a good smelling candle that Paula never let me light. Fuck it. She's not here! I light that candle and place it gingerly on a square of tinfoil.

The candle doesn't relax me. You can't have fire safety drummed into you for over twenty years and then relax with a candle. I blow it out and resort to the last-ditch anti-panic maneuver: cardio.

Barf.

I go down the three flights of stairs at my usual pace, but I climb back up at a quick clip (for me). I do it one more time, this time going up the stairs at my usual shuffling pace, since I'm out of energy.

By some magic, five minutes of stairs calms me down. The therapist had said that fight-or-flight released chemicals that are there to power us up to run from predators and that we have to give those chemicals something to do. If we just sit down and try to stay calm, our insides turn into an anxiety pinball machine.

The downside is that this is just a temporary fix. I still need to deal with the monster below the surface: the truth that I hurt Lise.

At seven twenty-seven in the evening, I stand at Lise's doorway. Is it weird to be early? Wouldn't being exactly on time be weirder? I sniff my pits to see if I'm stinky from those stairs, and that's when Lise opens the door. "We have a camera doorbell," she says, pointing.

"That's new." Did I pick my wedgie earlier? I don't remember if that was up here in camera view or lower down on the stairs.

"Can we talk?" she asks. She leads me halfway down the stairwell and we both sit on the dirty step, but I don't complain. I'll do whatever she wants.

"Lise, I'm so sorr—"

"No, Zillah, can I go first? You remember when I told you about the time with the hummus? When my mom made me vomit in public?"

"Yeah. Of course."

"What you did was worse."

I want to reassure her that I know. That she doesn't need to tell me. But I *don't* really know. I'll never know how that felt. I just let my tears stream down my face and look at my knees.

She says, "Afterwards, every time I left the apartment, I felt like every-one was staring at me. Like, I know it doesn't make sense, you know? But I had this feeling that you knowing made everyone know. Like all my secrets were out and everyone was staring. Everyone was judging the weird girl."

"That's—" I don't have an appropriate adjective. "It sucks. I'm so sorry," I say quietly.

"And I just didn't want to leave at all. It was like the early 2020s all over again."

"Fuck."

"It wore off a little. I went outside again, but I didn't like it. You know?"

"Yeah."

We sit in silence together. I hear two dogs outside barking, and I wonder if they're messaging the dogs in our building about some threat, like USPS.

"I practiced my apology like a thousand times," I say.

"Let's hear it."

A good apology has three pieces. What you did wrong, how it affects the person, and how you'll avoid being such a tool in the future. And no "buts."

"I'm so sorry I invaded your privacy like that. Listening in on your therapy was the creepiest move ever, and I get that it ruined your trust for me and hurt you and embarrassed you. I don't expect you to forgive me. I just want you to know that I know I was wrong and I'm going to have my first therapy appointment really soon. And I've been more, um, mindful about privacy ever since." I picture Ben's composition notebook. "You didn't deserve any of that. It was a shitty thing to do."

"But why? Why did you do it?"

I stand up and bounce on my toes a little while holding on to the rail. I face away from her and say, "I don't *know*. It was like, I was so alone and so stuck in my stupid, sucky, crappy life. And then I heard you be so brave—" She interrupts with a harumph. "—so brave to talk to a real therapist. And so brave to want to *change* things. You were willing to do the scariest things to change. You were stuck, too, but you were doing something about it." I pause and wipe my face. "It was amazing. I couldn't stop listening, even though I knew it was wrong." I sit down again and look for a dry spot on my sleeves. "If I hadn't listened in, I never would have tried to make changes myself. I was just going to follow Paula's rules, marry Cliff, and I don't know what else. But it would have sucked. You changed all that for me."

"That was a good apology," she says after a while.

"Thanks."

"One small silver lining," Lise starts. I perk up, but she continues, "Minuscule. You still messed up. The tiny silver lining is that it was like having my worst fears happen and then surviving it. Like, you heard the worst stuff about me ever and you still liked me."

"I do still like you. A lot. And if I ever, ever break your trust again, you can burn all my hoodies and spit in my water bottle."

"I missed you."

"Same." I lean into her. "I have a hundred questions. What did you do in Indy?" I ask.

"Missed my dog and spent time with our dad."

"Dads," I say darkly. "Was it awkward?"

"The thing about absent dads is that they have no clue how to be a dad. They just have no practice," she says. "I have to just tell mine exactly what to do. I say, 'Dad, on my birthday, I want you to text me to arrange a time for a call, and when we talk, you need to ask some open-ended questions. Here's a list of suggestions.' If I waited for him to figure it out, we'd never connect."

"But doesn't that feel shitty? You telling exactly what you need?"

"You'd think so, right? But it still feels good when he does it. And he's learned a lot." She picks at some of the pilled thread on her sweater. "When I was in middle school, I used to test him. I'd just stay silent on FaceTime and see what he'd do."

"What happened?"

"He failed every time. This is better."

But my dad is more than absent. He left me behind in a bad situation. Maybe even neglectful. He saved his own ass and let me flail.

Well, it will be a good topic for my therapist.

"Oh!" she says so loudly I jump and hit my elbow on the wall. "Sorry," she says while I rub at my funny bone. "Ben said you have big news."

So, I use my most dramatic storytelling prowess to tell the Tale of Sausage.

"No fair! I should have been there. Are you going to eat more?"

I've been wondering the same thing. I thought about going to the store yesterday to buy a pack of those veggie sausages and to just *look* at strawberries, but what if there was some magic to eating food with Ben? What if I choke on it by myself or pick a disgusting strawberry by accident?

"I'm still deciding," I say.

"Please let me feed you something good. I have so many ideas of foods you might like. Or at least just look at more food with me? You owe me."

"I don't—" 'I don't like this' is what I want to say, but I'm too nervous about our tenuous reunion to risk assertiveness.

"Just consider it. You don't have to say yes right now."

We talk about other things. Graphic design. Her old haunts in Indianapolis. Ben. Halsted. Vivian.

I feel more solid about the friendship when we say goodbye. I float home on a cloud.

When I put away my phone to go to sleep, I glance at the wall that separates me from Lise. I bet there's some kind of adhesive sound baffling I could put up. I could ask Cliff for suggestions.

"Goodnight, Lise," I whisper.

Chapter Fifty-Seven

The next morning, I wake up to texts from Lise. `"When can I come over and bring snacks?"`

"Give me thirty minutes," I respond.

Great. Here we go. I'm mottled with red nervousness again.

I take a shower and try lots of deep breathing. "You don't have to eat anything you don't want to eat," I remind myself. "You can be a little uncomfortable."

Lise brings me a charcuterie board in the style of the 2024 "girl dinner" trend. "It's got a lot of my favorite snacks in really small quantities," she explains, "and if you keep it in the fridge under plastic wrap, you don't have to do anything special. What do you think? It's just a little bit of each thing, so no pressure."

Yeah right. We sit at my kitchen table, and I try to make my leg stop bouncing. My heart is racing and I twist my napkin around and around my fingers.

There are fresh grapes, dried fruit, a few kinds of cheese, some unfamiliar mottled meats, olives, tiny tomatoes, cucumber slices, and a ramekin of mysterious white dip with green stuff in it.

"What do you think," she asks again. "Too much?"

With our reunion so recent, I want to please her.

But.

All of it looks disgusting.

"I don't know, Lise. It might have been a fluke."

"How about the cheddar cheese? We can just hold it and sniff it, okay? And if you take a bite, you can spit it out right away, right?"

I pick up a piece of cheese.

"Just hold it until your fight-or-flight recedes, okay? Even if it takes a while."

I expect to stay panicky for a long time. Like, at least 20 minutes. But it actually doesn't take long.

"I think I'm okay. How long was that?"

"Less than a minute? Good! Let's smell it."

I smell it, but then because I'm sick of drawing this out, I take a bite too.

Hmm. It's soft on my teeth, but kind of firm like I'm chomping through dried up play dough. I grab a cracker and eat that while there's still some cheese in my mouth. Ohmygod the combination is so good. The crunch and the smoothness together. I can't tell where the saltiness is coming from, but it's lovely.

"Food 13," I say. "Thanks, Lise."

And then we move on to grapes.

Chapter Fifty-Eight

Over the next days, at every meal, while I'm hungry before I eat my usual foods, I try at least one new thing. I eat a sliver of cheddar cheese. A blueberry. A dried apricot. Avocado. Most of this is from Lise's gifts, but I eat some food with her at her place. If any of her family is around, they praise me like I'm Halsted learning to shake or lie down. The first time I eat a scrambled egg, Ben shouts, "Lise! Mom! Come look at this!" He spins me around and kisses the top of my head. Pleasing them all is so motivating.

"Sorry for mooching so much," I tell Vivian.

"Psh! Now we're even for you taking care of our barkity-boo while we were away." How many terms for dog can she come up with, I wonder.

I keep my new foods listed on a spreadsheet. Someday I'll serve my kids toast with raspberry preserves and be able to say, I had that the first time with my friend Lise back on this day.

It's still hard, though. I have to pep myself up with reminders that I can spit the food out, and that I can tolerate a bit of suffering. By Sunday night, I've done this five times in a row, sometimes eating two or three new foods at one go. And I'm going to keep going.

Now I'm less driven by rage and more by excitement. Although there's still an unhealthy dose of fear mixed in.

Paula and I text a few times a day. We message impersonal things like "Isn't it sunny out today?" and "Don't forget to put out the recycling." We finally talk on Saturday, two weeks after getting home from Myrtle Beach.

"You wouldn't believe Bethany's newest kick," she says as soon as I pick up the phone.

"Oh my gosh, what?"

"Macrame!" she says with glee.

"Is she a gazillion years old? Macrame!" I marvel.

We're immediately united by our shared amusement at Bethany's serial hobbyism. I know Bethany would forgive us. She's been a good sport about our teasing in the past, and this is for a good cause. Much better than Paula and I being cold and hesitant with each other.

"Tell me about the groups. Anyone interesting? Is it like on TV?" I sit on our sofa with my socked feet wrapped under me. I spin a nearby PokéStop while I listen.

"Zillah, you wouldn't believe how much these people like to talk. I'm the only one with manners. And the therapists are so annoying. Especially Stephanie. Oh! And Sarah. She's the one I texted you about who keeps wanting me to put internet dating on my fear hierarchy."

"That's hilarious. I wish I could see it."

"Right? How are things at home?"

"I have some news. I ate some new food." I hold my breath to see how she reacts.

"I knew you could. See? Once you wanted to, you did."

I want to argue with her, tell her how hard it is every time I risk putting a new food in my mouth. How I still clutch a napkin for spitting each time. How it's her fault for making food scary. But my goal for this call is warmth and next steps.

"I'll show you when I see you," I say. We share a brief, but loving goodbye. I hug my knees and send her some telepathic good vibes.

I keep up my method of trying a new food with every meal, even though sometimes it's only a condiment or a different variety of something I've had before. I can do it on my own, now. Eating without an audience is helpful because I don't feel guilty spitting out. It's rare that I reject something, but it happens. Like pickles.

I'm learning about what I like and dislike. I added a rating column to my spreadsheet to help me keep track. Sometimes food textures are so different from what I'm used to that I immediately want to spit it out. It's like my brain is saying, "This isn't food." So, unless it's acutely disgusting, I try to sit with it for a few seconds. I can handle a few seconds of discomfort. I ask myself what I notice. This helped with American cheese. I thought it would be waxy when I unwrapped it and was shocked when I chomped down into soft heaven.

The other big step I've taken with new foods is combining them. At first, I used the original ten as food testing helpers. When I wanted to try ketchup, french fries were a natural delivery system. Same with cream cheese (on a bagel), and banana slices (in Cheerios, like on the box). But I'm up to adding two new foods to get a third new food. Like eggs + cheese = an omelet. Well, Ben is doing the cooking for me. And sometimes Lise. Even Vivian joins in.

And the biggest win: smoothies. They go down easy. If I get too much in my head about them ('how many Yuck Foods are in there at the same time?' I hear in Paula's voice), I look at my phone while I suck it down. I know distracted eating is bad for health and mindfulness, but a picky eater's gotta start somewhere.

And my poop! I don't even need a stool softener anymore. Shitting is a delight.

I wonder what my iron level will be at my next blood draw.

There were so many parties I left early or skipped altogether because they seemed too food-focused for comfort. I used to dread staying at friends' houses too long out of fear of being there at dinner time. I must have said "no thanks" when offered a treat a hundred times throughout my life. How much did I miss out on?

Chapter Fifty-Nine

"Can I stop by your office to say hi sometime soon?" I text Cliff. I don't want any confusion about my motives, so I text again, "I want to share some updates about us Scrivens."

He sends me the thumbs up, which is too vague for my comfort. I would have preferred an exact day and time window that would be appropriate. But I get what I get.

I visit on a Wednesday and bring a container of mini muffins from the store. It's a great ice breaker. We skip right over preliminaries.

"What's this?" he asks.

"Banana nut muffins," I say. "Want to see a magic trick?" I pull off the muffin top from one and pop it in my mouth. "Made it disappear!" I say thickly.

"Zillah! What?"

I share how I've started eating new food and even pull up my spreadsheet on my phone to show him my progress. "I'm up to 87 new foods," I say.

"Can I see?" he asks. I hand over my phone and finish the muffin I had mauled while I watch him scroll through some of the list. He makes a variety of noises, and I hold back from interrogating. I want to know which food made him say, "Woah," and which ones made him laugh.

He hands back my phone and says, "You've never had fried rice?"

"Yeah, not 'til last week. It's so good. Have you had it?"

"Uh, yeah. I've had my fair share of fried rice." He takes a bite of a muffin and says, "Way to go, Z."

I ask about his family and his new hairstyle. Eventually we hug good-bye, without making plans to hang out. It's good to know there's affection there. In all, we followed the campsite rule and left each other better than we started.

Chapter Sixty

The first time I see Paula in person, after Myrtle Beach, is another three weeks later at Aunt Bethany's house for lunch. We had prepped for my visit with care. We scheduled it for a Saturday afternoon so that Paula would be relaxed. Well, relaxed for a Scriven.

I have a key to Bethany's and am used to letting myself in, but I ring the bell out of a weird sense of formality. Plus, I want to be led inside by someone instead of shouting around until I find my loved ones.

Bethany comes to the door and accepts the two plasticware containers I hand her and gives me a side hug. Paula follows Bethany to the entryway and gasps, "Your hair!" I forgot that my new hairstyle would make a great icebreaker. I've grown adjusted to the visual shock in the mirror. It's a pixy-ish undercut I've wanted for ages but couldn't get while panning on a real estate internship. "You look like an elf or nymph from that Shakespeare play," Paula says. "Can I touch it?"

I let her run her hands through the top, longish bits, and say, "Be sure to touch the shaved part on the side. It's soft."

Paula says, "Do you wear sunscreen on these short parts? I can see your scalp through the hair. Unless you wear a hat outside? No, you wouldn't want to cover it up! I bet there's sunscreen that's made for scalps. Don't you think that should be a product?"

Bethany herds us to her dining room and says, "They sell moisturizer for the space between your left toes. I am one hundred percent sure that there's scalp sunscreen for sale."

Aunt Bethany gets things ready for lunch while we set the table and attempt a naturalish flow of conversation.

The lunch will be make-your-own chicken burritos. Smart. Paula can have tortillas and chicken if she wants. Bethany puts out the contribution I brought: veggies and hummus. She moves the carrot sticks and cucumbers to a yellow Fiestaware plate and scoops the hummus from the other container into a blue Fiestaware bowl. I always love these bright colors and how they're mismatched until the table has enough on there that it's a serendipitous mosaic.

Paula has the expression of someone who was the first to catch the whiff of a silent-but-deadly fart.

"The chicken needs more time," Bethany says. "Maybe we can munch on the hummus?"

"Yeah, but let me drizzle a bit of this on, first," I say as I pull a small container of olive oil from my backpack.

"You carry vials of oil?" Paula asks.

"Ben made me promise I'd serve it this way."

"The cook?" Paula asks.

"Yeah," I mumble as I concentrate on drizzling a small line of oil on the hummus instead of spilling a large pool like during my first attempt the day before. When I'm done, I screw the cap back on and say, "He's a chef at Newell's."

"Did he make this?" Aunt Bethany asks.

"I helped!" I say. That pulls the three of us together for a moment since "I helped" in a sing-song voice was an inside joke from when Aunt Bethany and I had once set a small kitchen fire while trying to deep fry homemade nuggets.

"Sounds like you're spending a lot of time with this Ben," Paula says.

My cheeks get warm while I say, "Yeah, I guess I am. But his sister is like my best friend, so he's always around."

Bethany, ever the peacekeeper, says, "It's good you have nice neighbors right there while Paula's been here."

"You should have them over when I'm back next week," Paula says. I take this as an olive branch and give her hand a little squeeze.

Our texts and calls have been mostly warm, but she often throws barbs about my career plans, breaking up with Cliff, and my search for a cheap apartment with Lise for next fall. She gives me a little smile, but her sour look returns as more of the colorful bowls and plates arrive on the table with a variety of burrito fixings. She pulls back from the table bit by bit until she's as far back in her chair as possible. She clenches her jaw and twists her cloth napkin around and around her thumb.

Aunt Bethany ignores Paula's signs of distress, and I follow the directions she had given me earlier, "Eat like you would with anyone else. Be nice, but don't change anything to make her less anxious."

"No accommodation and no reassurance?" I had said, familiar with a saying I'd learned from Lise.

"Right, Zillah! Good." I'm happy to take the brownie points.

So, I eat hummus for the second time ever under Paula's watchful eye. It has special significance for me since Lise and I had dubbed it "Hummus: The Final Frontier." Both of us had managed to eat it the day before, although Lise had been too nervous to enjoy it. But she'd eaten it *without* upchucking.

Success.

Plus, seeing Ben be proud of us was a visual I'll carry with me for a long time.

Now, on *Hummus: The Final Frontier Day 2*, Paula's eyes follow the path my cucumber slice makes as it becomes a hummus vehicle. I drop a chunk of hummus on the table and pick it up with my fingers and pop it in my mouth. Not polite behavior, but I follow Bethany's directions and act like I would with anyone else. I may have learned excellent table manners, but I rarely use them these days.

The hummus is delicious.

As Ben had promised, it's even better after a night in the fridge. He said he needs to introduce me to additional sources of protein on behalf of the chicken population. Saving chickens is an easy excuse he makes for inviting me over or, on a few occasions when Lise is occupied (or claims she's occupied), coming to my place to cook for me. He then stays for a movie or goes with me to an exhibit if there's something interesting in town. We're moving slowly toward each other, but there's a clear trajectory.

With appetizers in my stomach, I feel better about the world.

From the kitchen where she's finishing lunch preparations, Bethany asks me about my work prospects. "I've got a couple things going," I say. "I've been making money on Fiverr selling graphic design packages to restaurants and small businesses. I have good ratings so far, but I'm not charging enough yet to earn a living." I pull out my phone while I talk and navigate to my storefront to show Paula. Bethany takes a quick break to peek over her shoulder. "But it's good practice and I can do it while I'm watching shows." Or pretending to pay attention in my econ class.

"You made all of this?" Paula asks. Is she actually impressed?

"Yeah," I say. "And I'm gonna interview for contract work on a design team for the fall. It barely pays at all but will be really good on my resume."

Six months ago, the piecemeal jobs would have seemed like failures. But I'm excited about them. And scared. I have that universal feeling of being an imposter, but Dr. Underwood had assured me that the summer Bootcamp will help "get your sea legs".

"So, no appraisal certification?" Paula asks.

"No." I think back to a piece of advice from a psychologist on TikTok: You don't owe anybody your detailed logic. Every explanation is a door to an argument.

We even discuss Paula's job. For a couple of weeks, she's been back as a half-time teleworker so she could finish the IOP month and fortunately had enough with my contribution to make rent. She'd also spent some time looking at other jobs to see if a change might be good. "But I'm coming back to Sid and the clinic when I'm back in Lakeview next week," she says. "I'll think about other jobs next year. Maybe."

"Makes sense," Bethany chimes in. "With Zillah moving out in the fall, it's a lot of change all at once."

Conversation lags whenever Bethany's out of the room, as though Paula and I are only safe to talk when we have a third party as buffer.

When Bethany serves the chicken, we discuss politics. A safe topic upon which all three of us agree. We make our burritos, and Paula watches as I add a bit of everything to mine. I haven't tried cooked green peppers yet, so I'm excited to have something new. I try one with my fork before I eat it in my burrito so I can get a better sense of its taste.

Paula follows the progression of my fork and the pepper, like she had with the cucumber and hummus.

Delicious.

My burrito has chicken, sauteed green peppers and onions, pico de gallo, and shredded cheese. I watch Bethany wrap hers and she shows me her technique with mine.

"You don't have to—" Paula says, then stops herself.

"I don't have to what?" I ask. Bethany gives me a look I recognize as "Leave it alone".

"You don't have to be polite," she continues.

"I'm not," I say.

"I mean you don't have to eat anything you don't want to eat," she explains. "Bethany doesn't mind. You just eat what you want."

Bethany nods. "That's right. Zillah. Just eat what you want."

"Oh." I say. "Um, okay." I look at all the colorful dishes. A buffet of things I never would have tried a few months ago. I could die happy with a meal like this in my stomach. "This is what I want."

Paula sits forward in her chair and even looks comfortable. "You're brave, my doll." Then, to Bethany, "How did I make such a brave daughter?"

"I'm not brave."

Bethany says, "Brave is being scared, but doing it anyway. Look at you."

We finish our meal. Even Paula eats about a third of a burrito. There's awkwardness, but sweet moments, too. A bit of passive-aggressiveness from both Paula and me, but nothing too egregious.

It's a start. An *amuse bouche* that entices the three of us to make plans for another meal next weekend. I'm glad to be well-fed for this afternoon. Now that it's UIC's spring break, I'm doing chores around the apartment for Alexi. He always keeps me busy on my school breaks since Paula and I never go anywhere. And he gives us a little discount on rent, which was especially helpful this year. After I move out, Paula will have to pay rent on her own, but she's going to move to a one-bedroom on the other side of the courtyard as soon as one becomes available in the fall.

Lise helps me this afternoon while I wax and then polish the wooden windowsills and bannisters in all the stairwells. She's not so great with manual labor and following directions, but she keeps me entertained while I show off my excellent housework skills.

My alarm goes off at 3:45, reminding me of my appointment.

"Want to come over after?" she asks.

"I dunno," I say. "I may be all blubbery and emotional."

Lise heads out and I slide my hand along the smooth railing up to my place. It's slick and perhaps dangerously frictionless. But humans are pretty good at walking up and down stairs. And it looks sophisticated like it belongs at The Willows Hotel.

I have just enough time to scrub under my nails and wash my hands. I sign into the meeting and gulp some water to calm my nerves.

Right on time, the therapist I've picked signs on, too. She looks older than her profile picture and has less make-up than in her introductory video. But I like the way she looks — comfortable and dimpled when she smiles.

"Hi Zillah. Good to meet you. Before we get started, let's discuss confidentiality."

Acknowledgements

So many people helped this book come to life. Above all, I thank my daughter, Eleanor Kinn, who asked me a few years ago whether I had ever thought about writing a book. That conversation in a pool during spring break got Picky started. Eleanor then encouraged me every step of the way by discussing character attributes, tricky plot points, and pop culture. She read chapters, brainstormed names (she came up with "Zillah"), and even drew concept art of the main characters. Thanks to Eleanor, instead of a lonely task, writing this novel was an adventure. I am so freaking lucky.

I've been fortunate to have help from professional writers and editors as well as clinicians. Thank you to Anna Barrett (www.the-writers-space.com), Kate Burke, Ronit Wagman, my cover designer Kari Brownlie (https://karibrownlie.co.uk/) and everyone at Kennedy Creek Press. Thank you also to therapists Lauren Hanely and Jenna Schloss for reading my manuscript from the clinical perspective (for both sensitivity and accuracy).

I'm also grateful to two of my besties, Jennifer Miller and Stephanie Fox, who read early chapters and reminded me over bagels at the San Francisco Street Bakery that success is not necessarily defined by a single, shared metric. Jacqueline Collette read a complete draft and suggested an entire series about these characters, praise that warmed me and gave me some exciting ideas. My other book-loving friends gave me moral support and patiently listened to my shenanigans: Sarah Clifthorne; Tish Conway-Cranos; Meghan Duffie; Jennifer Kassakian Anderson; Suzanne LiaBraaten; Kelly Morgan; Kimberly Newell; Jane O'Sullivan;

Brenda Polster; Stefanie Powell; Hilary Seidel; and Amy Underwood. There are so many of you, and listing you all here makes me think, "Damn! What a good life!"

My partner, husband, and best friend Jason Kinn is always up for supporting my latest projects and this one was no different (even though he mostly wanted to talk about Halsted). Ben's peeing-on-a-log obsession is 100% borrowed from Jason, with permission. Noah, my oldest human child, taught me everything I know about video games, confidence, and staying humble. Thank you, Noah, for keeping me grounded. I'm cooking some latkes for you right now.

To close, I want to acknowledge two phenomenal mothers in my life. Thank you to Cathleen Kinn, who introduced me to many of my favorite authors and is so generous with her love and support. Finally, thank you to my mom Nina Shecter for encouraging independence and exploration. She graciously allowed me to use some of her verbal habits for Paula, even though they are such opposites (How do you like that one?). Nina always delights in her kids' growth and was thrilled for me when I started expanding my diet in my twenties. I hope these traits stay in our family like heirlooms.

Literary Book Club Questions

1. How would you describe *PICKY* to someone who hasn't read it yet? What kind of novel is it, really?

2. Zillah is twenty-three and "stuck." In what ways is she stuck emotionally, practically, and relationally?

3. Food plays a central role in the book without it being a "food novel." How does the author use food symbolically?

4. How does the novel explore the idea of fear as something that can be inherited?

5. How would you describe the mother–daughter relationship at the heart of the book?

6. In what ways does pickiness function as protection? In what ways does it become a prison?

7. How does humor operate in the novel? Did it ever surprise you?

8. Were there moments where the tone shifted noticeably (from light to serious, or vice versa)? How did that affect your reading?

9. How does the novel portray adulthood?

10. How are romantic relationships treated in the novel? What purpose does Zillah's relationship serve in her arc?

11. Did you find Zillah a reliable narrator? Why or why not?

12. What scenes felt especially vivid or memorable to you?

13. How does the pacing of the novel support Zillah's emotional journey?

14. Were there any moments you found uncomfortable or challenging to read? Why?

15. What expectations did you bring into the book, and how did the novel meet or subvert them?

16. How does the author balance compassion for the characters with honest portrayal of their flaws?

17. Did any secondary characters stand out to you? What role do they play thematically?

18. How does *PICKY* engage with mental health without becoming didactic?

19. What do you think the title *PICKY* ultimately refers to?

20. What do you think lingers after the final page? What is the book asking readers to sit with?

Personal & Reflective Book Club Questions

1. Do you consider yourself picky in any area of life (food, relationships, routines, environments)? Where did that come from?

2. How did the book make you feel about your own relationship with food?

3. Did any of Zillah's food rules or habits feel familiar to you, even if your experiences are different?

4. How did your family talk about food, fear, or risk when you were growing up?

5. Were there "unspoken rules" in your household that shaped how you move through the world now?

6. Did the novel prompt any empathy shifts for people you've labeled as "difficult," "anxious," or "rigid"?

7. What emotions came up for you while reading? Comfort, frustration, sadness, recognition?

8. Was there a moment where you felt protective of Zillah? A moment where you felt frustrated with her?

9. How do you personally distinguish between self-protection and avoidance?

10. Have you ever stayed in a situation longer than you wanted because it felt safer than change?

11. What does bravery look like in everyday life, according to this book?

12. Did the novel make you think differently about how fear is passed down in families?

13. How do you respond when someone you love limits themselves out of fear?

14. How does the book resonate with ideas of caretaking, obligation, or guilt in families?

15. Did any scenes spark memories from your own life?

16. How do you feel society treats adult "pickiness" or anxiety compared to childhood versions?

17. How did you react to the balance of humor and seriousness? Did it mirror how you cope in your own life?

18. If you were Zillah's friend, what advice would you want to give her?

19. What conversations do you wish people had more openly about fear, food, or family dynamics?

20. Did reading *PICKY* make you more compassionate toward yourself in any way?

Frequently Asked Questions

What kind of therapy is Lise doing?

Lise and her therapist are using Cognitive Behavioral Therapy with Exposure & Response Prevention (ERP). This is an evidence-based treatment that helps individuals select exposure activities related to fears or obsessions. The "response prevention" part means that the therapist helps the client learn how to just lean into the anxiety without their usual responses (like reassurance, distraction, or compulsions).

Exposures can be thinking a scary thought, like when Lise sat with the fear, "everyone thinks I'm weird," or much more active (perhaps Paula will one day touch dog poop and wait 30 seconds before washing her hand). The client engages in the exposure (by choice!), rates their anxiety on a scale of 1-10, and then waits until it's half that number *without* any reassurance, distraction, or compulsions. This takes up to 15 or twenty minutes, but usually less, because that's how long our nervous system response to fear lasts when we just naturally let it recede. It's not fun. But our brain eventually desensitizes to the exposure and we start thinking, "What's for lunch?"

Why is ERP so goofy?

We use humor and games when helping clients learn ERP to decrease the sense that "this is very serious work." If we lower the stakes and make it easier to talk about, then the treatment is much easier.

Do real therapists actually do weird games and activities like in *Picky*?

Oh yes! As a clinical psychologist, ERP is my favorite modality because we get to be creative, have fun, do disgusting and scary things, and then laugh about it with the client. We never push the client to take on more than they'd like; indeed, the client creates their fear hierarchy and selects the items they feel they can address.

You can learn more about ERP by consulting Dr. Google or by visiting my website (www.juliekinn.com) for readings and resources.

Do Paula and Zillah have ARFID?

ARFID, or Avoidant Restrictive Food Intake Disorder, is an eating disorder that features extremely limited dietary variety due to the individual's discomfort around food. They may be uncomfortable due to sensory input like taste or texture, previous negative experiences and fear of future negative experiences (like vomiting or panic), or just a lack of interest in eating. People with ARFID don't eat enough (or enough of the right things) to meet minimum nutritional needs. However, they aren't restricting their diets due to concerns about weight loss. ARFID is treated with Cognitive-Behavioral Therapy for Avoidant/Restrictive Food Intake Disorder (CBT-AR), which is similar to ERP and usually involves a dietician as well.

It's hard to know when someone might have ARFID or whether they are just extremely picky. Bottom line, I leave it up to the reader to determine why the Scriven family limits their diet to the Ten Foods. Maybe someone will write fanfiction with more of Paula's backstory or Zillah's childhood and we can all chew on it together.